Doctor Faustus

DISCARD

WEST GEORGIA REGIONAL LIBRARY SYSTEM
Neva Lomason Memorial Library

Christopher Marlowe

DOCTOR FAUSTUS

Edited and with an Introduction by Sylvan Barnet

A SIGNET CLASSIC

SIGNET CLASSIC
Published by the Penguin Group
Penguin Books USA Inc., 375 Hudson Street,
New York, New York 10014, U.S.A.
Penguin Books Ltd, 27 Wrights Lane,
London W8 5TZ, England
Penguin Books Australia Ltd, Ringwood,
Victoria, Australia
Penguin Books Canada Ltd, 10 Alcorn Avenue,
Toronto, Ontario, Canada M4V 3B2
Penguin Books (N.Z.) Ltd, 182–190 Wairau Road,
Auckland 10, New Zealand

Penguin Books Ltd, Registered Offices:
Harmondsworth, Middlesex, England

Published by Signet Classic, an imprint of New American Library,
a division of Penguin Books USA Inc.

First Signet Classic Printing, May, 1969
27   26   25   24   23   22   21   20

Copyright © 1969 by Sylvan Barnet
All rights reserved

Cover painting, "Portrait of a Man," by Albrecht Dürer,
Prado, Madrid. Courtesy Scala New York/Florence, Art Resource.

"Dr. Faustus at Stratford-upon-Avon, 1968" Copyright © 1969
by John Russell Brown. Used by permission of the author.

 REGISTERED TRADEMARK—MARCA REGISTRADA

Library of Congress Catalog Card Number: 70-78795

Printed in the United States of America

If you purchased this book without a cover you should be aware that this book is stolen
property. It was reported as "unsold and destroyed" to the publisher and neither the
author nor the publisher has received any payment for this "stripped book."

Contents

Introduction

The historical Doctor Faustus apparently was a man
of shreds and patches, a disreputable astrologer and
necromancer known chiefly in German inns. Possibly he
was the Johannes Faust who was granted a B.A. in divinity at Heidelberg in 1509, but even this is uncertain; his
only well-attested accomplishment is a cruel practical
joke: imprisoned, in exchange for wine he offered to show
a chaplain how to remove hair from his face without a
razor; the chaplain provided the wine and Faustus provided the chaplain with a salve of arsenic, which removed
not only the hair but the flesh. Around this charlatan
there accumulated a host of legends, including some which
earlier had been associated with Simon Magus, who had
sought to buy the gift of the Holy Spirit, and who was
said to have flown through the air until Peter caused him
to fall to his death. The uninspired material and the un-
inspiring hero that Marlowe inherited can be seen in his
source, the so-called English Faust-book, printed in large
part at the rear of this volume; but Doctor Faustus owes
his eternal life to Marlowe and to Goethe rather than to
his own accomplishments.

In the Faust-book the legends concerning Faustus were
gathered together and unified by the idea that pride will
have a fall. The arrogant and powerful Faustus of the
legends is at last carried off by devils. Nor does Marlowe
neglect the moral. The Chorus early tells us that Faustus
flourished

> Till swoll'n with cunning, of a self-conceit,
> His waxen wings did mount above his reach
> And melting, heavens conspired his overthrow!

And at the end of the play the Chorus returns to summarize:

> Faustus is gone: regard his hellish fall,
> Whose fiendful fortune may exhort the wise
> Only to wonder at unlawful things,
> Whose deepness doth entice such forward wits
> To practice more than heavenly power permits.

His fortune, in short, teaches us to adhere to traditional Christian behavior rather than to practice the unlawful things that exceptional minds give themselves to. This is a simple enough moral, and perhaps some such reading of the play inspired the late Professor R. M. Dawkins to his epigram: the play tells "the story of a Renaissance man who had to pay the medieval price for being one." And because Faustus has so often been seen as the symbol of the Renaissance, it seems reasonable here to try to sketch some of the qualities of the Renaissance.

In 1860 Jacob Burckhardt published his *Civilization of the Renaissance in Italy;* it is scarcely an exaggeration to say that all subsequent discussions of the Renaissance are footnotes to Burckhardt. Burckhardt argued—as Renaissance men themselves had argued—that the Renaissance marked "the discovery of the world and of man." Put a little differently, the Renaissance saw the emergence of the individual: private man made his way through a world in which the traditional sanctions—especially medieval *humilitas*—no longer operated powerfully. (It is no accident that Marlowe's towering Faustus is born of "parents base of stock.") In England, the dissolution of the monasteries meant that one-fifth of England's land was put up for sale, and much of it was acquired by merchants and lawyers. Capitalism, with its attendant colonialism, double-entry bookkeeping, and technological advances— notably printing—made for a relatively open society in

hich a young man of humble origins could rise to wealth
nd power. The Renaissance, indeed, is the age that saw
.e birth of literature as a profession. Chaucer had been
n amateur author, writing his books after-hours, but
penser, Shakespeare, Jonson, Milton, and, of course,
Marlowe, were professionals who carved out their careers
vith their pens. Moreover, none of these men came from
n aristocratic family: Spenser's father was a tailor,
hakespeare's a dealer in farm commodities, Jonson's
tepfather a bricklayer, Milton's father a scrivener, and
Marlowe's a prosperous shoemaker. This is not to say
hat the old aristocratic families and the old authorities
eased to exist, or that the Renaissance is simply anti-
.uthoritarian. One can find innumerable statements, in the
»est and the worst Renaissance writers, that support
.uthority (Marlowe's Chorus in *Doctor Faustus* is a case
n point), but the fact remains that during the Renaissance
nan's horizons became bigger and there was a widespread
.ense that the traditional authorities were no longer ade-
juate. Burckhardt's remark about "the discovery of the
vorld and of man" can most obviously be supported by
·eference first to the geographical explorations, which
·xtended man's outer world, and second to the revival of
•agan classical learning, which extended man's inner
vorld. Portrait painting offers additional evidence of
nan's heightened discovery of himself and his attempt to
·ecord his personality and his achievements on earth. In
.he Middle Ages there are pictures of faces, but there is
scarcely anything that can be called portraiture; it is not
until the Renaissance that we find painters sufficiently
materialistic to be concerned with the physical looks
(rather than only the spiritual or regal qualities) of their
sitters. Yet another index, and one especially relevant to
Doctor Faustus, is the concept of wisdom. For the Middle Ages, the highest wisdom was knowledge of divine
things, which was achieved through God's grace, bestowed
in revelation. In the Renaissance, however, one finds
abundant deprecation of the contemplative life rooted in
faith, and abundant praise of the active life, of the study
of political and social man. The monasteries that the

Middle Ages built harbor (it was held in the Renaissance) idlers, caterpillars of the commonwealth, men who must be fools because they lack the experience of the world. Milton's disparagement of "cloistered virtue" is only the best-known of many Renaissance statements to the same effect, insisting that the *vita contemplativa* is inferior to the *vita activa*. The family man, the soldier, and especially the statesman, who serves a prince and his community rather than God, acquire esteem; the paradigm of virtue is no longer the doctor of theology.

Marlowe himself, according to popular report, scoffed at the traditional pieties. Shortly before his death he was accused of saying "that the first beginning of religion was only to keep men in awe." The point is not the truth or falsity of the accusation; the point is that in the Renaissance a way of life that is not centered in God becomes a believable possibility. Modern readers who feel that the charges against Marlowe must have had at least some truth behind them tend to hear in *Doctor Faustus* the heretical Marlowe, glorifying unfettered aspiration, attacking traditional sanctities, and only adding an unconvincing pious ending as a sop to conventional belief. Faustus the magician is not a worshiper of God, but an operator who manages to impose his will on the material world. He is, in short, an applied scientist, rejoicing in power rather than in contemplation, and, in this view, he is a symbol of the Renaissance, that second great attempt (after Periclean Athens) to free the mind from dogma and, by means of reason and experiment, to understand phenomena in terms of cause and effect.

But there is another way of looking at Faustus, Marlowe, and the Renaissance. One can see the Renaissance as the period in which man's thinking took a bad turn and entered upon the course it still pursues. In this view, unappeasable curiosity catastrophically banished intuition and faith. Etienne Gilson in *Les idées et les lettres* puts it thus: "The difference between the Renaissance and the Middle Ages was not a difference by addition but by subtraction. The Renaissance, as it has been described to us, was not the Middle Ages plus man, but the Middle Ages inus God, and the tragedy is that in losing God the Renaissance was losing man himself." Some Renaissance texts themselves can be summoned to support Gilson's charge that secularism diminished man's possibilities. For example, John Lyly's Euphues in 1579 asked himself, "Is Aristotle more dear to thee with his books, than Christ with his blood?" Faustus, of course, centers his life on the quest for knowledge, and for the power that knowledge confers, rather than on God. Marlowe is careful to show us that in his egoism Faustus deludes himself into thinking that magic, which means control over nature, is "heavenly," and that, for example, Helen's kiss—or rather, worse yet, the kiss of a demon impersonating Helen—confers immortality. Faustus' unwillingness, or inability, to see things as they evidently are, to see evil as evil, is nicely indicated early in the play, when Mephostophilis first appears. Faustus says,

> I charge thee to return and change thy shape,
> Thou art too ugly to attend on me.
> Go, and return an old Franciscan friar:
> That holy shape becomes a devil best.

There is a crude anti-Catholic joke here, of course, but there is more: the speech reveals Faustus' perverse simplification of reality by fiddling with surface matters. Several of his other speeches make this point unambiguously. In I.iii, for example, Faustus jauntily asserts that

> This word "damnation" terrifies not me
> For I confound hell in Elysium:
> My ghost be with the old philosophers!

This superficiality is too much even for Mephostophilis, who, agitated by the memory of the vision of the God that he lost through pride and insolence, is moved to pity the man whom he has come to capture:

> Think'st thou that I who saw the face of God
> And tasted the eternal joys of heaven

> Am not tormented with ten thousand hells
> In being deprived of everlasting bliss?
> O Faustus, leave these frivolous demands
> Which strikes a terror to my fainting soul!

Faustus replies:

> What, is great Mephostophilis so passionate
> For being deprivèd of the joys of heaven?
> Learn thou of Faustus manly fortitude
> And scorn those joys thou never shalt possess.

We do not have to wait until later in the play, when we
see Faustus' jauntiness give way to cringing, to hear in
these words not only scorn and arrogance but a foolish
rejection of traditional wisdom. Similarly, the trivial end
to which on the whole Faustus puts his magic—the "belly
cheer" that includes satisfying his palate and his lust—
reveal Faustus' reduction of spiritual realities to physical
states. The spectacle of the Seven Deadly Sins, for instance, moves him to exclaim, "O, how this sight doth
delight my soul," whereas a wiser man (i.e., one not
merely learned but imbued with faith and drawing upon
instinct as well as intellect) would reject this activity as
diminishing rather than nourishing. At his lowest, Doctor
Faustus sounds almost like the absurd old Doctor in
Italian popular comedy, pedantic, gluttonous, amorous,
and thoroughly foolish.

But of course there is another side, too. Faustus' aspira-
tions are curiously mixed: he studies medicine so that he
may "heap up gold," but he also would "make men to
live eternally." In him we occasionally hear the voice of
the Renaissance humanist, the man refreshed by the great-
ness of the pagan past and anxious to live an ampler life
than his father had lived. Faustus, for example, has "made
blind Homer sing" to him, an accomplishment especially
resonant when we recall that Petrarch (1304–74), one
of the first humanists, failed to master Greek and had to
be content with Homer's epics in Latin versions. Most
notable, of course, is the famous apostrophe to Helen:

we can say that the speech is mistaken (Helen cannot con-
fer immortality) and that images of destruction under-
mine the opulence, but the fact remains that Marlowe's
ability as a poet infuses in Faustus an unmistakable
grandeur that is not wholly eradicated by conmmon-sense
reflections:

> Was this the face that launched a thousand ships
> And burnt the topless towers of Ilium?
> Sweet Helen, make me immortal with a kiss.
> Her lips suck forth my soul. See where it flies!
> Come Helen, come, give me my soul again.
> Here will I dwell, for heaven is in these lips
> And all is dross that is not Helena.

We can go through the text and find abundant evidence
that Faustus is foolish and corrupt, but we ought not to
deny that at times his imaginings capture our imagination
and evoke awe, or at least rapt attention rather than
censure. His ideals are corrupted, but they reveal an
abundance of energy that makes Faustus indisputably
greater (not better, of course) than any of the other
mortals in the play. The danger in reading the play is that
we will see only either the heroic humanist or the fool;
we may have difficulty in understanding that Faustus can
be both.

Reinhold Niebuhr, in *Beyond Tragedy,* has an interesting discussion of the corruption that is inherent in man's
highest social values. Man, he points out (and Faustus is
a good example), "is constantly tempted to forget the
finiteness of his cultures and civilisation and to pretend
a finality for them which they do not have. Every civilisation and every culture is thus a Tower of Babel." When
Faustus, longing to perform great deeds, says, "This night
I'll conjure though I die therefor," we hear an urgency
that cannot be denied, but this urgent claim itself denies
other claims, lacks the finality it pretends to, and will
finally be blasted. An extended quotation from Niebuhr—
even though it is not specifically concerned with *Doctor
Faustus*—will make clear the tragic ambiguity.

Man is mortal. That is his fate. Man pretends not to be mortal. That is his sin. Man is a creature of time and place, whose perspectives and insights are invariably conditioned by his immediate circumstances. But man is not merely the prisoner of time and place. He touches the fringes of the eternal. He is not content to be merely American man, or Chinese man, or bourgeois man, or man of the twentieth century. He wants to be man. He is not content with his truth. He seeks *the* truth. His memory spans the ages in order that he may transcend his age. His restless mind seeks to comprehend the meaning of all cultures so that he may not be caught within the limitations of his own.

Thus man builds towers of the spirit from which he may survey larger horizons than those of his class, race and nation. This is a necessary human enterprise. Without it man could not come to his full estate. But it is also inevitable that these towers should be Towers of Babel, that they should pretend to reach higher than their real height; and should claim a finality which they cannot possess. The truth man finds and speaks is, for all of his efforts to transcend himself, still his truth. The "good" which he discovers is, for all of his efforts to disassociate it from his own interest and interests, still his "good." The higher the tower is built to escape unnecessary limitations of the human imagination, the more certain it will be to defy necessary and inevitable limitations. Thus sin corrupts the highest as well as the lowest achievements of human life. Human pride is greatest when it is based upon solid achievements; but the achievements are never great enough to justify its pretensions. This pride is at least one aspect of what Christian orthodoxy means by "original sin." It is not so much an inherited corruption as an inevitable taint upon the spirituality of a finite creature, always enslaved to time and place, never completely enslaved and always under the illusion that the measure of his emancipation is greater than it really is.*

* Reprinted from *Beyond Tragedy* by Reinhold Niebuhr, pp. 28–30, by permission of Charles Scribner's Sons.

Niebuhr's reference to enslavement brings up yet another matter. We can say that Faustus makes a choice, and that he is responsible for his choice, but there is in the play a suggestion—sometimes explicit, sometimes only very dimly implicit—that Faustus comes to destruction not merely through his own actions but through the actions of a hostile cosmos that entraps him. In this sense, too, there is something of everyman in Faustus. The story of Adam, for instance, insists on Adam's culpability; Adam, like Faustus, made himself, rather than God, the center of his existence. And yet, despite the traditional expos: tions, one cannot entirely suppress the common-sense response that if the Creator knew Adam would fall, the Creator rather than Adam is responsible for the fall; Adam ought to have been created of better stuff. To what degree is Faustus, or any tragic hero, victimized? Lear sees himself "more sinned against than sinning," Othello sees himself as one "ensnared" by a "demi-devil," and there are similar statements in almost all of the major tragedies, from Aeschylus' *Prometheus Bound* onward. It can be argued, of course, that the devils cannot control Faustus; they can only come to him when he has laid himself open to them. Mephostophilis says something to this effect when he explains that he has come to Faustus not because Faustus' invocation is compelling, but because Faustus has made himself vulnerable to attack:

> . . . when we hear one rack the name of God,
> Abjure the Scriptures and his savior Christ,
> We fly in hope to get his glorious soul.
> Nor will we come unless he use such means
> Whereby he is in danger to be damned.
> Therefore the shortest cut for conjuring
> Is stoutly to abjure the Trinity
> And pray devoutly to the prince of hell.

This suggests that the devils are not so much independent external creatures as they are aspects of Faustus himself, symbols perhaps of his pride. On the other hand, one can argue that given Faustus' character—his extraordinary abilities that can find no satisfaction in the trivial pursuits of ordinary men—he is not entirely responsible for his actions. He clearly is of a nature different from that of his fellow scholars, whose attainments are far beneath his, and it is not at all evident that such a nature could find satisfaction and fulfill itself in the allowed activities. Faustus' initial speech, in which he masters and tires of four branches of learning, each of which would normally require a lifetime—the liberal arts, medicine, law, and divinity—suggests that he is the victim of the intellectual abilities that were given to him by his Creator.

There are, moreover, some passages that explicitly say that Faustus is trapped—although they do not entirely obliterate our sense that we are watching a man who freely acts and who then reaps the consequences of his actions. For example, while Faustus signs the bond, giving his soul to Lucifer, Mephostophilis in an aside says, "What will not I do to obtain his soul!" Even more explicit is Mephostophilis' confession, late in the play, that he has ensnared Faustus' soul. To Faustus' charge, " 'Twas thy temptation/Hath robbed me of eternal happiness," Mephostophilis replies,

> I do confess it Faustus, and rejoice.
> 'Twas I, that when thou wert i' the way to heaven
> Dammed up thy passage. When thou took'st the book
> To view the scriptures, then I turned the leaves
> And led thine eye.

One can trace this voice of motiveless malignity (Coleridge's description of Iago) through such figures as Iago, and Aaron in *Titus Andronicus,* back to the Vice of medieval drama, but to call attention to the literary tradition does not diminish the voice itself. Again, one can say that to some degree the diabolic voices are aspects of Faustus himself, like the Good and Bad Angels, and the Old Man, but one cannot entirely dismiss the personages as shadowy allegoric representations of Faustus; these personages have their independent reality too.

Moreover, the idea that Faustus is in some measure

rapped is implicitly strengthened by the stage business at the beginning of V.ii, and perhaps at the beginning of I.iii. To take the more certain episode first: the stage direction at V.ii reads thus: "Enter Lucifer, Belzebub, and Mephostophilis." The ensuing dialogue suggests that they rise through a trapdoor and then climb to a playing area above the main stage, so that like cosmic powers they gaze down upon their plaything beneath them:

> Thus from infernal Dis do we ascend
> To view the subjects of our monarchy,
> Those souls which sin seals the black sons of hell.
> 'Mong which as chief, Faustus, we come to thee,
> Bringing with us lasting damnation
> To wait upon thy soul. The time is come
> Which makes it forfeit.

Possibly in I.iii also, where Lucifer and four devils enter and remain unseen while Faustus seeks to conjure them up, the devils are above; but even if they merely hover on one side of the main stage, their presence and Faustus' ignorance of them suggests that they dominate him, or at least that they lie in wait for him.

But perhaps we need not worry too much about whether Faustus trapped himself or was trapped by diabolic creatures (though it seems reasonable to say that the play suggests not an *either-or* situation, but *both/and*); it is a tragic play, and tragic plays are not philosophic treatises on the freedom of the will. Still, a reader or a spectator—at least if he has been corrupted by too much education—inevitably tries to make sense out of his experiences and is reluctant merely to have the experience itself. What sense, then, can we make out of *Doctor Faustus?* The "meaning" of the play, of course, is the play itself; any paraphrase, and certainly any reduction to a moral tag, inevitably simplifies the work. The play "means" what it says, beginning with the Chorus' first entry and concluding with its final exit. Still, if we stand back from the play, perhaps we can see in it something rather like what Sir Philip Sidney, writing at about the time that Marlowe was beginning his theatrical career, suggested could be found in all tragedies: a depiction of "the uncertainty of this world, and upon how weak foundation gilden roofs are builded." This depiction, Sidney says, evokes wonder (his word is "admiration," used with a suggestion of its Latin meaning) and pity. Perhaps we can say that the protagonist's vitality and the cosmic order's power both evoke wonder. That the protagonist is destroyed by the vitality that brings him into conflict with the order is pitiful. Perhaps, then, we can amplify Professor Dawkins' epigram (Faustus is "a Renaissance man who had to pay the medieval price for being one") into something along these lines: doubtful of traditional authority, anxious to exert himself to the fullest, Faustus drove himself—and was driven—into experiences that were exhilarating but that brought him into conflict with a basic law of life. His displays of pride and will evoke both wonder and pity; there is something magnificent about Faustus, but his magnificence is corrupt because it is founded on egoism rather than on love and service, and so the magnificence is destroyed by the moral order with which it conflicts. Faustus partly willingly and partly blindly rejects the inherent limitations of life, thereby becoming both hero and villain. Let the last words be Marlowe's: Faustus dies with "fearful shrieks," yet his limbs are given due burial because "he was a scholar once admired/For wondrous knowledge." His gifts were indisputable, and, as indisputably, they destroyed him:

> Cut is the branch that might have grown full straight
> And burnèd is Apollo's laurel bough
> That sometime grew within this learnèd man.

SYLVAN BARNET
Tufts University

Biographical note: Christopher Marlowe (1564–1593) was born in Canterbury the year of Shakespeare's birth.

ike Shakespeare, he was of a prosperous middle-class
amily, but unlike Shakespeare he went to a university,
Corpus Christi College, Cambridge, where he received the
achelor's degree in 1584 and the master's degree in 1587.
The terms of his scholarship implied that he was prepar-
ing for the clergy but he did not become a clergyman.
hortly before he received his M.A. the University seems
to have wished to withhold it, apparently suspecting him
of conversion to Roman Catholicism, but the Queen's
Privy Council intervened on his behalf, stating that he
had done her majesty good service" and had been em-
ployed "in matters touching the benefit of his country."
His precise service is unknown. After Cambridge Marlowe
vent to London, where he apparently lived a turbulent
life (he had two brushes with the law and he was said to
be disreputable) while pursuing a career as dramatist. He
wrote seven plays—the dates of which are uncertain—
before he was yet again in legal difficulties: he was ar-
ested in 1593, accused of atheism. He was not imprisoned, and before his case could be decided he was
lead, having been stabbed in a tavern while quarreling
over the bill.

Doctor Faustus

[Speaking Characters

Chorus
Doctor Faustus
Wagner, his student and servant
Good Angel
Bad Angel
Valdes } *magicians*
Cornelius
Three Scholars
Lucifer, prince of devils
Mephostophilis, a devil
Robin, a Clown
Belzebub, a devil
Pride
Covetousness
Envy
Wrath } *the Seven Deadly Sins*
Gluttony
Sloth
Lechery
Dick, a clown
Pope Adrian
Raymond, King of Hungary
Bruno, rival Pope appointed by the Emperor
Two Cardinals
Archbishop of Rheims
Friars
Vintner
Martino
Frederick } *gentlemen at the Emperor's court*
Benvolio
The German Emperor, Charles the Fifth
Duke of Saxony
Two Soldiers   *Duke of Vanholt*
Horse-courser, a clown   *Duchess of Vanholt*
Carter, a clown   *Servant*
Hostess of a Tavern   *Old Man*

Mute Characters

Darius of Persia, Alexander the Great, Alexander's Paramour, Helen of Troy, Devils, Piper, Cardinals, Monks Friars, Attendants, Soldiers, Servants, Two Cupids]

[Prologue] *Enter Chorus.*°

Not marching in the fields of Trasimene°
Where Mars did mate° the warlike Carthagens,
Nor sporting in the dalliance of love
In courts of kings where state° is overturned,
Nor in the pomp of proud audacious deeds   5
Intends our muse° to vaunt° his heavenly verse.
Only this, gentles—We must now perform
The form of Faustus' fortunes, good or bad:
And now to patient judgments we appeal
And speak for Faustus in his infancy.   10
Now is he born of parents base of stock
In Germany within a town called Rhode;°
At riper years to Wittenberg he went
Whereas° his kinsmen chiefly brought him up.
So much he profits in divinity   15
That shortly he was graced° with doctor's name,
Excelling all, and sweetly can dispute
In th' heavenly matters of theology;
Till swoll'n with cunning, of a self-conceit,°
His waxen wings° did mount above his reach   20

rologue s.d. **Chorus** a single actor (here, perhaps, Wagner,
austus' servant-student)   1 **Trasimene** Lake Trasimene, site of one
f Hannibal's victories over the Romans, 217 B.C. (Marlowe is not
nown to have written on this subject, though lines 3–4 may refer
› his *Edward II*, and line 5 to his *Tamburlaine*)   2 **Mars did mate**
e., the Roman army encountered   4 **state** government   6 **muse**
oet   6 **vaunt** proudly display   12 **Rhode Roda**   14 **Whereas** where
5 **graced** (alluding to the official "grace" permitting the student to
ke his degree)   19 **cunning, of a self-conceit** ingenuity, born of
rrogance   20 **waxen wings** (alluding to Icarus, who flew by means
f wings made of feathers waxed to a framework; despite the warning
f his father, Icarus soared too near the sun, the wax melted, and he
lunged to his death)

23

And melting, heavens conspired his overthrow!
For falling to a devilish exercise
And glutted now with learning's golden gifts
He surfeits upon cursèd necromancy:°
25   Nothing so sweet as magic is to him
Which he prefers before his chiefest bliss°—
And this the man that in his study sits.

                                                    Exit

[I.i] *Faustus in his study.*°

Faustus. Settle thy studies Faustus, and begin
To sound the depth of that thou wilt profess.°
Having commenced,° be a divine in show—
Yet level° at the end of every art
5   And live and die in Aristotle's works.
Sweet *Analytics,*° 'tis thou hast ravished me.
Bene disserere est finis logices.°
Is to dispute well logic's chiefest end?
Affords this art no greater miracle?
10   Then read no more, thou has attained that end.
A greater subject fitteth Faustus' wit:°
Bid *on kai me on*° farewell, and Galen° come:
Be a physician Faustus, heap up gold,
And be eternized for some wondrous cure.
15   *Summum bonum medicinae sanitas,*°
The end of physic° is our body's health.
Why Faustus hast thou not attained that end?
Are not thy bills° hung up as monuments

24 **necromancy** (literally divination by means of the spirits of th
dead, but here probably equivalent to black magic)   26 **prefers b**
fore his chiefest bliss sets above his hope of salvation   **I.i.s.d. Faustu**
in his study (probably at his last line the Chorus drew back a curtai
at the rear of the stage, disclosing Faustus)   2 **profess** study an
teach   3 **commenced** taken a degree   4 **level** aim   6 **Analytics** tit
of two treatises by Aristotle on logic   7 **Bene . . . logices** the en
(i.e., purpose) of logic is to argue well (Latin)   11 **wit** intelligenc
12 **on kai me on** being and not being (Greek)   12 **Galen** Gree
authority on medicine, 2nd century A.D.   15 **Summum . . . sanita**
health is the greatest good of medicine (Latin, translated fro
Aristotle's *Nichomachean Ethics*)   16 **physic** medicine   18 **bills** pr
scriptions

Whereby whole cities have escaped the plague
And thousand desperate maladies been cured?   20
Yet art thou still but Faustus and a man.
Could'st thou make men to live eternally
Or being dead raise them to life again,
Then this profession were to be esteemed.
Physic farewell! Where is Justinian?°   25
Si una eademque res legatur duobus, alter rem, alter
    valorem rei, et cetera.°
A petty case of paltry legacies.
Exhereditare filium non potest pater, nisi°—
Such is the subject of the *Institute*   30
And universal body of the law!
This study fits a mercenary drudge
Who aims at nothing but external trash,
Too servile and illiberal for me.
When all is done, divinity is best.   35
Jerome's Bible,° Faustus, view it well.
Stipendium peccati mors est.° Ha! *Stipendium et*
    cetera. The reward of sin is death? That's hard:
    Si peccasse negamus, fallimur, et nulla est in
    nobis veritas.° If we say that we have no sin, we   40
    deceive ourselves, and there is no truth in us.
    Why, then belike, we must sin, and so conse-
    quently die.
Ay, we must die an everlasting death.
What doctrine call you this? *Che serà, serà:*°   45
What will be, shall be! Divinity, adieu!

25 **Justinian** Roman emperor and authority on law (483–565) who
ordered the compilation of the *Institutes* (see line 30)   26–27 **Si** ...
et cetera if one thing is willed to two persons, one of them shall have
the thing itself, the other the value of the thing, and so forth (Latin)
29 **Exhereditare** ... **nisi** a father cannot disinherit his son unless
(Latin)   36 **Jerome's Bible** the Latin translation made by St. Jerome
(c.340–420)   37 **Stipendium** ... **est** the wages of sin is death
(Romans 6:23; if Faustus had gone on to read the rest of the verse,
he would have found that "the gift of God is eternal life through
Jesus Christ our Lord")   39–40 **Si** ... **veritas** from I John 1:8,
translated in the next two lines; Faustus neglects the following verse:
"If we confess our sins, He is faithful and just to forgive us our sins,
and to cleanse us from all unrighteousness"   45 **Che serà, serà** (Italian, translated in the first half of the next line)

These metaphysics° of magicians
And negromantic° books are heavenly;
Lines, circles, letters, characters—
50   Ay, these are those that Faustus most desires.
O, what a world of profit and delight,
Of power, of honor, and omnipotence
Is promised to the studious artisan!°
All things that move between the quiet° poles
55   Shall be at my command: emperors and kings
Are but obeyed in their several provinces
But his dominion that exceeds in this°
Stretcheth as far as doth the mind of man:
A sound magician is a demi-god!
60   Here tire my brains to get° a deity!

Enter Wagner.

Wagner, commend me to my dearest friends,
The German Valdes and Cornelius.
Request them earnestly to visit me.

Wagner. I will, sir.   *Exit.*

65   *Faustus.* Their conference° will be a greater help to me
Than all my labors, plod I ne'er so fast.

Enter the [Good] Angel and [the Evil] Spirit.°

Good Angel. O Faustus, lay that damnèd book aside
And gaze not on it lest it tempt thy soul
And heap God's heavy wrath upon thy head!
70   Read, read the Scriptures— that° is blasphemy!

Bad Angel. Go forward Faustus, in that famous art

---

47 **metaphysics** subjects lying beyond (or studied after) physics   48
negromantic black magical (though probably here also associated
with "necromantic," i.e., concerned with raising the spirits of the
dead)   53 **artisan** i.e., expert   54 **quiet** motionless   57 **this** i.e., magic
60 **get** beget   65 **conference** conversation   67 s.d. **Spirit** Bad Angel,
devil (the two angels probably enter the stage from separate doors)
70 **that** i.e., the book of magic

Wherein all nature's treasure is contained.
Be thou on earth as Jove is in the sky,
Lord and commander of these elements!

Exeunt Angels.

Faustus. How am I glutted with conceit of this!°   75
Shall I make spirits fetch me what I please?
Resolve me of° all ambiguities?
Perform what desperate enterprise I will?
I'll have them fly to India° for gold,
Ransack the ocean for orient° pearl,   80
And search all corners of the new-found world
For pleasant fruits and princely delicates;
I'll have them read me strange philosophy
And tell the secrets of all foreign kings;
I'll have them wall all Germany with brass   85
And make swift Rhine circle fair Wittenberg;
I'll have them fill the public schools° with silk
Wherewith the students shall be bravely° clad.
I'll levy soldiers with the coin they bring
And chase the Prince of Parma° from our land   90
And reign sole king of all the provinces!
Yea, stranger engines for the brunt° of war
Than was the fiery keel° at Antwerp bridge
I'll make my servile spirits to invent.

Enter Valdes and Cornelius.

Come German Valdes and Cornelius   95
And make me blest with your sage conference.
Valdes, sweet Valdes, and Cornelius,
Know that your words have won me at the last
To practice magic and concealèd arts.

---

75 **conceit of this** i.e., the conception of being a magician   77 **Resolve me of** explain to me   79 **India** either the West Indies (America)
or the East Indies   80 **orient** lustrous and precious   87 **public
schools** universities   88 **bravely** splendidly   90 **Prince of Parma**
Spanish governor-general of the Low Countries during 1579–92
92 **brunt** assault   93 **fiery keel** burning ship sent by the Netherlanders in 1585 against a bridge erected by Parma to blockade Antwerp
(Antwerp here is an adjective, not genetive)

100   Philosophy is odious and obscure,
       Both law and physic are for petty wits,
       Divinity is basest of the three—
       Unpleasant, harsh, contemptible, and vile.
       'Tis magic, magic, that hath ravished me!
105   Then, gentle friends, aid me in this attempt
       And I, that have with subtle syllogisms
       Graveled° the pastors of the German church
       And made the flow'ring pride of Wittenberg
       Swarm to my problems° as th' infernal spirits
110   On sweet Musaeus° when he came to hell,
       Will be as cunning as Agrippa° was,
       Whose shadows made all Europe honor him.

    Valdes. Faustus, these books, thy wit, and our ex-
         perience
       Shall make all nations to canonize us.
115   As Indian Moors° obey their Spanish lords,
       So shall the spirits of every element
       Be always serviceable to us three:
       Like lions shall they guard us when we please,
       Like Almain rutters° with their horsemen's staves
120   Or Lapland giants trotting by our sides;
       Sometimes like women or unwedded maids
       Shadowing° more beauty in their airy brows
       Than has the white breasts of the queen of love;
       From Venice shall they drag huge argosies
125   And from America the golden fleece
       That yearly stuffs old Philip's° treasury,
       If learnèd Faustus will be resolute.

    Faustus. Valdes, as resolute am I in this
       As thou to live; therefore object it not.

130 *Cornelius.* The miracles that magic will perform

---

107 **Graveled** confounded   109 **problems** questions proposed for
disputation   110 **Musaeus** legendary Greek poet   111 **Agrippa** Cornelius Agrippa of Nettesheim (1486–1535), German author of *De
occulta philosophia,* a survey of Renaissance magic; Agrippa was
believed to have raised spirits ("shadows") from the dead   115 **Indian Moors** American Indians   119 **Almain rutters** German caval-
rymen   122 **Shadowing** sheltering   126 **Philip** King Philip II of
Spain (1527–98)

Will make thee vow to study nothing else.
He that is grounded in astrology,
Enriched with tongues, well seen° in minerals,
Hath all the principles magic doth require.
Then doubt not Faustus but to be renowned   *135*
And more frequented for this mystery°
Than heretofore the Delphian oracle.°
The spirits tell me they can dry the sea
And fetch the treasure of all foreign wracks,
Yea, all the wealth that our forefathers hid   *140*
Within the massy° entrails of the earth.
Then tell me Faustus, what shall we three want?°

Faustus. Nothing, Cornelius. O, this cheers my soul!
Come, show me some demonstrations magical
That I may conjure° in some bushy grove   *145*
And have these joys in full possession.

Valdes. Then haste thee to some solitary grove,
And bear wise Bacon's° and Albanus'° works,
The Hebrew Psalter, and New Testament;
And whatsoever else is requisite   *150*
We will inform thee ere our conference cease.

Cornelius. Valdes, first let him know the words of art,
And then, all other ceremonies learned,
Faustus may try his cunning by himself.

Valdes. First I'll instruct thee in the rudiments,   *155*
And then wilt thou be perfecter than I.

Faustus. Then come and dine with me, and after meat
We'll canvass every quiddity° thereof,
For ere I sleep I'll try what I can do:
This night I'll conjure though I die therefor!   *160*
                              Exeunt omnes.°

---

133 well seen skilled   **136 frequented for this mystery** resorted to for
this art   **137 Delphian oracle** oracle of Apollo at Delphi   **141 massy**
massive   **142 want** lack   **145 conjure** raise spirits   **148 Bacon** Roger
Bacon, medieval friar and scientist   **148 Albanus** perhaps Pietro
d'Abano, medieval writer on medicine and philosophy   **158 canvass
every quiddity** discuss every essential detail   **160 s.d. omnes** all
(Latin)

[I.ii] *Enter two Scholars.*

1 Scholar. I wonder what's become of Faustus that
was wont to make our schools ring with *sic probo.*°

Enter Wagner.

2 Scholar. That shall we presently° know. Here comes
his boy.°

5 *1 Scholar.* How now sirrah,° where's thy master?

Wagner. God in heaven knows.

1 Scholar. Why, dost not thou know then?

Wagner. Yes, I know, but that follows not.

1 Scholar. Go to° sirrah, leave your jesting and tell us
10 where he is.

Wagner. That follows not by force of argument, which
you, being licentiates,° should stand upon;° therefore acknowledge your error and be attentive.

2 Scholar. Then you will not tell us?

15 *Wagner.* You are deceived, for I will tell you. Yet if
you were not dunces,° you would never ask me
such a question. For is he not *corpus naturale?*
And is not that *mobile?*° Then wherefore should
you ask me such a question? But that I am by
20 nature phlegmatic,° slow to wrath, and prone to
lechery—to love, I would say—it were not for you

I.ii.2 **sic probo** thus I prove it (Latin)   3 **presently** at once   4 **boy**
servant (an impoverished student)   5 **sirrah** (term of address used to
an inferior)   9 **Go to** (exclamation of impatience)   12 **licentiates**
possessors of a degree preceding the master's degree   12 **stand upon**
make much of   16 **dunces** (1) fools (2) hairsplitters   17–18 **corpus
naturale . . . mobile** natural matter . . . movable (Latin, scholastic
definition of the subject-matter of physics)   20 **phlegmatic** sluggish

to come within forty foot of the place of execution°
—although I do not doubt but to see you both
hanged the next sessions.° Thus, having triumphed
over you, I will set my countenance like a precisian°   25
and begin to speak thus: Truly, my dear brethren,
my master is within at dinner, with Valdes and
Cornelius, as this wine, if it could speak, would
inform your worships; and so, the Lord bless you,
preserve you, and keep you, my dear brethren.   30

                                                  Exit.

1 Scholar. O Faustus, then I fear that which I have
    long suspected,
That thou art fall'n into that damnèd art
For which they two are infamous through the world.

2 Scholar. Were he a stranger, not allied to me,
The danger of his soul would make me mourn.   35
But come, let us go and inform the rector.°
It may be his grave counsel may reclaim him.

1 Scholar. I fear me nothing will reclaim him now.

2 Scholar. Yet let us see what we can do.   *Exeunt.*

[I.iii] *Thunder. Enter Lucifer and four Devils.°*
    Faustus to them with this speech.

Faustus. Now that the gloomy shadow of the night,
Longing to view Orion's° drizzling look,
Leaps from th' antarctic world unto the sky
And dims the welkin° with her pitchy breath,
Faustus, begin thine incantations   5
And try if devils will obey thy hest,

2 **the place of execution** the place of action, i.e., the dining room
with quibble on gallows)   24 **sessions** sittings of a court   25 **pre-
sian** Puritan (Wagner goes on to parody the style of the Puritans)
6 **rector** head of the university   I.iii.s.d. **Enter . . . Devils** (they are
visible to Faustus; perhaps they enter through a trapdoor and climb
to the upper playing area, as implied in V.ii.s.d.)   2 **Orion** constella-
tion appearing at the beginning of winter, associated with rain
welkin sky

Seeing thou hast prayed and sacrificed to them.
Within this circle° is Jehovah's name
Forward and backward anagrammatized,
10   Th' abbreviated names of holy saints,
Figures of every adjunct to° the heavens,
And characters of signs and erring stars,°
By which the spirits are enforced to rise:
Then fear not, Faustus, to be resolute
15   And try the utmost magic can perform.   *Thunder.*
Sint mihi dei Acherontis propitii! Valeat numen
triplex Iehovae! Ignei, aerii, aquatici, spiritus, sal-
vete! Orientis princeps, Belzebub inferni ardentis
monarcha, et Demogorgon, propitiamus vos ut ap-
20   *pareat et surgat Mephostophilis! Quid tu moraris?*
Per Iehovam, Gehennam, et consecratam aquam
quam nunc spargo, signumque crucis quod nunc
facio, et per vota nostra, ipse nunc surgat nobis
dicatus Mephostophilis!°

Enter a Devil.°

25   I charge thee to return and change thy shape,
Thou art too ugly to attend on me.
Go, and return an old Franciscan friar:
That holy shape becomes a devil best.   *Exit Devil.*
I see there's virtue in my heavenly words.
30   Who would not be proficient in this art?

---

8 circle circle the conjuror draws around him on the ground, to call
the spirits and to protect himself from them   **11 adjunct to** heavenly body fixed to   **12 signs and erring stars** signs of the Zodiac and
planets   **16–24 Sint . . . Mephostophilis** may the gods of the lower
region be favorable to me. Away with the trinity of Jehovah. Hail,
spirits of fire, air, water. Prince of the east, Belzebub monarch of
burning hell, and Demogorgon, we pray to you that Mephostophilis
may appear and rise. Why do you delay? By Jehovah, Gehenna, and
the holy water which now I sprinkle, and the sign of the cross which
now I make, and by our vows, may Mephostophilis himself now rise
to serve us (Latin)   **24 s.d. Devil** (the word "dragon" oddly appears,
after "surgat Mephostophilis," in the preceding conjuration. It makes
no sense in the sentence, and it has therefore been omitted from the
present text, but perhaps it indicates that a dragon briefly appears
at that point, or perhaps the devil referred to in the present stage
direction is disguised as a dragon)

How pliant is this Mephostophilis,
Full of obedience and humility,
Such is the force of magic and my spells.

Enter Mephostophilis.

Mephostophilis. Now Faustus, what wouldst thou have
    me do?

Faustus. I charge thee wait upon me whilst I live   35
    To do whatever Faustus shall command,
    Be it to make the moon drop from her sphere
    Or the ocean to overwhelm the world.

Mephostophilis. I am a servant to great Lucifer
    And may not follow thee without his leave.   40
    No more than he commands must we perform.

Faustus. Did not he charge thee to appear to me?

Mephostophilis. No, I came now hither of mine own
    accord.

Faustus. Did not my conjuring raise thee? Speak.

Mephostophilis. That was the cause, but yet *per acci-
    dens:*°   45
    For when we hear one rack° the name of God,
    Abjure the Scriptures and his savior Christ,
    We fly in hope to get his glorious° soul.
    Nor will we come unless he use such means
    Whereby he is in danger to be damned.   50
    Therefore the shortest cut for conjuring
    Is stoutly to abjure the Trinity
    And pray devoutly to the prince of hell.

Faustus. So Faustus hath already done, and holds this
    principle,
    There is no chief but only Belzebub: 55
    To whom Faustus doth dedicate himself.
    This word "damnation" terrifies not me

_____

45 **per accidens** the immediate (but not ultimate) cause (Latin)   46
rack torture   48 **glorious** (1) splendid (2) presumptuous

For I confound hell in Elysium:°
My ghost° be with the old° philosophers!
60 But leaving these vain trifles of men's souls,
Tell me, what is that Lucifer thy lord?

Mephostophilis. Arch-regent and commander of al
spirits.°

Faustus. Was not that Lucifer an angel once?

Mephostophilis. Yes Faustus, and most dearly loved
of God.

65 *Faustus.* How comes it then that he is prince of devils?

Mephostophilis. O, by aspiring pride and insolence
For which God threw him from the face of heaven

Faustus. And what are you that live with Lucifer?

Mephostophilis. Unhappy spirits that fell with Lucifer
70 Conspired against our God with Lucifer,
And are forever damned with Lucifer.

Faustus. Where are you damned?

Mephostophilis. In hell.

Faustus. How comes it then that thou art out of hell?

75 *Mephostophilis.* Why this is hell, nor am I out of it
Think'st thou that I who saw the face of God
And tasted the eternal joys of heaven
Am not tormented with ten thousand hells
In being deprived of everlasting bliss?
80 O Faustus, leave these frivolous demands
Which strikes° a terror to my fainting soul!

Faustus. What, is great Mephostophilis so passionate
For being deprivèd of the joys of heaven?
Learn thou of Faustus manly fortitude

---

58 **confound hell in Elysium** do not distinguish between hell and
Elysium   59 **ghost** spirit   59 **old** i.e., pre-Christian   62 **spirits** devil
81 **strikes** (it is not unusual to have a plural subject—especially when
it has a collective force—take a verb ending in -s)   82 **passionate**
emotional

And scorn those joys thou never shalt possess.   *85*
Go bear these tidings to great Lucifer:
Seeing Faustus hath incurred eternal death
By desperate thoughts against Jove's deity,
Say he surrenders up to him his soul
So he will spare him four and twenty years,   *90*
Letting him live in all voluptuousness,
Having thee ever to attend on me,
To give me whatsoever I shall ask,
To tell me whatsoever I demand,
To slay mine enemies and to aid my friends   *95*
And always be obedient to my will.
Go and return to mighty Lucifer
And meet me in my study at midnight,
And then resolve° me of thy master's mind.

Mephostophilis. I will, Faustus.   *100*

Faustus. Had I as many souls as there be stars
I'd give them all for Mephostophilis.
By him I'll be great emperor of the world,
And make a bridge through° the moving air
To pass the ocean with a band of men;   *105*
I'll join the hills that bind the Afric shore
And make that country continent to° Spain,
And both contributary to my crown;
The Emperor shall not live but by my leave,
Nor any potentate of Germany.   *110*
Now that I have obtained what I desired
I'll live in speculation° of this art
Till Mephostophilis return again.   *Exit.*
                         [*Exeunt Lucifer and Devils.*]

[I.iv] *Enter Wagner and [Robin] the Clown.*°

Wagner. Come hither, sirrah boy.

Robin. Boy! O, disgrace to my person! Zounds,° boy
   in your face! You have seen many boys with such
   pickadevants,° I am sure.

5   *Wagner.* Sirrah, hast thou no comings in?°

Robin. Yes, and goings out too, you may see sir.

Wagner. Alas, poor slave! See how poverty jests in his
   nakedness. I know the villain's out of service, and
   so hungry that I know he would give his soul to
10   the devil for a shoulder of mutton, though it were
   blood-raw.

Robin. Not so, neither! I had need to have it well
   roasted, and good sauce to it, if I pay so dear, I
   can tell you.

15   *Wagner.* Sirrah, wilt thou be my man and wait on me?
   And I will make thee go like *Qui mihi discipulus.*°

Robin. What, in verse?

Wagner. No, slave, in beaten° silk and stavesacre.°

Robin. Stavesacre? That's good to kill vermin! Then
20   belike, if I serve you I shall be lousy.

Wagner. Why, so thou shalt be, whether thou dost it
   or no; for sirrah, if thou dost not presently bind
   thyself to me for seven years, I'll turn all the lice

I.iv.s.d. **Clown** buffoon   2 **Zounds** by God's wounds   4 **pickade**
vants pointed beards   5 **comings in** income (the Clown then quibbles
on "goings out," i.e., expenses and also holes in his clothes through
which his body pokes)   16 **Qui mihi discipulus** one who is my
disciple, i.e., like the servant of a learned man (the Latin is the
beginning of a poem, familiar to Renaissance schoolboys, on proper
behavior)   18 **beaten** embroidered (leading to the quibble on the
sense "hit")   18 **stavesacre** preparation from seeds of delphinium
used to kill vermin

about thee into familiars° and make them tear thee
in pieces.   25

Robin. Nay sir, you may save yourself a labor, for
they are as familiar with me as if they paid for their
meat and drink, I can tell you.

Wagner. Well sirrah, leave your jesting and take these
guilders.°   30

Robin. Yes marry° sir, and I thank you too.

Wagner. So, now thou art to be at an hour's warning
whensoever and wheresoever the devil shall fetch
thee.

Robin. Here, take your guilders, I'll none of 'em!   35

Wagner. Not I, thou art pressed.° Prepare thyself, for
I will presently raise up two devils to carry thee
away. Banio! Belcher!

Robin. Belcher! And° Belcher come here I'll belch
him. I am not afraid of a devil!   40

Enter two Devils.

Wagner. How now sir, will you serve me now?

Robin. Ay, good Wagner, take away the devil then.

Wagner. Spirits, away! [*Exeunt Devils.*] Now sirrah,
follow me.

Robin. I will sir! But hark you master, will you teach   45
me this conjuring occupation?

Wagner. Ay sirrah, I'll teach thee to turn thyself to a
dog or a cat or a mouse or a rat or anything.

Robin. A dog or a cat or a mouse or a rat? O brave°
Wagner!   50

---

4 **familiars** attendant demons   30 **guilders** Dutch coins   31 **marry**
indeed (a mild oath, from "by the Virgin Mary")   36 **pressed** en-
listed into service   39 **And if**   49 **brave** splendid

Wagner. Villain, call me Master Wagner. And see tha
you walk attentively, and let your right eye be
always diametrally° fixed upon my left heel, tha
thou mayst *quasi vestigiis nostris insistere.*°

55 *Robin.* Well sir, I warrant you.   *Exeunt*

[II.i] *Enter Faustus in his study.*

Faustus. Now, Faustus, must thou needs be damned
Canst thou not be saved!
What boots° it then to think on God or heaven
Away with such vain fancies, and despair—
5   Despair in God and trust in Belzebub!
Now go not backward. Faustus, be resolute!
Why waver'st thou? O something soundeth in mine
ear,
"Abjure this magic, turn to God again."
Ay, and Faustus will turn to God again.
10   To God? He loves thee not;
The god thou serv'st is thine own appetite
Wherein is fixed the love of Belzebub!
To him I'll build an altar and a church
And offer lukewarm blood of newborn babes!

Enter the two Angels.

15 *Bad Angel.* Go forward, Faustus, in that famous art.

Good Angel. Sweet Faustus, leave that execrable art.

Faustus. Contrition, prayer, repentance, what of these?

Good Angel. O, they are means to bring thee unto
heaven.

Bad Angel. Rather illusions, fruits of lunacy,
20   That make men foolish that do use them most.

53 diametrally directly   **54 quasi vestigiis nostris insistere** as if to
step in our footsteps   **II.i.3 boots** avails

Good Angel. Sweet Faustus, think of heaven and
  heavenly things.

Bad Angel. No Faustus, think of honor and of wealth.
                                        Exeunt Angels.

Faustus. Wealth!
  Why, the signory of Emden° shall be mine!
  When Mephostophilis shall stand by me   25
  What power can hurt me? Faustus, thou art safe.
  Cast no more doubts! Mephostophilis, come,
  And bring glad tidings from great Lucifer.
  Is't not midnight? Come Mephostophilis,
  Veni, veni, Mephostophile!°   30

                Enter Mephostophilis.

Now tell me, what saith Lucifer thy lord?

Mephostophilis. That I shall wait on Faustus whilst
    he lives,
  So he will buy my service with his soul.

Faustus. Already Faustus hath hazarded that for thee.

Mephostophilis. But now thou must bequeath it
    solemnly   35
  And write a deed of gift with thine own blood,
  For that security craves Lucifer.
  If thou deny it I must back to hell.

Faustus. Stay Mephostophilis and tell me
  What good will my soul do thy lord?   40

Mephostophilis. Enlarge his kingdom.

Faustus. Is that the reason why he tempts us thus?

Mephostophilis. *Solamen miseris socios habuisse
    doloris.°*

---

4 signory of Emden lordship of the rich German port at the mouth
f the Ems   30 Veni, veni, Mephostophile come, come, Mephos-
ophilis (Latin)   43 Solamen . . . doloris misery loves company
Latin)

Faustus. Why, have you any pain that torture other?

Mephostophilis. As great as have the human souls of
45   men.
    But tell me, Faustus, shall I have thy soul—
    And I will be thy slave and wait on thee
    And give thee more than thou hast wit to ask?

Faustus. Ay Mephostophilis, I'll give it him.°

Mephostophilis. Then, Faustus, stab thy arm cou-
50   rageously
    And bind thy soul that at some certain day
    Great Lucifer may claim it as his own.
    And then be thou as great as Lucifer!

Faustus. Lo, Mephostophilis, for love of thee
55   Faustus hath cut his arm and with his proper° blood
    Assures° his soul to be great Lucifer's,
    Chief lord and regent of perpetual night.
    View here this blood that trickles from mine arm
    And let it be propitious for my wish.

60 *Mephostophilis.* But Faustus,
    Write it in manner of a deed of gift.

Faustus. Ay so I do—But Mephostophilis,
    My blood congeals and I can write no more.

Mephostophilis. I'll fetch thee fire to dissolve it
    straight.   *Exit*

65 *Faustus.* What might the staying of my blood portend?
    Is it unwilling I should write this bill?°
    Why streams it not that I may write afresh:
    "Faustus gives to thee his soul"? O there it stayed
    Why shouldst thou not? Is not thy soul thine own?
70   Then write again: "Faustus gives to thee his soul."

    Enter Mephostophilis with the chafer° of fire.

44 other others   49 him i.e., to Lucifer   55 proper own   56 As-
sures conveys by contract   66 bill contract   70 s.d. chafer portable
grate

Mephostophilis. See Faustus, here is fire. Set it° on.

Faustus. So, now the blood begins to clear again.
　　Now will I make an end immediately.

Mephostophilis. [*aside*] What will not I do to obtain
　　his soul!

Faustus. Consummatum est!° This bill is ended:　　　75
　　And Faustus hath bequeathed his soul to Lucifer.
　　—But what is this inscription on mine arm?
　　Homo fuge!° Whither should I fly?
　　If unto God, He'll throw me down to hell.
　　My senses are deceived, here's nothing writ.　　　80
　　O yes, I see it plain! Even here is writ
　　Homo fuge! Yet shall not Faustus fly!

Mephostophilis. [*aside*] I'll fetch him somewhat to
　　delight his mind.　　　　　　　　　　　　　*Exit.*

　　*Enter Devils giving crowns and rich apparel to
　　　　Faustus. They dance and then depart.*

　　　　　　Enter Mephostophilis.

Faustus. What means this show? Speak, Mepho-
　　stophilis.

Mephostophilis. Nothing Faustus, but to delight thy
　　mind　　　　　　　　　　　　　　　　　　　85
　　And let thee see what magic can perform.

Faustus. But may I raise such spirits when I please?

Mephostophilis. Ay Faustus, and do greater things
　　than these.

Faustus. Then, Mephostophilis, receive this scroll,
　　A deed of gift of body and of soul:　　　　　　90

---

71 **It** i.e., the receptacle containing the congealed blood　　75 **Consummatum est** it is finished (Latin; a blasphemous repetition of
Christ's words on the Cross; see John 19:30)　　78 **Homo fuge** fly,
man (Latin)

But yet conditionally that thou perform
All covenants and articles between us both.

Mephostophilis. Faustus, I swear by hell and Lucifer
To effect all promises between us both.

95 *Faustus.* Then hear me read it, Mephostophilis:
"On these conditions following:
First, that Faustus may be a spirit° in form and
substance.
Secondly, that Mephostophilis shall be his servant
100 and be by him commanded.
Thirdly, that Mephostophilis shall do for him and
bring him whatsoever.
Fourthly, that he shall be in his chamber or house
invisible.
105 Lastly, that he shall appear to the said John Faustus
at all times in what form or shape soever he
please:
I, John Faustus of Wittenberg, Doctor, by these
presents, do give both body and soul to Lucifer,
110 prince of the east, and his minister Mephostophilis, and furthermore grant unto them that,
four and twenty years being expired, and these
articles above written being inviolate,° full power
to fetch or carry the said John Faustus, body and
115 soul, flesh, blood, or goods, into their habitation
wheresoever.

By me John Faustus.

Mephostophilis. Speak Faustus, do you deliver this as
your deed?

Faustus. Ay, take it, and the devil give thee good of it!

Mephostophilis. So now Faustus, ask me what thou
120 wilt.

Faustus. First will I question with thee about hell.
Tell me, where is the place that men call hell?

97 **spirit** evil spirit, devil (but to see Faustus as transformed now into
a devil deprived of freedom to repent is to deprive the remainder of
the play of much of its meaning)   113 **inviolate** unviolated

Mephostophilis. Under the heavens.

Faustus. Ay, so are all things else, but whereabouts?

Mephostophilis. Within the bowels of these elements   125
  Where we are tortured and remain forever.
  Hell hath no limits nor is circumscribed
  In one self place, but where we are is hell,
  And where hell is there must we ever be.
  And to be short, when all the world dissolves   130
  And every creature shall be purified
  All places shall be hell that is not heaven!

Faustus. I think hell's a fable.

Mephostophilis. Ay, think so still—till experience
  change thy mind!

Faustus. Why, dost thou think that Faustus shall be
  damned?   135

Mephostophilis. Ay, of necessity, for here's the scroll
  In which thou hast given thy soul to Lucifer.

Faustus. Ay, and body too; but what of that?
  Think'st thou that Faustus is so fond° to imagine
  That after this life there is any pain?   140
  No, these are trifles and mere old wives' tales.

Mephostophilis. But I am an instance to prove the
    contrary,
  For I tell thee I am damned and now in hell!

Faustus. Nay, and this be hell, I'll willingly be
  damned—
  What, sleeping, eating, walking, and disputing?   145
  But leaving this, let me have a wife, the fairest maid
    in Germany, for I am wanton and lascivious and
    cannot live without a wife.

Mephostophilis. Well Faustus, thou shalt have a wife.
    He fetches in a woman Devil [with fireworks].

Faustus. What sight is this?   150

139 fond foolish

Mephostophilis. Now Faustus, wilt thou have a wife?

Faustus. Here's a hot whore indeed! No, I'll no wife.

Mephostophilis. Marriage is but a ceremonial toy,°
                                    [*Exit She-devil.*]
   And if thou lovest me, think no more of it.
155   I'll cull thee out° the fairest courtesans
   And bring them every morning to thy bed.
   She whom thine eye shall like thy heart shall have,
   Were she as chaste as was Penelope,°
   As wise as Saba,° or as beautiful
160   As was bright Lucifer before his fall.
   Here, take this book and peruse it well.
   The iterating° of these lines brings gold;
   The framing° of this circle on the ground
   Brings thunder, whirlwinds, storm, and lightning;
165   Pronounce this thrice devoutly to thyself,
   And men in harness° shall appear to thee,
   Ready to execute what thou command'st.

Faustus. Thanks Mephostophilis for this sweet book.
   This will I keep as chary as my life.   *Exeunt.*°

[II.ii] *Enter Faustus in his study and Mephostophilis.*

Faustus. When I behold the heavens, then I repent
   And curse thee, wicked Mephostophilis,
   Because thou has deprived me of those joys.

Mephostophilis. 'Twas thine own seeking Faustus,
   thank thyself.
5   But think'st thou heaven is such a glorious thing?

---

153 **toy** trifle   155 **cull thee out** select for you   158 **Penelope** wife
of Ulysses, famed for her fidelity   159 **Saba** the Queen of Sheba
162 **iterating** repetition   163 **framing** drawing   166 **harness** armor
169s.d. **Exeunt** (a scene following this stage direction has probably
been lost. Earlier Wagner hired the Clown; later the Clown is an
ostler possessed of one of Faustus' conjuring books. Possibly, then,
the lost scene was a comic one, showing the Clown stealing a book
and departing)

I tell thee, Faustus, it is not half so fair
As thou or any man that breathe on earth.

Faustus. How prov'st thou that?

Mephostophilis. 'Twas made for man; then he's more
excellent.

Faustus. If heaven was made for man, 'twas made for
me!   10
I will renounce this magic and repent.

Enter the two Angels.

Good Angel. Faustus, repent: yet° God will pity thee!

Bad Angel. Thou art a spirit: God cannot pity thee!

Faustus. Who buzzeth in mine ears I am a spirit?
Be I a devil, yet God may pity me—   15
Yea, God will pity me if I repent.

Bad Angel. Ay, but Faustus never shall repent.
                                        Exit Angels.

Faustus. My heart is hardened, I cannot repent.
Scarce can I name salvation, faith, or heaven,
Swords, poison, halters, and envenomed steel   20
Are laid before me to dispatch myself.
And long ere this I should have done the deed
Had not sweet pleasure conquered deep despair.
Have not I made blind Homer sing to me
Of Alexander's love and Oenon's° death?   25
And hath not he° that built the walls of Thebes
With ravishing sound of his melodious harp
Made music with my Mephostophilis?
Why should I die then or basely despair?
I am resolved, Faustus shall not repent!   30

I.ii.12 yet still, even now   25 Alexander . . . Oenone Paris, also
called Alexander, was Oenone's lover, but he later deserted her for
Helen of Troy, causing the Trojan War, the subject of Homer's
Iliad   26 he Amphion, whose music charmed stones to form the
walls of Thebes

Come Mephostophilis, let us dispute again
And reason of divine astrology.
Speak, are there many spheres above the moon?
Are all celestial bodies but one globe
35   As is the substance of this centric° earth?

Mephostophilis. As are the elements, such° are th
    heavens,
Even from the moon unto the empyreal orb
Mutually folded in each others' spheres,
And jointly move upon one axle-tree,
40   Whose terminè° is termed the world's wide pole.
Nor are the names of Saturn, Mars, or Jupiter
Feigned but are erring stars.°

Faustus. But have they all one motion,
Both *situ et tempore?*°

45 *Mephostophilis.* All move from east to west in fou
and twenty hours upon the poles of the world bu
differ in their motions upon the poles of the zodiac

Faustus. These slender questions Wagner can decide
Hath Mephostophilis no greater skill?
50   Who knows not the double motion of the planets?
That the first is finished in a natural day.°
The second thus: Saturn in thirty years;
Jupiter in twelve; Mars in four; the sun, Venus, and
    Mercury in a year; the moon in twenty-eigh
55   days. These are freshmen's suppositions.° Bu
tell me, hath every sphere a dominion or *intelligentia?*°

Mephostophilis. Ay.

Faustus. How many heavens or spheres are there?

---

35 **centric** central   36 **such** i.e., separate but combined; the idea i
that the heavenly bodies are separate but their spheres are con
centric ("folded"), and all—from the nearest (the moon) to the
farthest ("the empyreal orb" or empyrean)—move on one axletree
40 **terminè** end, extremity   42 **erring stars** planets   44 **situ et tempore** in place and in time   51 **natural day** twenty-four hours   5
suppositions premises   56 **dominion or intelligentia** governing ange
or intelligence (believed to impart motion to the sphere)

Mephostophilis. Nine: the seven planets, the firma-   60
ment, and the empyreal heaven.

Faustus. But is there not *coelum igneum et crystallinum?*°

Mephostophilis. No Faustus, they be but fables.

Faustus. Resolve me then in this one question. Why   65
are not conjunctions, oppositions, aspects, eclipses
all at one time,° but in some years we have more,
in some less?

*Mephostophilis. Per inaqualem motum respectu
totius.*°   70

Faustus. Well, I am answered. Now tell me, who made
the world?

Mephostophilis. I will not.

Faustus. Sweet Mephostophilis, tell me.

Mephostophilis. Move° me not, Faustus!   75

Faustus. Villain, have not I bound thee to tell me
anything?

Mephostophilis. Ay, that is not against our kingdom.
This is. Thou art damned. Think thou of hell!

Faustus. Think, Faustus, upon God, that made the
world.   80

Mephostophilis. Remember this!   *Exit.*

Faustus. Ay, go accursèd spirit to ugly hell!
'Tis thou hast damned distressèd Faustus' soul.—
Is't not too late?

Enter the two Angels.

Bad Angel. Too late.   85

2–63 **coelum igneum et crystallinum** a heaven of fire and a crystal-
ne sphere (Latin)   67 **at one time** i.e., at regular intervals   69–70 **Per
. . totius** because of unequal speed within the system (Latin)   75
Move anger

Good Angel. Never too late, if Faustus will repen

Bad Angel. If thou repent, devils will tear thee i
pieces.

Good Angel. Repent, and they shall never raze° th
skin.   *Exeunt Angel*

Faustus. O Christ, my savior, my savior!
90   Help to save distressèd Faustus' soul.

Enter Lucifer, Belzebub, and Mephostophilis.

Lucifer. Christ cannot save thy soul, for He is jus
There's none but I have interest in° the same.

Faustus. O, what art thou that look'st so terribly?

Lucifer. I am Lucifer
95   And this is my companion prince in hell.

Faustus. O Faustus, they are come to fetch thy sou

Belzebub. We are come to tell thee thou dost injure us

Lucifer. Thou call'st on Christ contrary to th
promise.

Belzebub. Thou should'st not think on God.

Lucifer.   Think on the Devi
100 *Belzebub.* And his dam° too.

Faustus. Nor will Faustus henceforth. Pardon him fo
this,
And Faustus vows never to look to heaven!
Never to name God or to pray to Him,
To burn His Scriptures, slay His ministers,
105 And make my spirits pull His churches down.

Lucifer. So shalt thou show thyself an obedien
servant,
And we will highly gratify thee for it.

88 **raze** scratch   92 **interest in** legal claim on   100 **dam** mother

Belzebub. Faustus, we are come from hell in person
to show thee some pastime. Sit down and thou shalt
behold the Seven Deadly Sins° appear to thee in   *110*
their own proper shapes and likeness.

Faustus. That sight will be as pleasant to me as Paradise was to Adam the first day of his creation.

Lucifer. Talk not of Paradise or creation but mark
the show. Go Mephostophilis, fetch them in.   *115*

Enter the Seven Deadly Sins [led by a Piper].

Belzebub. Now Faustus, question them of their names
and dispositions.

Faustus. That shall I soon. What art thou, the first?

Pride. I am Pride. I disdain to have any parents. I
am like to Ovid's flea,° I can creep into every cor-   *120*
ner of a wench: sometimes, like a periwig I sit upon
her brow; next, like a necklace I hang about her
neck; then, like a fan of feathers I kiss her; and
then, turning myself to a wrought smock,° do what
I list—But fie, what a smell is here! I'll not speak a   *125*
word more for a king's ransom unless the ground be
perfumed and covered with cloth of arras.°

Faustus. Thou art a proud knave indeed. What art
thou, the second?

Covetousness. I am Covetousness, begotten of an old   *130*
churl in a leather bag;° and might I now obtain
my wish, this house, you and all, should turn to
gold that I might lock you safe into my chest. O
my sweet gold!

Faustus. And what art thou, the third?   *135*

---

10 **Seven Deadly Sins** (so called because they cause spiritual death;
they are Pride, Covetousness, Envy, Wrath, Gluttony, Sloth,
lechery)   120 **Ovid's flea** flea in *Carmen de pulce,* a lewd poem
mistakenly attributed to Ovid   124 **wrought smock** decorated petti-
coat   127 **cloth of arras** Flemish cloth used for tapestries   131
leather bag moneybag (?)

Envy. I am Envy, begotten of a chimney-sweeper and
an oyster-wife.° I cannot read and therefore wish
all books burned. I am lean with seeing others eat.
O, that there would come a famine over all the
140   world that all might die and I live alone! Then thou
shouldst see how fat I'd be. But must thou sit and
I stand? Come down, with a vengeance!

Faustus. Out, envious wretch! But what art thou, the
fourth?

145   *Wrath.* I am Wrath. I had neither father nor mother.
I leapt out of a lion's mouth when I was scarce an
hour old and ever since have run up and down the
world with these case° of rapiers, wounding myself
when I could get none to fight withal. I was born
150   in hell! And look to it, for some of you shall be
my father.

Faustus. And what art thou, the fifth?

Gluttony. I am Gluttony. My parents are all dead, and
the devil a penny they have left me, but a small
155   pension: and that buys me thirty meals a day and
ten bevers,° a small trifle to suffice nature. I come
of a royal pedigree. My father was a gammon° of
bacon, and my mother was a hogshead of claret
wine. My godfathers were these: Peter Pickled
160   herring and Martin Martlemas-beef.° But my god-
mother, O, she was an ancient gentlewoman: her
name was Margery March-beer.° Now Faustus,
thou hast heard all my progeny,° wilt thou bid me
to supper?

165   *Faustus.* Not I.

Gluttony. Then the devil choke thee!

136–37 **chimney-sweeper . . . oyster-wife** i.e., dirty and smell
148 **these case** this pair   156 **bevers** snacks (literally drinks)   15
gammon haunch   160 **Martlemas-beef** cattle slaughtered at Martin
mas (11 November) and salted for winter consumption   162 **March**
beer strong beer brewed in March   163 **progeny** ancestry

Faustus. Choke thyself, glutton! What art thou, the
    sixth?

Sloth. Heigh-ho!° I am Sloth. I was begotten on a
    sunny bank. Heigh-ho, I'll not speak a word more   *170*
    for a king's ransom.

Faustus. And what are you, Mistress Minx, the
    seventh and last?

Lechery. Who, I, I sir? I am one that loves an inch
    of raw mutton° better than an ell of fried stockfish,°   *175*
    and the first letter of my name begins with Lechery.

Lucifer. Away to hell, away! On, piper!
                            Exeunt the Seven Sins.

Faustus. O, how this sight doth delight my soul!

Lucifer. But Faustus, in hell is all manner of delight.

Faustus. O, might I see hell and return again safe,   *180*
    how happy were I then!

Lucifer. Faustus, thou shalt. At midnight I will send
        for thee.
    Meanwhile peruse this book and view it thoroughly,
    And thou shalt turn thyself into what shape thou
        wilt.

Faustus. Thanks mighty Lucifer.   *185*
    This will I keep as chary° as my life.

Lucifer. Now Faustus, farewell.

Faustus. Farewell great Lucifer. Come Mephostoph-
    ilis.   *Exeunt omnes several° ways.*

---

169 **Heigh-ho** (a yawn or tired greeting)   174–75 **inch of raw mutton**
., penis ("mutton" in a bawdy sense commonly alludes to a
rostitute, but since here the speaker is a woman, the allusion must
e to a male)   175 **an ell of . . . stockfish** forty-five inches of dried
d   186 **chary** carefully   188 s.d. **several** various

[II.iii] *Enter [Robin] the Clown.*

Robin. What, Dick, look to the horses there till
    come again! I have gotten one of Doctor Faustu:
    conjuring books, and now we'll have such knaver
    as't passes.

Enter Dick.

5 *Dick.* What, Robin, you must come away and wal
    the horses.

Robin. I walk the horses? I scorn't, 'faith. I have othe
    matters in hand. Let the horses walk themselve
    an° they will. [*Reading*] A *per se°*—a; t, h, e—the
10   o *per se*—o; deny orgon—gorgon.° Keep furthe
    from me, O thou illiterate and unlearned hostle:

Dick. 'Snails,° what hast thou got there, a book? Why
    thou canst not tell ne'er a word on't.

Robin. That thou shalt see presently. Keep out of th
15   circle, I say, lest I send you into the hostry° with
    vengeance.

Dick. That's like, 'faith! You had best leave you
    foolery, for an my master come, he'll conjure yo
    'faith.

20 *Robin.* My master conjure me? I'll tell thee what. A
    my master come here, I'll clap as fair a pair c
    horns° on's head as e'er thou sawest in thy lif

Dick. Thou need'st not do that, for my mistress hat
    done it.

II.iii. 9 an if   9 per se by itself (Latin; the idea is, "A by itself spel'
A")   10 deny orgon—gorgon (Robin is trying to read the nam
"Demogorgon")   12 'Snails by God's nails   15 hostry hostelry, in
22 horns (as the next speech indicates, horns were said to ador
the head of a man whose wife was unfaithful)

Robin. Ay, there be of us here that have waded as   25
    deep into matters as other men—if they were dis-
    posed to talk.

Dick. A plague take you! I thought you did not sneak
    up and down after her for nothing. But I prithee
    tell me in good sadness° Robin, is that a conjuring   30
    book?

Robin. Do but speak what thou't have me to do, and
    I'll do't. If thou't dance naked, put off thy clothes,
    and I'll conjure thee about presently. Or if thou't
    go but to the tavern with me, I'll give thee white   35
    wine, red wine, claret wine, sack,° muscadine,
    malmsey, and whippincrust°—hold-belly-hold. And
    we'll not pay one penny for it.

Dick. O brave! Prithee let's to it presently, for I am
    as dry as a dog.   40

Robin. Come then, let's away.   *Exeunt.*

[III] *Enter the Chorus.*

Learnèd Faustus,
To find the secrets of astronomy
Graven in the book of Jove's high firmament,
Did mount him up to scale Olympus' top:
Where, sitting in a chariot burning bright   5
Drawn by the strength of yokèd dragons' necks,
He views the clouds, the planets, and the stars,
The tropics, zones,° and quarters of the sky,
From the bright circle° of the hornèd moon
Even to the height of *primum mobile:*°   10
And whirling round with this circumference
Within the concave compass of the pole,
From east to west his dragons swiftly glide

30 in good sadness seriously   36 sack sherry   37 whippincrust il-
iterate pronunciation of "hippocras," a spiced wine   III Chorus
8 zones segments of the sky   9 circle orbit   10 primum mobile the
outermost sphere, the empyrean

And in eight days did bring him home again.
15 Not long he stayed within his quiet house
To rest his bones after his weary toil
But new exploits do hale him out again.
And mounted then upon a dragon's back,
That with his wings did part the subtle air,
20 He now is gone to prove cosmography,°
That measures coasts and kingdoms of the earth,
And as I guess will first arrive at Rome
To see the Pope and manner of his court
And take some part of holy Peter's feast,
25 The which this day is highly solemnized.   *Exit.*

[III.i] *Enter Faustus and Mephostophilis.*

Faustus. Having now, my good Mephostophilis,
Passed with delight the stately town of Trier,°
Environed round with airy mountain tops,
With walls of flint, and deep-entrenchèd lakes,°
5 Not to be won by any conquering prince:
From Paris next, coasting the realm of France,
We saw the river Main fall into Rhine,
Whose banks are set with groves of fruitful vines:
Then up to Naples, rich Campania,
10 Whose buildings fair and gorgeous to the eye,
The streets straight forth and paved with finest
    brick,
Quarters the town in four equivalents.
There saw we learnèd Maro's° golden tomb,
The way he cut an English mile in length
15 Through° a rock of stone in one night's space.
From thence to Venice, Padua, and the rest,
In one of which a sumptuous temple stands
That threats the stars with her aspiring top,
Whose frame is paved with sundry colored stones

---

20 **prove cosmography** test maps, i.e., explore the universe   III.i.2
Trier German city on the Moselle, also known as Trèves   4 **deep-
entrenchèd lakes** moats   13 **Maro** Vergil (Publius Vergilius Maro,
70–19 B.C.)   15 **Through** (pronounced "thorough")

And roofed aloft with curious work in gold.   20
Thus hitherto hath Faustus spent his time.
But tell me now, what resting-place is this?
Hast thou, as erst I did command,
Conducted me within the walls of Rome?

Mephostophilis. I have, my Faustus, and for proof
    thereof   25
This is the goodly palace of the Pope,
And 'cause we are no common guests
I choose his privy chamber for our use.

Faustus. I hope his Holiness will bid us welcome.

Mephostophilis. All's one, for we'll be bold with his
    venison.   30
But now my Faustus, that thou may'st perceive
What Rome contains for to delight thine eyes,
Know that this city stands upon seven hills
That underprop the groundwork of the same:
Just through the midst runs flowing Tiber's stream   35
With winding banks that cut it in two parts,
Over the which four stately bridges lean°
That make safe passage to each part of Rome.
Upon the bridge called Ponte Angelo
Erected is a castle passing strong   40
Where thou shalt see such store of ordinance
As that the double cannons forged of brass
Do match the number of the days contained
Within the compass of one complete year,
Beside the gates and high pyramides°   45
That Julius Caesar brought from Africa.

Faustus. Now, by the kingdoms of infernal rule,
Of Styx, of Acheron, and the fiery lake
Of ever-burning Phlegethon,° I swear
That I do long to see the monuments   50
And situation of bright-splendent Rome.
Come therefore, let's away.

7 lean bend   45 pyramides obelisk (pronounced py - ràm - i - des)
48–49 Styx, Acheron, Phlegethon rivers of the underworld

Mephostophilis. Nay stay my Faustus. I know you'd
    see the Pope
55   And take some part of holy Peter's feast,
    The which this day with high solemnity,
    This day, is held through Rome and Italy
    In honor of the Pope's triumphant victory.

Faustus. Sweet Mephostophilis, thou pleasest me.
    Whilst I am here on earth let me be cloyed
60   With all things that delight the heart of man.
    My four and twenty years of liberty
    I'll spend in pleasure and in dalliance,
    That Faustus' name, whilst this bright frame doth
      stand,
    May be admirèd through the furthest land.

Mephostophilis. 'Tis well said, Faustus, come then
65   stand by me
    And thou shalt see them come immediately.

Faustus. Nay stay, my gentle Mephostophilis,
    And grant me my request, and then I go.
    Thou know'st, within the compass of eight days
70   We viewed the face of heaven, of earth, and hell
    So high our dragons soared into the air
    That looking down the earth appeared to me
    No bigger than my hand in quantity—
    There did we view the kingdoms of the world,
75   And what might please mine eye I there beheld.
    Then in this show let me an actor be
    That this proud Pope may Faustus' cunning see!

Mephostophilis. Let it be so, my Faustus, but first stay
    And view their triumphs° as they pass this way.
80   And then devise what best contents thy mind
    By cunning in thine art to cross the Pope
    Or dash the pride of this solemnity—
    To make his monks and abbots stand like apes
    And point like antics° at his triple crown,

---

79 **triumphs** spectacular displays   84 **antics** grotesque figures, buf-
foons

To beat the beads about the friars' pates,   85
Or clap huge horns upon the cardinals' heads,
Or any villainy thou canst devise—
And I'll perform it, Faustus. Hark, they come!
This day shall make thee be admired° in Rome!

Enter the Cardinals and Bishops, some bearing
crosiers, some the pillars; Monks and Friars singing
their procession; then the Pope and Raymond King of
Hungary, with Bruno° led in chains.

Pope. Cast down our footstool.

Raymond.   Saxon Bruno, stoop,   90
Whilst on thy back his Holiness ascends
Saint Peter's chair and state° pontifical.

Bruno. Proud Lucifer, that state belongs to me—
But thus I fall to Peter, not to thee.

Pope. To me and Peter shalt thou grov'lling lie   95
And crouch before the papal dignity!
Sound trumpets then, for thus Saint Peter's heir
From Bruno's back ascends Saint Peter's chair!

A flourish° while he ascends.

Thus as the gods creep on with feet of wool
Long ere with iron hands they punish men,   100
So shall our sleeping vengeance now arise
And smite with death thy hated enterprise.
Lord Cardinals of France and Padua,
Go forthwith to our holy consistory°
And read amongst the statutes decretal°   105
What by the holy council held at Trent°
The sacred synod° hath decreed for him

89 **admired** wondered at   89s.d. **Raymond King of Hungary . . .**
Bruno (unhistorical figures; Bruno is the emperor's nominee for the
papal throne)   92 **state** throne   98s.d. **flourish** trumpet fanfare
104 **consistory** i.e., meeting-place of the papal consistory or senate
105 **statutes decretal** i.e., ecclesiastical laws   106 **council held at**
Trent (intermittently from 1545 to 1563)   107 **synod** council

That doth assume the papal government
Without election and a true consent.
110   Away, and bring us word with speed!

1 Cardinal. We go my lord.   *Exeunt [two] Cardinals.*

Pope. Lord Raymond—   *[Talks to him apart.]*

Faustus. Go haste thee, gentle Mephostophilis,
Follow the cardinals to the consistory
115   And as they turn their superstitious books
Strike them with sloth and drowsy idleness
And make them sleep so sound that in their shapes
Thyself and I may parley with this Pope,
This proud confronter of the Emperor!
120   —And in despite of all his holiness
Restore this Bruno to his liberty
And bear him to the states of Germany!

Mephostophilis. Faustus, I go.

Faustus. Dispatch it soon.
125   The Pope shall curse that Faustus came to Rome.
             Exit Faustus and Mephostophilis.

Bruno. Pope Adrian, let me have some right of law:
I was elected by the Emperor.

Pope. We will depose the Emperor for that deed
And curse the people that submit to him.
130   Both he and thou shalt stand excommunicate
And interdict from church's privilege
And all society of holy men.
He grows too proud in his authority,
Lifting his lofty head above the clouds,
135   And like a steeple overpeers the church.
But we'll pull down his haughty insolence.
And as Pope Alexander,° our progenitor,°
Trod on the neck of German Frederick,
Adding this golden sentence to our praise:

137 **Pope Alexander** Pope Alexander III (d. 1181) compelled the
Emperor Frederick Barbarossa to kneel before him   137 **progenitor**
predecessor

"That Peter's heirs should tread on emperors   *140*
And walk upon the dreadful adder's back,
Treading the lion and the dragon down,
And fearless spurn the killing basilisk"°—
So will we quell that haughty schismatic
And by authority apostolical   *145*
Depose him from his regal government.

Bruno. Pope Julius swore to princely Sigismond,
For him and the succeeding Popes of Rome,
To hold the emperors their lawful lords.

Pope. Pope Julius did abuse the church's rites   *150*
And therefore none of his decrees can stand.
Is not all power on earth bestowed on us?
And therefore though we would, we cannot err.
Behold this silver belt whereto is fixed
Seven golden keys fast sealed with seven seals   *155*
In token of our sevenfold power from heaven
To bind or loose, lock fast, condemn, or judge,
Resign° or seal, or whatso pleaseth us.
Then he and thou and all the world shall stoop—
Or be assurèd of our dreadful curse   *160*
To light as heavy as the pains of hell.

Enter Faustus and Mephostophilis like the cardinals.

Mephostophilis. [*aside*] Now tell me Faustus, are we
    not fitted well?

Faustus. [*aside*] Yes Mephostophilis, and two such
    cardinals
Ne'er served a holy Pope as we shall do.
But whilst they sleep within the consistory   *165*
Let us salute his reverend Fatherhood.

Raymond. Behold my lord, the cardinals are returned.

Pope. Welcome grave fathers, answer presently,°
What have our holy council there decreed

143 **basilisk** fabulous monster said to kill with a glance   158 **Resign**
unseal   168 **presently** immediately

170   Concerning Bruno and the Emperor
      In quittance of° their late conspiracy
      Against our state and papal dignity?

      Faustus. Most sacred patron of the church of Rome,
      By full consent of all the synod
175   Of priests and prelates it is thus decreed:
      That Bruno and the German Emperor
      Be held as lollards° and bold schismatics
      And proud disturbers of the church's peace.
      And if that Bruno by his own assent,
180   Without enforcement of the German peers,
      Did seek to wear the triple diadem
      And by your death to climb Saint Peter's chair,
      The statutes decretal have thus decreed:
      He shall be straight condemned of heresy
185   And on a pile of fagots burnt to death.

      Pope. It is enough. Here, take him to your charge
      And bear him straight to Ponte Angelo
      And in the strongest tower enclose him fast.
      Tomorrow, sitting in our consistory
190   With all our college of grave cardinals
      We will determine of his life or death.
      Here, take his triple crown along with you
      And leave it in the church's treasury.
      Make haste again,° my good lord cardinals,
195   And take our blessing apostolical.

      Mephostophilis. [*aside*] So, so! Was never devil thus
          blessed before.

      Faustus. [*aside*] Away sweet Mephostophilis, be gone!
      The cardinals will be plagued for this anon.
          Exeunt Faustus and Mephostophilis [*with Bruno*].

      Pope. Go presently and bring a banquet forth,
200   That we may solemnize Saint Peter's feast
      And with Lord Raymond, King of Hungary,
      Drink to our late and happy victory.   *Exeunt.*

---

171 **quittance of** requital for   177 **lollards** heretics   194 **again** i.e.,
to return

[III.ii] *A sennet° while the banquet is brought in, and*
then enter Faustus and Mephostophilis in their
own shapes.

Mephostophilis. Now Faustus, come prepare thyself
    for mirth.
  The sleepy cardinals are hard at hand
  To censure Bruno, that is posted hence,
  And on a proud-paced steed as swift as thought
  Flies o'er the Alps to fruitful Germany,   *5*
  There to salute the woeful Emperor.

Faustus. The Pope will curse them for their sloth today
  That slept both Bruno and his crown away.
  But now, that Faustus may delight his mind
  And by their folly make some merriment,   *10*
  Sweet Mephostophilis, so charm me here
  That I may walk invisible to all
  And do whate'er I please unseen of any.

Mephostophilis. Faustus, thou shalt. Then kneel down
    presently,
      Whilst on thy head I lay my hand   *15*
      And charm thee with this magic wand.
      First wear this girdle, then appear
      Invisible to all are here:
      The planets seven, the gloomy air,
      Hell, and the Furies' forkèd hair,°   *20*
      Pluto's blue fire, and Hecat's° tree
      With magic spells so compass thee
      That no eye may thy body see.
  So Faustus, now for all their holiness,
  Do what thou wilt, thou shalt not be discerned.   *25*

III.ii.s.d. **sennet** set of notes played on a trumpet signaling an ap-
proach or a departure   20 **Furies' forkèd hair** (the hair of the Furies
consisted of snakes, whose forked tongues may be implied here)
21 **Hecat** Hecate, goddess of magic (possibly her "tree" is the
gallows-tree, but possibly "tree" is a slip for "three," Hecate being
the triple goddess of heaven, earth, and hell)

Faustus. Thanks Mephostophilis. Now friars, take
     heed
   Lest Faustus make your shaven crowns to bleed.

Mephostophilis. Faustus, no more. See where the
     cardinals come.

*Enter Pope [and Friars] and all the Lords [with King
Raymond and the Archbishop of Rheims]. Enter the
[two] Cardinals with a book.*

Pope. Welcome lord cardinals. Come, sit down.
30   Lord Raymond, take your seat. Friars, attend,
       And see that all things be in readiness
       As best beseems this solemn festival.

1 Cardinal. First may it please your sacred Holiness
       To view the sentence of the reverend synod
35   Concerning Bruno and the Emperor.

Pope. What needs this question? Did I not tell you
       Tomorrow we would sit i' th' consistory
       And there determine of his punishment?
       You brought us word, even now, it was decreed
40   That Bruno and the cursèd Emperor
       Were by the holy council both condemned
       For loathèd lollards and base schismatics.
       Then wherefore would you have me view that
         book?

1 Cardinal. Your Grace mistakes. You gave us no
     such charge.

45 *Raymond.* Deny it not; we all are witnesses
       That Bruno here was late delivered you
       With his rich triple crown to be reserved
       And put into the church's treasury.

Both Cardinals. By holy Paul we saw them not.

50 *Pope.* By Peter you shall die
       Unless you bring them forth immediately.

Hale them to prison, lade their limbs with gyves.°
False prelates, for this hateful treachery
Cursed be your souls to hellish misery.
    [Exeunt Attendants with two Cardinals.]

Faustus. So, they are safe. Now Faustus, to the feast.   55
The Pope had never such a frolic guest.

Pope. Lord Archbishop of Rheims, sit down with us.

Archbishop. I thank your Holiness.

Faustus. Fall to,° the devil choke you an you spare!

Pope. Who's that spoke? Friars, look about.   60
Lord Raymond, pray fall to. I am beholding
To the Bishop of Milan for this so rare a present.

Faustus. *[aside]* I thank you, sir! *[Snatches the dish.]*

Pope. How now! Who snatched the meat from me?
Villains, why speak you not?   65
My good Lord Archbishop, here's a most dainty
   dish
Was sent me from a cardinal in France.

Faustus. *[aside]* I'll have that too!   *[Snatches the dish.]*

Pope. What lollards do attend our Holiness
That we receive such great indignity!   70
Fetch me some wine.

Faustus. *[aside]* Ay, pray do, for Faustus is adry.

Pope. Lord Raymond, I drink unto your Grace.

Faustus. *[aside]* I pledge your Grace.
    [Snatches the goblet.]

Pope. My wine gone too? Ye lubbers, look about   75
And find the man that doth this villainy,
Or by our sanctitude you all shall die.
I pray, my lords, have patience at this troublesome
   banquet.

52 gyves fetters   59 Fall to set to work (here, as commonly, "start eating")

80 *Archbishop.* Please it your Holiness, I think it be
       some ghost crept out of purgatory, and now is come
       unto your Holiness for his pardon.

    Pope. It may be so:
       Go then, command our priests to sing a dirge
85   To lay the fury of this same troublesome ghost.
                                    [*Exit Attendant.*]

    [*The Pope crosses himself before eating.*]

    Faustus. How now! Must every bit be spicèd with a
       cross?
       Nay then, take that!   [*Strikes the Pope.*]

    Pope. O, I am slain! Help me my lords!
       O come and help to bear my body hence.
90   Damned be this soul forever for this deed.
                        Exeunt the Pope and his train.

    Mephostophilis. Now Faustus, what will you do now?
       For I can tell you, you'll be cursed with bell, book,
       and candle.°

    Faustus. Bell, book, and candle. Candle, book, and
       bell.
95   Forward and backward, to curse Faustus to hell!

    *Enter the Friars, with bell, book, and candle
               for the dirge.*

    1 Friar. Come brethren, let's about our business with
       good devotion.
       Cursèd be he that stole his Holiness' meat from the
       table.
             Maledicat Dominus!°
       Cursèd be he that struck his Holiness a blow on
100   the face.

***

92–93 **bell, book, and candle** implements used in excommunicating
(the bell was tolled, the book closed, the candle extinguished)   99
Maledicat Dominus may the Lord curse him (Latin)

Maledicat Dominus!
                    [*Faustus strikes a Friar.*]
Cursèd be he that took Friar Sandelo a blow on the
    pate.
    Maledicat Dominus!
Cursèd be he that disturbeth our holy dirge.
    Maledicat Dominus!   *105*
Cursèd be he that took away his Holiness' wine.
    Maledicat Dominus!

[*Faustus and Mephostophilis*] *beat the Friars, fling
    fireworks among them and exeunt.*

[III.iii] *Enter* [*Robin the*] *Clown and Dick with a cup.*

Dick. Sirrah Robin, we were best look that your devil
    can answer the stealing of this same cup, for the
    vintner's boy follows us at the hard heels.°

Robin. 'Tis no matter, let him come! An he follow
    us I'll so conjure him as he was never conjured in   *5*
    his life, I warrant him. Let me see the cup.

                    Enter Vintner.

Dick. Here 'tis. Yonder he comes. Now Robin, now
    or never show thy cunning.

Vintner. O, are you here? I am glad I have found you.
    You are a couple of fine companions!° Pray,   *10*
    where's the cup you stole from the tavern?

Robin. How, how! We steal a cup? Take heed what
    you say. We look not like cup-stealers, I can tell
    you.

Vintner. Never deny't, for I know you have it, and   *15*
    I'll search you.

III.iii.3 **at the hard heels** hard at heel, closely   10 **companions** fel-
lows (contemptuous)

Robin. Search me? Ay, and spare not! [*Aside*] Hold
   the cup, Dick.—Come, come. Search me, search
   me.   [*Vintner searches him.*]

20 *Vintner.* Come on sirrah, let me search you now.

Dick. Ay ay, do do. [*Aside*] Hold the cup, Robin.—
   I fear not your searching. We scorn to steal your
   cups, I can tell you.   [*Vintner searches him.*]

Vintner. Never outface me for the matter, for sure the
25   cup is between you two.

Robin. Nay, there you lie! 'Tis beyond us both.°

Vintner. A plague take you. I thought 'twas your
   knavery to take it away. Come, give it me again.

Robin. Ay, much! When, can you tell?° [*Aside*] Dick,
30   make me a circle and stand close at my back and
   stir not for thy life. Vintner, you shall have your
   cup anon. [*Aside*] Say nothing, Dick! O *per se,* o;
   Demogorgon, Belcher, and Mephostophilis!

Enter Mephostophilis. [*Exit Vintner.*]

Mephostophilis. You princely legions of infernal rule,
35   How am I vexèd by these villains' charms!
   From Constantinople have they brought me now
   Only for pleasure of these damnèd slaves.

Robin. By lady sir, you have had a shrewd° journey
   of it. Will it please you to take a shoulder of mutton
40   to supper and a tester° in your purse and go back
   again?

Dick. Ay, I pray you heartily, sir. For we called you
   but in jest, I promise you.

Mephostophilis. To purge the rashness of this cursèd
   deed,

26 **beyond us both** (apparently Robin has managed to place the cup
at some distance from where he now stands)   29 **When, can you tell**
(a scornful reply)   38 **shrewd** bad   40 **tester** sixpence

First be thou turnèd to this ugly shape,   45
For apish° deeds transformèd to an ape.

Robin. O brave! An ape! I pray sir, let me have the
carrying of him about to show some tricks.

Mephostophilis. And so thou shalt. Be thou transformed to a dog and carry him upon thy back.   50
Away, be gone!

Robin. A dog! That's excellent. Let the maids look
well to their porridge-pots, for I'll into the kitchen
presently. Come Dick, come.
                              Exeunt the two Clowns.

Mephostophilis. Now with the flames of ever-burning
fire   55
I'll wing myself and forthwith fly amain
Unto my Faustus, to the Great Turk's court.   *Exit.*

[IV] *Enter Chorus.*

When Faustus had with pleasure ta'en the view
Of rarest things and royal courts of kings,
He stayed his course and so returnèd home,
Where such as bare his absence but with grief,
I mean his friends and nearest companions,   5
Did gratulate° his safety with kind words.
And in their conference° of what befell
Touching his journey through the world and air
They put forth questions of astrology
Which Faustus answered with such learnèd skill   10
As they admired and wondered at his wit.
Now is his fame spread forth in every land.
Amongst the rest the Emperor is one,
Carolus the Fifth,° at whose palace now
Faustus is feasted 'mongst his noblemen.   15
What there he did in trial of his art
I leave untold, your eyes shall see performed. *Exit.*

46 apish (1) foolish (2) imitative IV Chorus   6 gratulate express joy
in   7 conference discussion   14 Carolus the Fifth Charles V (1500–
58), Holy Roman Emperor

[IV.i] *Enter Martino and Frederick at several° doors.*

Martino. What ho, officers, gentlemen!
  Hie to the presence° to attend the Emperor.
  Good Frederick, see the rooms be voided straight,°
  His Majesty is coming to the hall.
5 Go back and see the state° in readiness.

Frederick. But where is Bruno, our elected Pope,
  That on a fury's back came post from Rome?
  Will not his Grace consort° the Emperor?

Martino. O yes, and with him comes the German
      conjurer,
10 The learnèd Faustus, fame of Wittenberg,
  The wonder of the world for magic art:
  And he intends to show great Carolus
  The race of all his stout progenitors
  And bring in presence of his Majesty
15 The royal shapes and warlike semblances
  Of Alexander and his beauteous paramour.°

Frederick. Where is Benvolio?

Martino.   Fast asleep, I warrant you.
  He took his rouse with stoups° of Rhenish wine
  So kindly yesternight to Bruno's health
20 That all this day the sluggard keeps his bed.

Frederick. See, see, his window's ope. We'll call to
  him.

Martino. What ho, Benvolio!

*Enter Benvolio above at a window, in his nightcap,
      buttoning.*

IV.i.s.d. **several** separate   2 **presence** presence-chamber   3 **voided
straight** emptied immediately   5 **state** chair of state, throne   8 **con-
sort** attend   16 **Alexander and his beauteous paramour** Alexander
the Great and his mistress Thaïs   18 **took his rouse with stoups** had
drinking bouts with full goblets

Benvolio. What a devil ail you two?

Martino. Speak softly sir, lest the devil hear you,
For Faustus at the court is late arrived 　　　　　*25*
And at his heels a thousand furies wait
To accomplish whatsoever the doctor please.

Benvolio. What of this?

Martino. Come, leave thy chamber first, and thou
　　shalt see
This conjurer perform such rare exploits 　　　　*30*
Before the Pope° and royal Emperor
As never yet was seen in Germany.

Benvolio. Has not the Pope enough of conjuring yet?
He was upon the devil's back late enough!
And if he be so far in love with him 　　　　　　*35*
I would he would post with him to Rome again.

Frederick. Speak, wilt thou come and see this sport?

Benvolio. 　　　　　　　　　　　　　Not I.

Martino. Wilt thou stand in thy window and see it
　　then?

Benvolio. Ay, and I fall not asleep i' th' meantime.

Martino. The Emperor is at hand, who comes to see 　*40*
What wonders by black spells may compassed be.

Benvolio. Well, go you attend the Emperor. I am
content for this once to thrust my head out at a
window, for they say if a man be drunk overnight
the devil cannot hurt him in the morning. If that 　*45*
be true, I have a charm in my head shall control
him as well as the conjurer, I warrant you.
　　　　　Exit [*Martino with Frederick. Benvolio
　　　　　　　remains at window*].°

31 the Pope i.e., Bruno　47s.d. Benvolio remains at window (because Benvolio does not leave the stage, this scene cannot properly
be said to be ended. But the present edition, following its predecessors
for convenience of reference, begins a new scene)

[IV.ii] *A sennet.° Charles the German Emperor,*
Bruno, [Duke of] Saxony, Faustus, Mephostophilis,
Frederick, Martino, and Attendants.

Emperor. Wonder of men, renowned magician,
    Thrice-learnèd Faustus, welcome to our court.
    This deed of thine in setting Bruno free
    From his and our professèd enemy,
5   Shall add more excellence unto thine art
    Than if by powerful necromantic spells
    Thou could'st command the world's obedience.
    For ever be beloved of Carolus!
    And if this Bruno thou hast late redeemed°
10   In peace possess the triple diadem
    And sit in Peter's chair despite of chance,
    Thou shalt be famous through all Italy
    And honored of the German Emperor.

Faustus. These gracious words, most royal Carolus,
15   Shall make poor Faustus to his utmost power
    Both love and serve the German Emperor
    And lay his life at holy Bruno's feet.
    For proof whereof, if so your Grace be pleased,
    The doctor stands prepared by power of art
20   To cast his magic charms that shall pierce through
    The ebon gates of ever-burning hell,
    And hale the stubborn furies from their caves
    To compass whatsoe'er your Grace commands.

Benvolio. Blood! He speaks terribly. But for all that
25   I do not greatly believe him. He looks as like a
    conjurer as the Pope to a costermonger.°

IV.ii.s.d. **sennet** trumpet fanfare (the absence of a verb in the rest
of the stage direction perhaps indicates that the Emperor and his
party do not enter but rather are "discovered," as Faustus may have
been discovered at the beginning of I.i, if the Chorus drew back a
curtain)   9 **redeemed** freed   26 **costermonger** fruit-seller

Emperor. Then Faustus, as thou late didst promise us,
   We would behold that famous conqueror
   Great Alexander and his paramour
   In their true shapes and state majestical,   30
   That we may wonder at their excellence.

Faustus. Your Majesty shall see them presently.—
   Mephostophilis away,
   And with a solemn noise of trumpets' sound
   Present before this royal Emperor   35
   Great Alexander and his beauteous paramour.

Mephostophilis. Faustus, I will.   [*Exit*.]

Benvolio. Well master doctor, an your devils come
not away quickly, you shall have me asleep presently. Zounds,° I could eat myself for anger to   40
think I have been such an ass all this while to stand
gaping after the devils' governor and can see nothing.

Faustus. I'll make you feel something anon if my art
fail me not!   45
   My lord, I must forewarn your Majesty
   That when my spirits present the royal shapes
   Of Alexander and his paramour,
   Your Grace demand no questions of the King
   But in dumb silence let them come and go.   50

Emperor. Be it as Faustus please; we are content.

Benvolio. Ay ay, and I am content too. And thou
bring Alexander and his paramour before the Emperor, I'll be Actaeon° and turn myself to a stag.

Faustus. [*aside*] And I'll play Diana and send you the   55
horns presently.

Sennet. Enter at one [*door*] *the Emperor Alexander,
at the other Darius.° They meet. Darius is thrown*

40 **Zounds** by God's wounds   54 **Actaeon** legendary hunter who
saw the naked goddess Diana bathing. She transformed him into a
stag, and he was torn to pieces by his own hounds   56s.d. **Darius**
King of Persia, defeated by Alexander in 334 B.C.

down. Alexander kills him, takes off his crown, an
offering to go out, his Paramour meets him. He en
braceth her and sets Darius' crown upon her hea
and coming back both salute the Emperor; who lea
ing his state offers to embrace them, which Faust
seeing suddenly stays him. Then trumpets cease an
music sounds.

My gracious lord, you do forget yourself.
These are but shadows, not substantial.

Emperor. O pardon me, my thoughts are so ravishe
60   With sight of this renownèd Emperor,
That in mine arms I would have compassed° hin
But Faustus, since I may not speak to them,
To satisfy my longing thoughts at full,
Let me this tell thee: I have heard it said
65   That this fair lady whilst she lived on earth,
Had on her neck a little wart or mole.
How may I prove that saying to be true?

Faustus. Your Majesty may boldly go and see.

Emperor. Faustus, I see it plain!
70   And in this sight thou better pleasest me
Than if I gained another monarchy.

Faustus. Away, be gone!   *Exit show*
See, see, my gracious lord, what strange beast i
yon that thrusts his head out at the window!

75 *Emperor.* O wondrous sight! See, Duke of Saxony,
Two spreading horns most strangely fastened
Upon the head of young Benvolio.

Saxony. What, is he asleep or dead?

Faustus. He sleeps my lord, but dreams not of hi
horns.

Emperor. This sport is excellent. We'll call and wak
80   him.
What ho, Benvolio!

61 compassed encompassed, embraced

envolio. A plague upon you! Let me sleep awhile.

mperor. I blame thee not to sleep much, having such a head of thine own.

xony. Look up Benvolio! 'Tis the Emperor calls.   85

envolio. The Emperor! Where? O zounds, my head!

mperor. Nay, and thy horns hold, 'tis no matter for thy head, for that's armed sufficiently.

austus. Why, how now Sir Knight? What, hanged by the horns?° This is most horrible! Fie fie, pull   90
in your head for shame! Let not all the world won-
der at you.

envolio. Zounds doctor, is this your villainy?

austus. Oh, say not so sir: The doctor has no skill,
No art, no cunning to present these lords   95
Or bring before this royal Emperor
The mighty monarch, warlike Alexander.
If Faustus do it, you are straight resolved
In bold Actaeon's shape to turn a stag.
And therefore my lord, so please your Majesty,   100
I'll raise a kennel of hounds shall hunt him so
As all his footmanship shall scarce prevail
To keep his carcass from their bloody fangs.
Ho, Belimote, Argiron, Asterote!

envolio. Hold, hold! Zounds, he'll raise up a kennel   105
of devils I think, anon. Good my lord, entreat for
me. 'Sblood,° I am never able to endure these torments.

mperor. Then good master doctor,
Let me entreat you to remove his horns.   110
He has done penance now sufficiently.

austus. My gracious lord, not so much for injury
done to me, as to delight your Majesty with some

89–90 **hanged by the horns** (the spreading horns prevent Benvolio om pulling his head inside of the window)   107 **'Sblood** by God's ood

mirth, hath Faustus justly requited this injuriou
115 knight; which being all I desire, I am content
remove his horns. Mephostophilis, transform hi
And hereafter sir, look you speak well of schola

Benvolio. [*aside*] Speak well of ye! 'Sblood, a
scholars be such cuckold-makers to clap horns
120 honest men's heads o' this order, I'll ne'er tru
smooth faces and small ruffs° more. But an I
not revenged for this, would I might be turned to
gaping oyster and drink nothing but salt water.
[*Exi*

Emperor. Come Faustus, while the Emperor lives,
125 In recompense of this thy high desert,
Thou shalt command the state of Germany
And live beloved of mighty Carolus.
Exeunt omne

[IV.iii] *Enter Benvolio, Martino, Frederick,
and Soldiers.*

Martino. Nay, sweet Benvolio, let us sway t
thoughts
From this attempt against the conjurer.

Benvolio. Away! You love me not to urge me thu
Shall I let slip° so great an injury
5 When every servile groom jests at my wrongs
And in their rustic gambols proudly say,
"Benvolio's head was graced with horns today"?
O, may these eyelids never close again
Till with my sword I have that conjurer slain!
10 If you will aid me in this enterprise,
Then draw your weapons and be resolute;
If not, depart. Here will Benvolio die
But° Faustus' death shall quit° my infamy.

114 injurious insulting   121 small ruffs (worn by scholars, in co
trast to the large ruffs worn by courtiers)   IV.iii.4 let slip ign
13 But unless   13 quit avenge

Frederick. Nay, we will stay with thee, betide what
    may,
  And kill that doctor if he come this way.   15

Benvolio. Then, gentle Frederick, hie thee to the grove
  And place our servants and our followers
  Close in an ambush there behind the trees.
  By this, I know, the conjurer is near.
  I saw him kneel and kiss the Emperor's hand   20
  And take his leave laden with rich rewards.
  Then soldiers, boldly fight. If Faustus die,
  Take you the wealth, leave us the victory.

Frederick. Come soldiers, follow me unto the grove.
  Who kills him shall have gold and endless love.   25
             Exit Frederick with the Soldiers.

Benvolio. My head is lighter than it was by th' horns—
  But yet my heart more ponderous than my head,
  And pants until I see that conjurer dead.

Martino. Where shall we place ourselves, Benvolio?

Benvolio. Here will we stay to bide the first assault.   30
  O, were that damnèd hell-hound but in place
  Thou soon should'st see me quit my foul disgrace.

           Enter Frederick.

Frederick. Close, close! The conjurer is at hand
  And all alone comes walking in his gown.
  Be ready then and strike the peasant° down!   35

Benvolio. Mine be that honor then! Now sword, strike
  home!
  For horns he gave I'll have his head anon.

    Enter Faustus with the false head.

Martino. See see, he comes.

35 peasant low fellow

Benvolio.   No words. This blow ends a|
                                            [*Strikes Faustus*
  Hell take his soul, his body thus must fall.

40 *Faustus.* O!

Frederick. Groan you, master doctor?

Benvolio. Break may his heart with groans! De|
  Frederick, see,
  Thus will I end his griefs immediately.

[*Cuts off Faustus' false head.*]

Martino. Strike with a willing hand! His head is of

45 *Benvolio.* The devil's dead, the furies now may laug|

Frederick. Was this that stern aspect, that aw|
  frown,
  Made the grim monarch of infernal spirits
  Tremble and quake at his commanding charms?

Martino. Was this that damnèd head whose heart con
  spired
50 Benvolio's shame before the Emperor?

Benvolio. Ay, that's the head, and here the body lie
  Justly rewarded for his villainies.

Frederick. Come let's devise how we may add mor
  shame
  To the black scandal of his hated name.

55 *Benvolio.* First, on his head in quittance of my wrong
  I'll nail huge forkèd horns and let them hang
  Within the window where he yoked me first
  That all the world may see my just revenge.

Martino. What use shall we put his beard to?

60 *Benvolio.* We'll sell it to a chimney-sweeper. It wi|
  wear out ten birchen brooms, I warrant you.

Frederick. What shall eyes do?

envolio. We'll put out his eyes, and they shall serve
for buttons to his lips to keep his tongue from
catching cold.   65

Martino. An excellent policy! And now sirs, having
divided him, what shall the body do?

> [*Faustus rises.*]

envolio. Zounds, the devil's alive again!

rederick. Give him his head for God's sake!

austus. Nay keep it. Faustus will have heads and
     hands,   70
Ay, all your hearts, to recompense this deed.
Knew you not, traitors, I was limited
For four and twenty years to breathe on earth?
And had you cut my body with your swords
Or hewed this flesh and bones as small as sand,   75
Yet in a minute had my spirit returned
And I had breathed a man made free from harm.
But wherefore do I dally my revenge?
Asteroth, Belimoth, Mephostophilis!

Enter Mephostophilis and other Devils.

Go horse these traitors on your fiery backs   80
And mount aloft with them as high as heaven,
Thence pitch them headlong to the lowest hell.
Yet stay, the world shall see their misery,
And hell shall after plague their treachery.
Go Belimoth, and take this caitiff° hence   85
And hurl him in some lake of mud and dirt:
Take thou this other, drag him through the woods
Amongst the pricking thorns and sharpest briars:
Whilst with my gentle Mephostophilis
This traitor flies unto some steepy rock   90
That rolling down may break the villain's bones
As he intended to dismember me.
Fly hence, dispatch my charge immediately!

rederick. Pity us, gentle Faustus, save our lives!

caitiff wretch

Faustus. Away!

95 *Frederick.*   He must needs go that the devil driv
                            Exeunt Spirits with the Knigl

Enter the ambushed Soldiers.

1 Soldier. Come sirs, prepare yourselves in readine
Make haste to help these noble gentlemen.
I heard them parley with the conjurer.

2 Soldier. See where he comes, dispatch, and kill
slave!

100 *Faustus.* What's here, an ambush to betray my li.
Then Faustus, try thy skill. Base peasants, stanc
For lo, these trees remove° at my command
And stand as bulwarks 'twixt yourselves and
To shield me from your hated treachery!
105 Yet to encounter this your weak attempt
Behold an army comes incontinent.°

Faustus strikes the door, and enter a Devil playing
a drum, after him another bearing an ensign, a
divers with weapons: Mephostophilis with firework
they set upon the Soldiers and drive them out.
[Exeunt all.]

[IV.iv] *Enter at several doors Benvolio, Frederic*
and Martino, their heads and faces bloody and b
smeared with mud and dirt, all having horns on the
heads.

Martino. What ho, Benvolio!

Benvolio.   Here! What, Frederick, h

Frederick. O, help me gentle friend. Where is Ma
tino?

102 **remove** move   106 **incontinent** immediately

Martino. Dear Frederick, here,
  Half smothered in a lake of mud and dirt,
  Through which the furies dragged me by the heels.   5

Frederick. Martino, see, Benvolio's horns again.

Martino. O misery! How now Benvolio?

Benvolio. Defend me, heaven! Shall I be haunted°
    still?

Martino. Nay fear not man, we have no power to kill.

Benvolio. My friends transformèd thus! O hellish
    spite,   10
  Your heads are all set with horns.

Frederick.   You hit it right:
  It is your own you mean. Feel on your head.

Benvolio. Zounds, horns again!

Martino.   Nay chafe° not man, we all are sped.°

Benvolio. What devil attends this damned magician,
  That spite of spite our wrongs are doubled?   15

Frederick. What may we do that we may hide our
    shames?

Benvolio. If we should follow him to work revenge
  He'd join long asses' ears to these huge horns
  And make us laughing-stocks to all the world.

Martino. What shall we then do, dear Benvolio?   20

Benvolio. I have a castle joining near these woods,
  And thither we'll repair and live obscure
  Till time shall alter this our brutish shapes.
  Sith° black disgrace hath thus eclipsed our fame,
  We'll rather die with grief than live with shame.   25
                            Exeunt omnes.

V.iv.8 **haunted** (the following line suggests that there is a quibble
on "hunted," Benvolio now resembling a stag)   13 **chafe** fret   13
sped done for, ruined (because of the horns)   24 **Sith** since

[IV.v] *Enter Faustus and the Horse-courser.*°

Horse-courser. I beseech your worship, accept of the
forty dollars.°

Faustus. Friend, thou canst not buy so good a hors
for so small a price. I have no great need to se
5   him, but if thou likest him for ten dollars mor
take him, because I see thou hast a good mind 1
him.

Horse-courser. I beseech you sir, accept of this. I a
a very poor man and have lost very much of lat
10   by horse-flesh,° and this bargain will set me u
again.

Faustus. Well, I will not stand° with thee. Give n
the money. Now sirrah, I must tell you that yo
may ride him o'er hedge and ditch and spare hi
15   not. But, do you hear, in any case ride him not in
the water.

Horse-courser. How sir, not into the water! Why, w
he not drink of all waters?°

Faustus. Yes, he will drink of all waters, but ride hi
20   not into the water: o'er hedge and ditch or whe
thou wilt, but not into the water. Go bid the hostl
deliver him unto you, and remember what I say.

Horse-courser. I warrant you sir. O joyful day! No
am I a made man forever.   *Ex*

Faustus. What art thou, Faustus, but a man co
25   demned to die?
Thy fatal time° draws to a final end;
Despair doth drive distrust into my thoughts.

IV.v.s.d. **Horse-courser** horse trader   2 **dollars** German coins
horse-flesh (the possibility of a quibble on "whores' flesh" is i
creased by "set me up" and "stand" in the ensuing dialogu
12 **stand** haggle   18 **drink of all waters** i.e., go anywhere   26 fat
time life span

Confound these passions with a quiet sleep.
Tush, Christ did call the thief upon the cross!°
Then rest thee Faustus, quiet in conceit.°   30

He sits to sleep.

Enter the Horse-courser wet.

Horse-courser. O what a cozening° doctor was this!
I riding my horse into the water, thinking some
hidden mystery had been in the horse, I had nothing under me but a little straw and had much ado
to escape drowning. Well, I'll go rouse him and   35
make him give me my forty dollars again. Ho,
sirrah doctor, you cozening scab! Master doctor,
awake and rise, and give me my money again, for
your horse is turned to a bottle° of hay. Master
doctor!   *He pulls off his leg.*   40
Alas, I am undone! What shall I do? I have pulled
off his leg.

Faustus. O help, help! The villain hath murdered me!

Horse-courser. Murder or not murder, now he has but
one leg I'll outrun him, and cast this leg into some   45
ditch or other.   [*Exit.*]

Faustus. Stop him, stop him, stop him!—Ha, ha, ha!
Faustus hath his leg again, and the horse-courser a
bundle of hay for his forty dollars.

Enter Wagner.

How now, Wagner? What news with thee?   50

Wagner. If it please you, the Duke of Vanholt doth
earnestly entreat your company, and hath sent some
of his men to attend you with provision fit for your
journey.

29 Christ . . . cross (in Luke 23:39–43 Christ promised one of the
thieves that he would be with Christ in paradise)   30 quiet in conceit with a quiet mind   31 cozening deceiving   39 bottle bundle

55 *Faustus*. The Duke of Vanholt's an honorable gentle
   man, and one to whom I must be no niggard of m
   cunning. Come, away!   *Exeun*

[IV.vi] *Enter* [*Robin the*] *Clown, Dick, Horse-courser
and a Carter.*

Carter. Come my masters, I'll bring you to the bes
beer in Europe. What ho, hostess! Where be thes
whores?

Enter Hostess.

Hostess. How now? What lack you? What, my ol
5 guests, welcome.

Robin. [*aside*] Sirrah Dick, dost thou know why
stand so mute?

Dick. [*aside*] No Robin, why is't?

Robin. [*aside*] I am eighteen pence on the score.
10 But say nothing. See if she have forgotten me.

Hostess. Who's this that stands so solemnly by him
self? What, my old guest!

Robin. O, hostess, how do you? I hope my score
stands still.

15 *Hostess*. Ay, there's no doubt of that, for methink
you make no haste to wipe it out.

Dick. Why hostess, I say, fetch us some beer!

Hostess. You shall, presently.—Look up into th' hal
there, ho!   *Exit*

20 *Dick*. Come sirs, what shall we do now till mine
hostess comes?

IV.vi.9 on the score in debt

Carter. Marry sir, I'll tell you the bravest tale how a
conjurer served me. You know Doctor Fauster?

Horse-courser. Ay, a plague take him! Here's some
on's have cause to know him. Did he conjure thee   25
too?

Carter. I'll tell you how he served me. As I was going
to Wittenberg t'other day with a load of hay, he
met me and asked me what he should give me for
as much hay as he could eat. Now sir, I thinking   30
that a little would serve his turn, bad him take as
much as he would for three farthings. So he presently gave me my money and fell to eating; and as
I am a cursen° man, he never left eating till he had
eat up all my load of hay.   35

All. O monstrous, eat a whole load of hay!

Robin. Yes yes, that may be, for I have heard of one
that has eat a load of logs.°

Horse-courser. Now sirs, you shall hear how villain-
ously he served me. I went to him yesterday to buy   40
a horse of him, and he would by no means sell him
under forty dollars. So sir, because I knew him to
be such a horse as would run over hedge and ditch
and never tire, I gave him his money. So, when I
had my horse, Doctor Fauster bade me ride him   45
night and day and spare him no time. "But," quoth
he, "in any case ride him not into the water." Now
sir, I thinking the horse had had some quality that
he would not have me know of, what did I but rid
him into a great river—and when I came just in   50
the midst, my horse vanished away and I sate strad-
dling upon a bottle of hay.

All. O brave doctor!

Horse-courser. But you shall hear how bravely I
served him for it. I went me home to his house,   55

and there I found him asleep. I kept ahallowing a
whooping in his ears, but all could not wake h
I seeing that, took him by the leg and never res
pulling till I had pulled me his leg quite off, a
60   now 'tis at home in mine hostry.°

Dick. And has the doctor but one leg then? Tha
excellent, for one of his devils turned me into
likeness of an ape's face.

Carter. Some more drink, hostess!

65   Robin. Hark you, we'll into another room and dri
awhile, and then we'll go seek out the doctor.

                                    Exeunt omn

[IV.vii] *Enter the Duke of Vanholt, his [Servan
Duchess, Faustus, and Mephostophilis.*

Duke. Thanks master doctor, for these pleasant sigh
Nor know I how sufficiently to recompense yo
great deserts in erecting that enchanted castle in t
air, the sight whereof so delighted me,
5   As nothing in the world could please me more.

Faustus. I do think myself, my good lord, highly re
ompensed in that it pleaseth your Grace to think t
well of that which Faustus hath performed.—B
gracious lady, it may be that you have taken
10   pleasure in those sights. Therefore I pray you t
me what is the thing you most desire to have:
it in the world it shall be yours. I have heard th
great-bellied° women do long for things are ra
and dainty.

15   Duchess. True master doctor, and since I find you
kind, I will make known unto you what my he
desires to have: and were it now summer, as it

60 **hostry** inn   IV.vii.13 **great-bellied** i.e., pregnant

January, a dead time of the winter, I would request
no better meat° than a dish of ripe grapes.

austus. This is but a small matter. Go Mephostoph-   20
ilis, away!   *Exit Mephostophilis.*
Madam, I will do more than this for your content.

Enter Mephostophilis again with the grapes.

Here, now taste ye these. They should be good,
For they come from a far country, I can tell you.

uke. This makes me wonder more than all the rest,   25
that at this time of the year when every tree is
barren of his fruit, from whence you had these ripe
grapes.

austus. Please it your Grace, the year is divided into
two circles° over the whole world, so that when it   30
is winter with us, in the contrary circle it is likewise
summer with them, as in India, Saba,° and such
countries that lie far east, where they have fruit
twice a year. From whence, by means of a swift
spirit that I have, I had these grapes brought as you   35
see.

uchess. And trust me, they are the sweetest grapes
that e'er I tasted.

*he Clowns [Robin, Dick, Carter, and Horse-courser]
bounce° at the gate within.*

uke. What rude disturbers have we at the gate?
Go pacify their fury, set it ope,   40
And then demand of them what they would have.

hey knock again and call out to talk with Faustus.

---

9 **meat** food   30 **two circles** i.e., the northern and the southern
emispheres (though later in the speech he talks of east and west
ather than of north and south)   38s.d. **bounce** knock

A Servant. Why, how now masters, what a coil°
there!
What is the reason° you disturb the Duke?

Dick. We have no reason for it, therefore a fig for hi

45 *Servant.* Why saucy varlets, dare you be so bold!

Horse-courser. I hope sir, we have wit enough to
more bold than welcome.

Servant. It appears so. Pray be bold elsewhere
And trouble not the Duke.

50 *Duke.* What would they have?

Servant. They all cry out to speak with Doct
Faustus.

Carter. Ay, and we will speak with him.

Duke. Will you sir? Commit° the rascals.

Dick. Commit with us! He were as good commit wi
55   his father as commit with us!

Faustus. I do beseech your Grace, let them come i
They are good subject for a merriment.

Duke. Do as thou wilt, Faustus, I give thee leave.

Faustus. I thank your Grace.

Enter [Robin] the Clown, Dick, Carter, and
Horse-courser.

Why, how now my good friend
60 'Faith, you are too outrageous; but come near,
I have procured your pardons. Welcome all.

Robin. Nay sir, we will be welcome for our mone

42 coil turmoil   43 reason (pronounced like "raisin," leading to t
quibble on "fig"; a "fig" here is an obscene contemptuous gestu
in which the hand is clenched and the thumb is thrust between t
first and second fingers, making the thumb resemble the stem of
fig, or a penis)   53 Commit imprison (Dick proceeds to quibble
the idea of committing adultery)

and we will pay for what we take. What ho, give's
half a dozen of beer here, and be hanged!

Faustus. Nay, hark you, can you tell me where you
　　are?　　　　　　　　　　　　　　　　　　　　　　65

Carter. Ay, marry can I, we are under heaven.

Servant. Ay, but Sir Sauce-box, know you in what
　　place?

Horse-courser. Ay ay, the house is good enough to
　　drink in. Zounds, fill us some beer, or we'll break
　　all the barrels in the house and dash out all your　　70
　　brains with your bottles.

Faustus. Be not so furious. Come, you shall have beer.
　　My lord, beseech you give me leave awhile;
　　I'll gage° my credit 'twill content your Grace.

Duke. With all my heart, kind doctor, please thyself.　　75
　　Our servants and our court's at thy command.

Faustus. I humbly thank your Grace.—Then fetch
　　some beer.

Horse-courser. Ay marry, there spake a doctor in-
　　deed! And 'faith, I'll drink a health to thy wooden
　　leg for that word.　　　　　　　　　　　　　　　　80

Faustus. My wooden leg? What dost thou mean by
　　that?

Carter. Ha, ha, ha, dost hear him Dick? He has for-
　　got his leg.

Horse-courser. Ay ay, he does not stand much upon°　　85
　　that.

Faustus. No, 'faith, not much upon a wooden leg.

Carter. Good lord, that flesh and blood should be so
　　frail with your worship! Do not you remember a
　　horse-courser you sold a horse to?　　　　　　　90

4 gage pledge　　85 **stand much upon** (quibble on "attach much importance to")

Faustus. Yes, I remember I sold one a horse.

Carter. And do you remember you bid he should no
ride into the water?

Faustus. Yes, I do very well remember that.

95 *Carter.* And do you remember nothing of your leg?

Faustus. No, in good sooth.

Carter. Then I pray remember your curtsy.°

Faustus. I thank you sir.

Carter. 'Tis not so much worth. I pray you tell me on
100 thing.

Faustus. What's that?

Carter. Be both your legs bedfellows every night to
gether?

Faustus. Would'st thou make a colossus° of me tha
105 thou askest me such questions?

Carter. No, truly sir, I would make nothing of you
but I would fain know that.

Enter Hostess with drink.

Faustus. Then I assure thee certainly they are.

Carter. I thank you, I am fully satisfied.

110 *Faustus.* But wherefore dost thou ask?

Carter. For nothing, sir, but methinks you should hav
a wooden bedfellow of one of 'em.

Horse-courser. Why, do you hear sir, did not I pul
off one of your legs when you were asleep?

115 *Faustus.* But I have it again now I am awake. Lool
you here sir.

97 **curtsy** (also called "a leg," hence there is a quibble on the Carter'
previous speech)   104 **colossus** huge statue in the harbor at Rhode
between whose legs ships were said to have sailed

ll. O horrible! Had the doctor three legs?

arter. Do you remember sir, how you cozened me
and eat up my load of—
                    Faustus charms him dumb.

ick. Do you remember how you made me wear an   120
ape's—   [*Faustus charms him.*]

orse-courser. You whoreson conjuring scab! Do you
remember how you cozened me with a ho—
                              [*Faustus charms him.*]

obin. Ha' you forgotten me? You think to carry it
away with your "hey-pass" and "re-pass"?° Do you   125
remember the dog's fa—   [*Faustus charms him.*]
                              Exeunt Clowns.

ostess. Who pays for the ale? Hear you master
doctor, now you have sent away my guests, I pray
who shall pay me for my a—
                    [*Faustus charms her.*] *Exit Hostess.*

uchess. My lord,   130
We are much beholding to this learnèd man.

uke. So are we madam, which we will recompense
With all the love and kindness that we may:
His artful sport drives all sad thoughts away.
                                          Exeunt.

V.i] *Thunder and lightning. Enter Devils with covered
shes: Mephostophilis leads them into Faustus' study.
            Then enter Wagner.*

'agner. I think my master means to die shortly. He
has made his will and given me his wealth: his
house, his goods, and store of golden plate—besides
two thousand ducats ready coined. I wonder what
he means. If death were nigh, he would not frolic   5
thus. He's now at supper with the scholars, where

5 **hey-pass, re-pass** conjuring expressions

there's such belly-cheer as Wagner in his life ne'
saw the like! And see where they come. Belike
the feast is done.°   *Ex*

Enter Faustus, Mephostophilis, and two or three
Scholars.

10 *1 Scholar.* Master Doctor Faustus, since our confe
ence about fair ladies, which was the beautifulest i
all the world, we have determined with ourselve
that Helen of Greece was the admirablest lady tha
ever lived. Therefore master doctor, if you will d
15 us so much favor as to let us see that peerless dam
of Greece, whom all the world admires for majest
we should think ourselves much beholding unt
you.

Faustus. Gentlemen,
20 For that I know your friendship is unfeigned,
It is not Faustus' custom to deny
The just request of those that wish him well:
You shall behold that peerless dame of Greece
No otherwise for pomp or majesty
25 Than when Sir Paris crossed the seas with her
And brought the spoils° to rich Dardania.°
Be silent then, for danger is in words.

Music sounds. Mephostophilis brings in Helen: sh
passeth over the stage.

2 Scholar. Was this fair Helen, whose admired wort
Made Greece with ten years' wars afflict poor Troy

30 *3 Scholar.* Too simple is my wit to tell her worth,
Whom all the world admires for majesty.

V.i.8 **Belike** most likely   1–9 **I think . . . done** (though printed a
prose in the quarto, as here, perhaps this speech should be verse, th
lines ending *shortly, wealth, plate, coined, nigh, supper, belly-chee*
like, done)   26 **spoils** booty (including Helen)   26 **Dardania** Troy

Scholar. Now we have seen the pride of nature's
   work,
We'll take our leaves, and for this blessèd sight
Happy and blest be Faustus evermore.

ustus. Gentlemen, farewell, the same wish I to you.   *35*
                  Exeunt Scholars.

Enter an Old Man.

ld Man. O gentle Faustus, leave this damnèd art,
This magic that will charm thy soul to hell
And quite bereave° thee of salvation.
Though thou hast now offended like a man,
Do not persever° in it like a devil.   *40*
Yet, yet, thou hast an amiable soul°
If sin by custom grow not into nature.
Then, Faustus, will repentance come too late!
Then, thou are banished from the sight of heaven!
No mortal can express the pains of hell!   *45*
It may be this my exhortation
Seems harsh and all unpleasant. Let it not.
For gentle son, I speak it not in wrath
Or envy of thee but in tender love
And pity of thy future misery: *50*
And so have hope that this my kind rebuke,
Checking° thy body, may amend thy soul.

ustus. Where art thou, Faustus? Wretch, what hast
     thou done!   *Mephostophilis gives him a dagger.*
Hell claims his right and with a roaring voice
Says "Faustus, come, thine hour is almost come!"   *55*
And Faustus now will come to do thee right!

ld Man. O stay, good Faustus, stay thy desperate
   steps!
I see an angel hover o'er thy head,
And with a vial full of precious grace

: **bereave** deprive   **40 persever** (accent on second syllable)   **41 an
niable soul** a soul worthy of love   **52 Checking** rebuking

60   Offers to pour the same into thy soul:
        Then call for mercy and avoid despair.

        Faustus. O friend,
            I feel thy words to comfort my distressèd soul:
            Leave me awhile to ponder on my sins.

65 *Old Man.* Faustus, I leave thee, but with grief of hear
            Fearing the enemy of thy hapless soul.   *Ex.*

        Faustus. Accursèd Faustus! Wretch, what hast tho
            done!
            I do repent, and yet I do despair:
            Hell strives with grace for conquest in my breas
70   What shall I do to shun the snares of death?

        Mephostophilis. Thou traitor Faustus, I arrest thy so
            For disobedience to my sovereign lord.
            Revolt,° or I'll in piecemeal tear thy flesh.

        Faustus. I do repent I e'er offended him.
75   Sweet Mephostophilis, entreat thy lord
            To pardon my unjust presumption,
            And with my blood again I will confirm
            The former vow I made to Lucifer.

        Mephostophilis. Do it then, Faustus, with unfeignè
            heart
80   Lest greater dangers do attend thy drift.

        Faustus. Torment, sweet friend, that base and agè
            man
            That durst dissuade me from thy Lucifer,
            With greatest torment that our hell affords.

        Mephostophilis. His faith is great. I cannot touch hi
            soul.
85   But what I may afflict his body with
            I will attempt, which is but little worth.

        Faustus. One thing, good servant, let me crave of the
            To glut the longing of my heart's desire:

73 **Revolt** return (to your allegiance)

That I may have unto my paramour
That heavenly Helen which I saw of late,   90
Whose sweet embraces may extinguish clear
Those thoughts that do dissuade me from my vow,
And keep mine oath I made to Lucifer.

Mephostophilis. This or what else my Faustus shall
    desire
Shall be performed in twinkling of an eye.   95

Enter Helen again, passing over between two Cupids.

Faustus. Was this the face that launched a thousand
    ships
And burnt the topless° towers of Ilium?°
Sweet Helen, make me immortal with a kiss.
Her lips suck forth my soul. See where it flies!
Come Helen, come, give me my soul again.   100
Here will I dwell, for heaven is in these lips
And all is dross that is not Helena.
I will be Paris, and for love of thee
Instead of Troy shall Wittenberg be sacked;
And I will combat with weak Menelaus°   105
And wear thy colors on my plumèd crest.
Yea, I will wound Achilles° in the heel
And then return to Helen for a kiss.
O, thou art fairer than the evening's air
Clad in the beauty of a thousand stars,   110
Brighter art thou than flaming Jupiter
When he appeared to hapless Semele,°
More lovely than the monarch of the sky
In wanton Arethusa's° azure arms,
And none but thou shalt be my paramour. *Exeunt.* 115

97 **topless** i.e., so tall their tops are beyond sight   97 **Ilium** Troy
105 **Menelaus** Greek king, deserted by Helen for Paris   107 **Achilles**
greatest of the Greek warriors   112 **Semele** beloved by Jupiter, who
promised to do whatever she wished; she asked to see him in his full
splendor, and the sight incinerated her   114 **Arethusa** a nymph,
here apparently loved by Jupiter, "the monarch of the sky"

[V.ii] *Thunder. Enter Lucifer, Belzebub, and*
Mephostophilis.°

Lucifer. Thus from infernal Dis° do we ascend
    To view the subjects of our monarchy,
    Those souls which sin seals the black sons of hell.
    'Mong which as chief, Faustus, we come to thee,
5   Bringing with us lasting damnation
    To wait upon thy soul. The time is come
    Which makes it forfeit.

Mephostophilis.   And this gloomy night
    Here in this room will wretched Faustus be.

Belzebub. And here we'll stay
10   To mark him how he doth demean himself.

Mephostophilis. How should he but in desperate lunacy?
    Fond° worldling, now his heart blood dries with
        grief,
    His conscience kills it, and his laboring brain
    Begets a world of idle fantasies
15   To overreach the devil; but all in vain:
    His store of pleasures must be sauced with pain!
    He and his servant Wagner are at hand.
    Both come from drawing Faustus' latest will.
    See where they come.

Enter Faustus and Wagner.

20 *Faustus.* Say Wagner, thou hast perused my will;
    How dost thou like it?

Wagner.   Sir, so wondrous well

V.ii.s.d. **Enter Lucifer, Belzebub, and Mephostophilis** (probably they
rise out of a trapdoor and ascend to the upper stage, Mephostophilis
descending to the main stage at line 93)   1 **infernal Dis** the underworld (named for its ruler)   12 **Fond** foolish

As in all humble duty I do yield
My life and lasting service for your love.

Enter the Scholars.

Faustus. Gramercies,° Wagner.—Welcome gentlemen.
[*Exit Wagner.*]

1 Scholar. Now worthy Faustus, methinks your looks
are changed.   25

Faustus. O gentlemen!

2 Scholar. What ails Faustus?

Faustus. Ah my sweet chamber-fellow, had I lived
with thee, then had I lived still!—But now must
die eternally. Look sirs, comes he not, comes he   30
not?

1 Scholar. O my dear Faustus, what imports this fear?

2 Scholar. Is all our pleasure turned to melancholy?

3 Scholar. He is not well with being over-solitary.

2 Scholar. If it be so, we'll have physicians and   35
Faustus shall be cured.

3 Scholar. 'Tis but a surfeit° sir, fear nothing.

Faustus. A surfeit of deadly sin that hath damned both
body and soul!

2 Scholar. Yet Faustus, look up to heaven and re-   40
member mercy is infinite.

Faustus. But Faustus' offense can ne'er be pardoned.
The serpent that tempted Eve may be saved, but
not Faustus! O gentlemen, hear with patience and
tremble not at my speeches. Though my heart pant   45
and quiver to remember that I have been a student
here these thirty years, O, would I had never seen
Wittenberg, never read book.—And what wonders

24 **Gramercies** thank you   37 **a surfeit** indigestion

I have done all Germany can witness, yea all the
50   world, for which Faustus hath lost both Germany
and the world, yea heaven itself—heaven, the seat
of God, the throne of the blessèd, the kingdom of
joy—and must remain in hell forever! hell, O hell
forever! Sweet friends, what shall become of
55   Faustus being in hell forever?

2 Scholar. Yet Faustus, call on God.

Faustus. On God, whom Faustus hath abjured? On
God, whom Faustus hath blasphemed? O my God,
I would weep, but the devil draws in my tears!
60   Gush forth blood instead of tears, yea life and soul!
O, he stays my tongue! I would lift up my hands,
but see, they hold 'em, they hold 'em!

All. Who, Faustus?

Faustus. Why, Lucifer and Mephostophilis. O gentle-
65   men, I gave them my soul for my cunning.

All. O, God forbid!

Faustus. God forbade it indeed, but Faustus hath done
it. For the vain pleasure of four and twenty years
hath Faustus lost eternal joy and felicity. I writ
70   them a bill with mine own blood. The date is expired. This is the time. And he will fetch me.

1 Scholar. Why did not Faustus tell us of this before,
that divines might have prayed for thee?

Faustus. Oft have I thought to have done so, but the
75   devil threatened to tear me in pieces if I named God
—to fetch me body and soul if I once gave ear to
divinity; and now 'tis too late! Gentlemen, away,
lest you perish with me.

2 Scholar. O, what may we do to save Faustus?

80   *Faustus.* Talk not of me but save yourselves and depart.

3 Scholar. God will strengthen me. I will stay with
Faustus.

Scholar. Tempt not God, sweet friend, but let us   85
into the next room and pray for him.

Faustus. Ay, pray for me, pray for me. And what
noise soever you hear, come not unto me, for nothing can rescue me.

Scholar. Pray thou, and we will pray that God may   90
have mercy upon thee.

Faustus. Gentlemen, farewell! If I live till morning, I'll
visit you. If not, Faustus is gone to hell.

1. Faustus, farewell!

Exeunt Scholars.

Mephostophilis. Ay, Faustus, now thou hast no hope
of heaven.
Therefore, despair! Think only upon hell,   95
For that must be thy mansion, there to dwell.

Faustus. O thou bewitching fiend, 'twas thy temptation
Hath robbed me of eternal happiness.

Mephostophilis. I do confess it Faustus, and rejoice.
'Twas I, that when thou wert i' the way to heaven   100
Dammed up thy passage. When thou took'st the
book
To view the Scriptures, then I turned the leaves
And led thine eye.
What, weep'st thou! 'Tis too late, despair, farewell!
Fools that will laugh on earth, most weep in hell.   105

Exit.

Enter the Good Angel and the Bad Angel at
several doors.

Good Angel. O Faustus, if thou hadst given ear to me
Innumerable joys had followèd thee.
But thou did'st love the world.

Bad Angel.   Gave ear to me,
And now must taste hell's pains perpetually.

Good Angel. O, what will all thy riches, pleasure
110   pomps
        Avail thee now?

Bad Angel.   Nothing but vex thee more,
        To want in hell, that had on earth such store.
                        Music while the throne° descend

Good Angel. O, thou hast lost celestial happiness,
        Pleasures unspeakable, bliss without end.
115   Had'st thou affected° sweet divinity,
        Hell or the devil had had no power on thee.
        Had'st thou kept on that way, Faustus behold
        In what resplendent glory thou had'st sat
        In yonder throne, like those bright shining saints,
120   And triumphed over hell! That hast thou lost.
                                [*Throne ascends*
        And now, poor soul, must thy good angel leav
                thee,
        The jaws of hell are open to receive thee.   *Ex*
                        Hell is discovere

Bad Angel. Now Faustus, let thine eyes with horr
                stare
        Into that vast perpetual torture-house.
125   There are the furies, tossing damnèd souls
        On burning forks. Their bodies boil in lead.
        There are live quarters° broiling on the coals,
        That ne'er can die: this ever-burning chair
        Is for o'er-tortured souls to rest them in.
130   These that are fed with sops of flaming fire
        Were gluttons and loved only delicates
        And laughed to see the poor starve at their gate
        But yet all these are nothing. Thou shalt see
        Ten thousand tortures that more horrid be.

135 *Faustus.* O, I have seen enough to torture me.

Bad Angel. Nay, thou must feel them, taste the sma
                of all:

112s.d. **throne** (symbolic of heaven) 115 **affected** preferred 1
quarters bodies

He that loves pleasure must for pleasure fall.
And so I leave thee Faustus, till anon:
Then wilt thou tumble in confusion.°   *Exit.*
                              The clock strikes eleven.

ustus. O Faustus!   140
Now hast thou but one bare hour to live
And then thou must be damned perpetually.
Stand still, you ever-moving spheres of Heaven
That time may cease and midnight never come:
Fair nature's eye, rise, rise again and make   145
Perpetual day, or let this hour be but a year,
A month, a week, a natural day—
That Faustus may repent and save his soul.
O lente lente currite noctis equi!°
The stars move still, time runs, the clock will strike: 150
The devil will come, and Faustus must be damned!
O, I'll leap up to my God! Who pulls me down?
See, see where Christ's blood streams in the firma-
   ment!
One drop of blood will save me. O my Christ!—
Rend not my heart for naming of my Christ!   155
Yet will I call on Him! O spare me, Lucifer!—
Where is it now? 'Tis gone: and see where God
Stretcheth out His arm and bends His ireful brows!
Mountains and hills, come, come and fall on me
And hide me from the heavy wrath of God!   160
No?
Then will I headlong run into the earth.
Gape earth! O no, it will not harbor me.
You stars that reigned at my nativity,
Whose influence hath allotted death and hell,   165
Now draw up Faustus like a foggy mist
Into the entrails of yon laboring cloud
That when you vomit forth into the air,
My limbs may issue from your smoky mouths—
But let my soul mount and ascend to heaven!   170
                              The watch strikes.

9 **confusion** destruction   149 **O . . . equi** slowly, slowly run, O
rses of the night (Latin, adapted from Ovid's *Amores*, I.xiii.40,
ere a lover regretfully thinks of the coming of the dawn)

O half the hour is passed! 'Twill all be passed and
O God,
If thou wilt not have mercy on my soul,
Yet for Christ's sake, whose blood hath ransom
    me,
175 Impose some end to my incessant pain!
Let Faustus live in hell a thousand years,
A hundred thousand, and at last be saved!
No end is limited to° damnèd souls!
Why wert thou not a creature wanting soul?
180 Or why is this immortal that thou hast?
O, Pythagoras' metempsychosis,° were that true
This soul should fly from me and I be changed
Into some brutish beast.
All beasts are happy, for when they die
185 Their souls are soon dissolved in elements.
But mine must live still° to be plagued in hell!
Cursed be the parents that engendered me!
No Faustus, curse thyself, curse Lucifer
That hath deprived thee of the joys of heaven.
               The clock strikes twelv
190 It strikes, it strikes! Now body, turn to air,
Or Lucifer will bear thee quick° to hell!
O soul, be changed into small water-drops
And fall into the ocean, ne'er be found.

      Thunder, and enter the Devils.

My God, my God! Look not so fierce on me!
195 Adders and serpents, let me breathe awhile!
Ugly Hell, gape not! Come not Lucifer!
I'll burn my books!—O Mephostophilis!
         Exeunt [Devils with Faustus.

178 limited to set for   181 metempsychosis transmigration of sou
(a doctrine held by Pythagoras, philosopher of the sixth century B.c
186 still always   191 quick alive   197s.d.Exeunt [Devils wi
Faustus] (possibly the devils drag Faustus into the "hell" that w
"discovered" at V.ii.122, and then toss his limbs onto the stage,
possibly the limbs are revealed in V.iii.6 by withdrawing a curtain
the rear of the stage)

[V.iii] *Enter the Scholars.*

1 Scholar. Come gentlemen, let us go visit Faustus,
For such a dreadful night was never seen
Since first the world's creation did begin!
Such fearful shrieks and cries were never heard!
Pray heaven, the doctor have escaped the danger.   *5*

2 Scholar. O, help us heaven, see, here are Faustus'
     limbs
All torn asunder by the hand of death!

3 Scholar. The devils whom Faustus served have torn
     him thus:
For 'twixt the hours of twelve and one, methought
I heard him shriek and call aloud for help,   *10*
At which self° time the house seemed all on fire
With dreadful horror of these damnèd fiends.

2 Scholar. Well gentlemen, though Faustus' end be
     such
As every Christian heart laments to think on,
Yet for he was a scholar once admired   *15*
For wondrous knowledge in our German schools,
We'll give his mangled limbs due burial;
And all the students, clothed in mourning black,
Shall wait upon° his heavy° funeral.   *Exeunt.*

Enter Chorus.

Cut is the branch that might have grown full straight
And burnèd is Apollo's laurel bough°
That sometime grew within this learnèd man.
Faustus is gone: regard his hellish fall,
Whose fiendful fortune may exhort the wise   *5*
Only to wonder at° unlawful things,

V.iii.11 **self** same   19 **wait upon** attend   19 **heavy** sad   Chorus 2
laurel bough symbol of wisdom, here associated with Apollo, god of
divination   6 **Only to wonder at** i.e., merely to observe at a distance, with awe

Whose deepness doth entice such forward wits
To practice more than heavenly power permits.

[*Exit.*]

Terminat hora diem; terminat Author opus.°

FINIS

---

9 **Terminat . . . opus** the hour ends the day; the author ends his work
(this Latin tag probably is not Marlowe's but the printer's, though
it is engaging to believe Marlowe wrote it, ending his play at midnight, the hour of Faustus' death)

Textual Note

The earliest edition of the play, entitled *The Tragicall History of D. Faustus,* was published in 1604, eleven years after Marlowe's death. It survives in only one copy. Possibly it had been preceded by an earlier edition, but because it is the first edition extant it is called the A-text. It was reprinted in 1609 (A2) and again in 1611 (A3), but these two editions have no independent authority, differing occasionally from A1 only by virtue of small errors that they introduce.

In 1616 a very different text was published, *The Tragicall History of the Life and Death of Doctor Faustus,* which, like the A-text of 1604, survives in only one copy. It is conventionally called the B-text, and it was reprinted several times in the seventeenth century. The B-text has:

some passages that are very close to A;

some episodes that are broadly parallel to A, but with little verbal similarity;

some deletions of A's material, especially of material that might be thought blasphemous;

approximately six hundred more lines than A; the last act is notably fuller in B, which has a final visit of the angels, and the discovery of Faustus' mangled body. But although longer than A, B lacks some material found in A.

Because it is known that a theatrical entrepreneur in 1602

paid William Birde and Samuel Rowley "for ther adi-
cyones in doctor fostes," it was believed until recently
that B contained the un-Marlovian additions, and that
A, the shorter text, was closer to Marlowe's own play
But recent studies, especially those of Leo Kirschbaum
(in *Library* XXVI [1945–46], 272–94) and W. W
Greg (*Marlowe's "Doctor Faustus" 1604–1616: Paralle
Texts*), have persuasively argued that B is probably closer
to Marlowe's play. Instead of B containing un-Marlovian
additions to an authentic text represented by A, A is now
seen as an abridged text, assembled by actors for a provincial performance. For some reason these actors did not
have the promptbook, and they were forced to rely on
their memories of the original production, which means
that they sometimes omitted authentic material, sometimes
amplified it, and sometimes merely misremembered it
slightly. That A shows signs of stage-production can be
seen, for example, in the relative abundance of connectives
and ejaculations, such as "Tell me," "Tut," "Tush," and
so forth. One cannot prove that Marlowe did not write
these, but when parallel sentences in B lack them, one
feels that they indicate actors' additions. Similarly, when
in A we find repetitions where in B we find variations,
we seem to hear actors simplifying their material. And
perhaps most important, A uses a simpler stage than B,
again evidence that A is an abridged and provincial
version. For example, A does not use a window in IV.ii,
or an upper stage in V.ii, nor in V.ii is there the descent
of a throne from heaven and the discovery of hell. And in
B, V.iii apparently uses the inner-stage but A lacks this
scene.

But even if it is agreed that A is an abridged version,
and that B is closer to Marlowe's final manuscript, one
cannot simply rely on B. There are places where B is
unquestionably indebted to A, which leads one to believe
that the printer's copy for B was a manuscript that at
times was illegible, driving the printer to turn to A for
some of his readings. Indeed, it is virtually certain that
the printer of B made use of A3 (1611). For example,
A1 has:

Fau. and what are you that liue with Lucifer?

Me. Unhappy spirits that fell with Lucifer,

but A3 slipped, altering "fell" to "liue" as in the previous line, and B follows the slip, printing

Unhappy spirits that liue with Lucifer.

Moreover, whoever prepared B for print occasionally engaged in censorship, deleting expressions that smacked of blasphemy. B prints, for example, "O mercy heauen," where A had printed "My God, my God." A, then, surely contains words that B inadvertently lost, and probably others that B deliberately censored. It may have a third value: if indeed it represents a performance, and if B is mostly based on Marlowe's manuscript, A may contain some revisions made by Marlowe at some time after he drafted the manuscript that is behind B. But it is a tricky business to say that this or that line in A sounds more Marlovian than the parallel line in B, and that therefore A sometimes supersedes B because it contains Marlowe's second thoughts.

In short: the exact nature of B is uncertain, and the precise degree to which it is inferior to A is therefore a matter of argument. But the problem is not comparable to What song the sirens sang, and What name Achilles assumed when he hid among the women, which at present are matters beyond all conjecture. There is plenty of evidence in behalf of the argument that B gets us much closer to Marlowe than A does. But shall an editor relentlessly follow B? Of course not; it has already been mentioned that B sometimes repeats an error of A3, and that B sometimes gives a censored version of A. The present editor, therefore, has occasionally drawn upon A, but has followed B whenever there was no compelling reason to depart from it. Take, for example, the very first two lines of the play:

Not marching now in fields of Thracimene,
Where Mars did mate the Cathaginians

(A)

Not marching in the fields of Thrasimen,
Where Mars did mate the warlike Carthagens

(B).

I have assumed that since B makes excellent sense, that
since it is not demonstrably derived from A or in need of
anything that A offers, it is what should be printed. But
elsewhere I have restored the "blasphemy" of A, which
B toned down, and I have occasionally adopted a reading
from A when there seemed to be cause to do so. For
example, A speaks of "foure stately bridges," but B
speaks of "two stately Bridges." Now, in this instance A
agrees with the source, *The Damnable Life,* and it would
be odd for the actors, in their memorial reconstruction,
independently to come up with a version closer to Marlowe's source. Moreover, B's "two" is probably a com-
positor's slip, because the word "two" appears in the
previous line:

> With winding bankes that cut it in two parts;
> Ouer the which two stately Bridges leane.

Given both of these arguments, it seems reasonable to
depart from B and to follow A, printing "four" instead of
"two," on the assumption that "four" is the word Marlowe
wrote.

The present text, then, follows B quite closely; emenda-
tions have been made relatively sparingly, but spelling has
been modernized. For example, "The fiery keele at Anwerpe bridge" is printed here as "The fiery keel at
Antwerp bridge"; but note that unlike most editions, the
present edition—though modernizing the spelling of
"Anwerpe"—does not emend to "Antwerp's." The word
here is an adjective, not genetive, and is comparable, for
example, to "Verona streets" in *Romeo and Juliet* III.i.90.
In addition to modernizing the spelling, I have modernized the punctuation, regularized speech prefixes (e.g.
"Good Angel" replaces "Good," and "Good A."), divided
a few lines of verse differently from B, and corrected
obvious typographical errors. For convenience in refer-

nce, act and scene divisions have been added, in square
brackets [ ], though no edition of the play was so
divided until relatively recent times. The divisions here
used are identical with those in Greg's important edition,
Marlowe's Doctor Faustus 1604–1616: Parallel Texts
(Oxford, 1950). Greg for convenience followed F. S.
Boas' edition of 1932, which unfortunately begins a new
scene at IV.i.48 because at that point the stage is cleared.
But in fact Benvolio remains "above at a window," and
he plays a part subsequently. Strictly speaking, then, we
do not get a new scene here, but, again, the divisions are
merely a matter of convenience. Other departures from B
are listed below; the adopted reading is given first, in
italic type, followed by the original reading, in roman
type. When the adopted reading comes from the A-text of
1604, that fact is indicated in square brackets.

Prologue   12 *Rhode* Rhodes

i.7 *logices* Logicis   12 *on kai me on* [1604] Oeconomy   26–27 *Si
. . . et cetera* [1616 prints as verse, with lines ending *duobus, &c*]
46 *legatur* legatus   29 *Exheriditare* Exhereditari   37–43 *Stipendium . . . die* [1616 prints as verse, with lines ending *&c, hard,
veritas, sinne, vs, sinne, die*]   79 *India* [1604] Indian   87 *silk
kill* 102–3 *Divinity . . . vile* [1604; 1616 omits]   109 *Swarm*
[1604] Sworne   112 *shadows* [1604] shadow   126 *stuffs* [1604]
stuff'd

ii.1–2 [as in 1604; 1616 prints as verse, with lines ending *wont,
probo*]

iii.12 *erring* [1604] euening   16 *dei* [1604] Dij   17 *aquatici*
Aquatani   20 *Mephostophilis . . . moraris* Mephostophilis Dragon,
quod tumeraris   21 *Gehennam* [1604] gehennan   24 *dicatus* di-
catis   45 *accidens* accident   52 *the Trinity* [1604] all godlinesse
79 *fell* [1604] liue   76 *who* [1604] that

iv.3–4 *such pickadevants* [1604] beards   54 *vestigiis nostris* vesti-
gias nostras

II.i.9 *Ay . . . again* [1604; 1616 omits]   10–11 *To . . . appetite* [as in
1604; 1616 prints as one line, with *Why* in place of *To God*]   20
en [1604] them   32 *Mephostophilis* [1604; 1616 omits]   54–56
O . . . Lucifer's [as in 1604; 1616 prints as two lines, ending *arme,
ucifers*]   79 *God* [1604] heauen   106 *form or shape* [1604] shape

and forme   115 *or goods* [1604; 1616 omits]   121 *will I* [1604]
I will   121 *with* [1604; 1616 omits]

II.ii.s.d. [preceded in 1616 by the following passage, attributed to
Wagner, which is an abbreviation of material that the Chorus speaks
immediately preceding Act III: Enter Wagner solus. Wag. Learned
Faustus/To know the secrets of Astronomy/Grauen in the booke of
Ioues high firmament,/Did mount himselfe to scale Olympus top,/
Being seated in a chariot burning bright,/Drawne by the strength
of yoaky Dragons necks,/He now is gone to proue Cosmography,/
And as I gesse will first arriue at Rome,/To see the Pope and manner
of his Court;/And take some part of holy Peters feast,/That to this
day is highly solemnized. Exit Wagner]   42 *erring* [1604] euening
43–44 *But . . . tempore* [1616 prints as one line]   55 *suppositions*
[1604] questions   83–84 *'Tis . . . late* [as in 1604; 1616 prints as one
line]   94–95 *I . . . hell* [1616 prints as one line]   103–5 *Never . . .
down* [1604; 1616 omits]

II.iii.1 *Robin* [1616 omits]

III Prologue 1–2 *Learnèd . . . astronomy* [as in 1604; 1616 prints as
one line]   8 *tropics* Tropick

III.i.7 *Rhine* [1604] Rhines   12 *Quarters . . . equivalents* [1604;
1616 omits]   16 *rest* [1604] East   37 *four* [1604] two   43 *match*
[1604] watch   77, 81 *cunning* comming   155 *keys* seales

III.ii.70–71 *That . . . wine* [1616 prints as one line]   78 *I . . . banquet*
[1616 prints as two lines, ending *this, banquet*]   90–91 *Now . . .
candle* [1616 prints as verse, with lines ending *tell you, Candle*]
100 *on* [1604; 1616 omits]   107 s.d. *fireworks* [1604] fire worke

IV Prologue 1–17 *When . . . performed* [1604; 1616 omits]

IV.ii.25 *like a* like   74 *the* [1616 omits]   90 *is* [1616 omits]

IV.iii.71 *all* call

IV.v.s.d. *Horse-courser* Horse-courser, and Mephostophilis

IV.vi.5 *guests* Guesse   60 *Dick* Clow[n, i.e., Robin]

IV.vii.38 s.d. *Clowns* Clowne   128 *guests* guesse

V.i.19–20 *Gentlemen . . . unfeigned* [1616 prints as one line]   2?
s.d. *sounds* [1604] sound   62–63 *O . . . soul* [1616 prints as one
line]   79 *Mephostophilis* [1604; 1616 omits]   81 *Faustus* [1604;
1616 omits]   93 *mine oath* [1604] my vow

V.ii.28–30 *Ah . . . not* [1616 prints as verse, lines ending *thee, eter-*
nally, not]   42–43 *But . . . saved* [1616 prints as verse, lines ending
pardoned, saued]   118 *sat* set   126 *boil* broyle   152 *my God*
[1604] heauen   153 *See . . . firmament* [1604; 1616 omits]   157–58
gone . . . brows [1604, which ends the lines with *gone, arme,*
browes] gone./And see a threatning Arme, an angry Brow   160
God [1604] heauen   161–62 *No . . . earth* [1616 prints as one line]
172–73 *O . . . soul* [1604, which prints it as one line] O, if my
soule must suffer for my sinne   174 *Yet . . . me* [1604; 1616 omits]
194 *My God, my God* [1604] O mercy heauen

The Source of *Doctor Faustus*

The *Historia von D. Iohan Fausten* (1587), an anonymous German prose volume, describes the career of a man who gave the devil his soul in exchange for twenty-four years of earthly power, and who at last, after performing miraculous feats and low practical jokes, was carried off to hell. A translation of this book was published in 1592: *The Historie of the damnable life, and deserued death of Doctor Iohn Faustus, Newly imprinted, and in conuenient places imperfect matter amended . . . and translated into English by P. F. Gent[leman] . . . 1592.* Although the translation is fairly close, it is far from slavish, and some of its departures found their way into Marlowe's play. (If his play was written before 1592, Marlowe must have had access to a manuscript of the translation, or there must have been an edition—now lost—earlier than 1592. It is simplest, however, to assume that Marlowe wrote the play shortly after the edition of 1592 was printed.) This translation, commonly called the English Faust-book, or *The Damnable Life*, contains most of the narrative material for Marlowe's play, including the comic business of hitting the pope, making a fool of the horse-courser, etc. One episode in the play, however, where Pope Adrian humiliates Bruno, the rival pope who has the support of the emperor, has no parallel in *The Damnable Life*, and apparently is indebted to a passage in John Foxe's *Acts and Monuments*.

The following selection from P. F.'s *Damnable Life* includes all of the material that Marlowe used, and a few other portions that provide transitions and help to convey the flavor. The spelling has been modernized and the punctuation occasionally altered.

from *The History of the Damnable Life and Deserved Death of Doctor John Faustus*

Of his parentage and birth. Chap. 1

John Faustus, born in the town of Rhode, lying in the province of Weimar in Germany, his father a poor husbandman and not able well to bring him up: but having an uncle at Wittenberg, a rich man and without issue, took this J. Faustus from his father and made him his heir, in so much that his father was no more troubled with him, for he remained with his uncle at Wittenberg where he was kept at the university in the same city to study divinity. But Faustus, being of a naughty mind and otherwise addicted, applied not his studies but took himself to other exercises, the which his uncle oftentimes hearing, rebuked him for it as Eli oft times rebuked his children for sinning against the Lord. Even so this good man labored to have Faustus apply his study of divinity that he might come to the knowledge of God and his laws. But it is manifest that many virtuous parents have wicked children, as Cain, Reuben, Absalom, and such like have been to their parents: so this Faustus having godly parents, and seeing him to be of a toward wit, were very desirous to bring him up in those virtuous studies, namely, of divinity. But he gave himself secretly to study necromancy and conjuration, in so much that few or none could perceive his profession.

But to the purpose. Faustus continued at study in the university and was by the rectors and sixteen masters afterwards examined how he had profited in his studies. And being found by them that none for his time were able to argue with him in divinity or for the excellency of his wisdom to compare with him, with one consent they made him Doctor of Divinity. But Doctor Faustus, within short time after he had obtained his degree, fell into such fantasies and deep cogitations that he was marked of many, and of the most part of the students was called the Speculator. And sometimes he would throw the Scriptures from him as though he had no care of his former profession, so that he began a very ungodly life, as hereafter more at large may appear. For the old proverb sayeth, Who can hold that will away? So, who can hold Faustus from the devil, that seeks after him with all his endeavor? For he accompanied himself with divers that were seen in those devilish arts and that had the Chaldean, Persian, Hebrew, Arabian, and Greek tongues, using figures, characters, conjurations, incantations, with many other ceremonies belonging to these infernal arts, as necromancy, charms, soothsaying, witchcraft, enchantment; being delighted with their books, words, and names so well that he studied day and night therein: in so much that he could not abide to be called Doctor of Divinity but waxed a worldly man and named himself an astrologian and a mathematician, and for a shadow sometimes a physician, and did great cures, namely with herbs, roots, waters, drinks, receipts, and clysters. And without doubt he was passing wise, and excellent perfect in the holy Scriptures; but he that knoweth his master's will and doth it not, is worthy to be beaten with many stripes. It is written, "No man can serve two masters," and "Thou shalt not tempt the Lord thy God." But Faustus threw all this in the wind and made his soul of no estimation, regarding more his worldly pleasure than the joys to come. Therefore at the day of judgment there is no hope of his redemption.

*How Doctor Faustus began to practice
in his devilish art, and how he
conjured the devil, making him to
appear and meet him on the morrow
at his own house. Chap. 2.*

You have heard before that all Faustus' mind was set to study the arts of necromancy and conjuration, the which exercise he followed day and night; and taking to him the wings of an eagle thought to fly over the whole world and to know the secrets of heaven and earth. For his speculation was so wonderful, being expert in using his vocabula, figures, characters, conjurations, and other ceremonial actions, that in all the haste he put in practice to bring the devil before him. And taking his way to a thick wood near to Wittenberg called in the German tongue Spisser Wald, that is in English the Spissers Wood (as Faustus would oftentimes boast of it among his crew being in his jollity), he came into the same wood toward evening into a crossway, where he made with a wand a circle in the dust, and within that many more circles and characters. And thus he passed away the time until it was nine or ten of the clock in the night. Then began Doctor Faustus to call for Mephostophiles the spirit, and to charge him in the name of Beelzebub to appear there personally without any long stay. Then presently the devil began so great a rumor in the wood as if heaven and earth would have come together with wind, the trees bowing their tops to the ground. Then fell the devil to blare as if the whole wood had been full of lions, and suddenly about the circle ran the devil as if a thousand wagons had been running together on paved stones. After this, at the four corners of the wood it thundered horribly with such lightnings as if the whole world, to his seeming, had been on fire. Faustus all this while half amazed at the devil's so long tarrying, and doubting whether he were best to abide any more such horrible conjurings, thought to leave his circle and depart. Whereupon the devil made him such music of all sorts as if the nymphs themselves had been in place, whereat Faustus was revived and stood stoutly in his circle aspecting his purpose and began again to conjure the spirit Mephostophiles in the name of the prince of devils to appear in his likeness, whereat suddenly over his head hung hovering in the air a mighty dragon. Then calls Faustus again after his devilish manner, at which there was a monstrous cry in the wood as if hell had been open and all the tormented souls crying to God for mercy. Presently not three fathoms above his head fell a flame in manner of a lightning and changed itself into a globe, yet Faustus feared it not but did persuade himself that the devil should give him his request before he would leave. Oftentimes after to his companions he would boast that he had the stoutest head (under the cope of heaven) at commandment, whereat they answered they knew none stouter than the Pope or Emperor. But Doctor Faustus said "The head that is my servant is above all on earth," and repeated certain words out of Saint Paul to the Ephesians to make his argument good: The prince of this world is upon earth and under heaven. Well, let us come again to his conjuration where we left him at his fiery globe. Faustus, vexed at the spirit's so long tarrying, used his charms with full purpose not to depart before he had his intent, and crying on Mephostophiles the spirit. Suddenly the globe opened and sprang up in height of a man; so burning a time, in the end it converted to the shape of a fiery man. This pleasant beast ran about the circle a great while and lastly appeared in manner of a gray friar, asking Faustus what was his request. Faustus commanded that the next morning at twelve of the clock he should appear to him at his house, but the devil would in no wise grant. Faustus began again to conjure him, in the name of Beelzebub, that he should fulfill his request, whereupon the spirit agreed, and so they departed each one his way.

The conference of Doctor Faustus
with the spirit Mephostophiles the
morning following at his own house. Chap. 3.

Doctor Faustus having commanded the spirit to be with him, at his hour appointed he came and appeared in his chamber, demanding of Faustus what his desire was. Then began Doctor Faustus anew with him to conjure him that he should be obedient unto him, and to answer him certain articles, and to fulfill them in all points.

1   That the spirit should serve him and be obedient unto him in all things that he asked of him from that hour until the hour of his death.

2   Farther, anything that he desired of him he should bring it to him.

3   Also, that in all Faustus' demands or interrogations, the spirit should tell him nothing but that which is true.

Hereupon the spirit answered and laid his case forth, that he had no such power of himself until he had first given his prince (that was ruler over him) to understand hereof and to know if he could obtain so much of his Lord. "Therefore speak farther that I may do thy whole desire to my prince, for it is not in my power to fulfill without his leave." "Show me the cause why," said Faustus. The spirit answered, "Faustus, thou shalt understand that with us it is even as well a kingdom as with you on earth. Yea, we have our rulers and servants, as I myself am one, and we name our whole number the legion; for although that Lucifer is thrust and fallen out of heaven through his pride and high mind, yet he hath notwithstanding a legion of devils at his commandment that we call the oriental princes; for his power is great and infinite. Also there is an host in meridie, in septentrio, in occidente; and for that Lucifer hath his kingdom under heaven, we must change and give ourselves unto men to serve them at their pleasure. It is also certain, we have never as yet opened unto any man the truth of our dwelling, neither of our ruling, neither what our power is; neither have we given any man any gift or learned him anything except he promise to be ours."

Doctor Faustus, upon this, arose where he sat and said, "I will have my request, and yet I will not be damned." The spirit answered, "Then shalt thou want thy desire, and yet art thou mine notwithstanding. If any man would retain thee it is in vain, for thine infidelity hath confounded thee."

Hereupon spake Faustus, "Get thee hence from me, and take Saint Valentine's farewell and Crisam with thee, yet I conjure thee that thou be here at evening, and bethink thyself on that I have asked thee, and ask thy prince's counsel therein." Mephostophiles the spirit, thus answered, vanished away, leaving Faustus in his study, where he sat pondering with himself how he might obtain his request of the devil without loss of his soul. Yet fully he was resolved in himself, rather than to want his pleasure, to do whatsoever the spirit and his lord should condition upon.

The second time of the spirit's appearing to Faustus in his house, and of their parley. Chap. 4.

Faustus continuing in his devilish cogitations, never moving out of the place where the spirit left him (such was his fervent love to the devil), the night approaching, this swift-flying spirit appeared to Faustus, offering himself with all submission to his service, with full authority from his prince to do whatsoever he would request if so be Faustus would promise to be his. "This answer I bring thee, and an answer must thou make by me again, yet will I hear what is thy desire because thou hast sworn me to be here at this time." Doctor Faustus gave him this answer, though faintly (for his soul's sake), that his request was none other but to become a devil, or at the least a limb of him, and that the spirit should agree unto these articles as followeth.

1   That he might be a spirit in shape and quality.

2   That Mephostophiles should be his servant and at his commandment.

3   That Mephostophiles should bring him anything and do for him whatsoever.

4   That at all times he should be in his house, invisible to all men except only to himself, and at his commandment to show himself.

5   Lastly, that Mephostophiles should at all times appear at his command, in what form or shape soever he would.

. Upon these points the spirit answered Doctor Faustus that all this should be granted him and fulfilled and more if he would agree unto him upon certain articles as followeth.

First, that Doctor Faustus should give himself to his Lord Lucifer, body and soul.

Secondly, for confirmation of the same he should make him a writing, written with his own blood.

Thirdly, that he would be an enemy to all Christian people.

Fourthly, that he would deny his Christian belief.

Fifthly, that he let not any man change his opinion, if so be any man should go about to dissuade or withdraw him from it.

Further, the spirit promised Faustus to give him certain years to live in health and pleasure, and when such years were expired that then Faustus should be fetched away; and if he should hold these articles and conditions that then he should have all whatsoever his heart would wish or desire; and that Faustus should quickly perceive himself to be a spirit in all manner of actions whatsoever. Hereupon Doctor Faustus' mind was so inflamed that he forgot his soul and promised Mephostophiles to hold all things as he had mentioned them. He thought the devil was not so black as they used to paint him, nor hell so hot as the people say, etc.

*The third parley between Doctor Faustus
and Mephostophiles about a conclusion. Chap. 5.*

After Doctor Faustus had made his promise to the devil, in the morning betimes he called the spirit before him and commanded him that he should always come to him like a friar, after the order of Saint Francis, with a bell in his hand like Saint Anthony, and to ring it once or twice before he appeared, that he might know of his certain coming. Then Faustus demanded the spirit, what was his name? The spirit answered, "My name is as thou sayest, Mephostophiles, and I am a prince, but servant to Lucifer; and all the circuit from Septentrio to the Meridian I rule under him." Even at these words was this wicked wretch Faustus inflamed, to hear himself to have gotten so great a potentate to be his servant; forgot the

Lord his maker and Christ his redeemer; became an
enemy unto all mankind. Yea, worse than the giants
whom the poets feign to climb the hills to make war with
the gods, not unlike that enemy of God and his Christ
that for his pride was cast into hell, so likewise Faustus
forgot that the high climbers catch the greatest falls and
that the sweetest meat requires the sourest sauce.

After a while, Faustus promised Mephostophiles to
write and make his obligation, with full assurance of the
articles in the chapter before rehearsed. A pitiful case,
Christian reader, for certainly this letter or obligation
was found in his house after his most lamentable end,
with all the rest of his damnable practices used in his
whole life. Therefore I wish all Christians to take an
example by this wicked Faustus and to be comforted in
Christ, contenting themselves with that vocation whereunto it hath pleased God to call them, and not to esteem
the vain delights of this life, as did this unhappy Faustus
in giving his soul to the devil. And to confirm it the more
assuredly, he took a small penknife and pricked a vein in
his left hand, and for certainty thereupon were seen on his
hand these words written as if they had been written with
blood, *O homo fuge:* whereat the spirit vanished, but
Faustus continued in his damnable mind, and made his
writing as followeth.

How Doctor Faustus set his blood in a saucer on warm ashes, and writ as followeth. Chap. 6.

I, Johannes Faustus, Doctor, do openly acknowledge
with mine own hand, to the greater force and strengthening of this letter, that since I began to study and speculate
the course and order of the elements I have not found
through the gift that is given me from above any such
learning and wisdom that can bring me to my desires. And
for that I find that men are unable to instruct me any
farther in the matter, now have I, Doctor John Faustus,
unto the hellish prince of Orient and his messenger
Mephostophiles given both body and soul upon such con-

dition that they shall learn me and fulfill my desire in all things as they have promised and vowed unto me, with due obedience unto me, according unto the articles mentioned between us.

Further, I covenant and grant with them by these presents that at the end of twenty-four years next ensuing the date of this present letter, they being expired, and I in the meantime during the said years be served of them at my will, they accomplishing my desires to the full in all points as we are agreed, that then I give them full power to do with me at their pleasure, to rule, to send, fetch, or carry me or mine, be it either body, soul, flesh, blood, or goods, into their habitation, be it wheresoever. And hereupon I defy God and his Christ, all the host of heaven, and all living creatures that bear the shape of God, yea all that lives; and again I say it, and it shall be so. And to the more strengthening of this writing, I have written it with mine own hand and blood, being in perfect memory, and hereupon I subscribe to it with my name and title, calling all the infernal, middle, and supreme powers to witness of this my letter and subscription.

> John Faustus, approved in the elements,
> and the spiritual doctor.

*The manner how Faustus proceeded with
his damnable life, and of the diligent
service that Mephostophiles used towards
him. Chap. 8.*

Doctor Faustus having given his soul to the devil, renouncing all the powers of heaven, confirming this lamentable action with his own blood, and having already delivered his writing not into the devil's hand, the which so puffed up his heart that he had forgot the mind of a man and thought rather himself to be a spirit. This Faustus dwelt in his uncle's house at Wittenberg, who died and bequeathed it in his testament to his cousin Faustus. Faustus kept a boy with him that was his scholar, an unhappy wag called Christopher Wagner, to whom this sport and life that he saw his master follow seemed pleasant. Faustus loved the boy well, hoping to make him as good or better seen in his devilish exercise than himself, and he was fellow with Mephostophiles. Otherwise Faustus had no more company in his house but himself, his boy, and his spirit, that ever was diligent at Faustus' command, going about the house clothed like a friar with a little bell in his hand, seen of none but Faustus. For his victual and other necessaries, Mephostophiles brought him at his pleasure from the Duke of Saxon, the Duke of Bavaria, and the Bishop of Salzburg; for they had many times their best wine stolen out of their cellars by Mephostophiles. Likewise their provision for their own table, such meat as Faustus wished for, his spirit brought him in. Besides that, Faustus himself was become so cunning that when he opened his window, what fowl soever he wished for came presently flying into his house, were it never so dainty. Moreover, Faustus and his boy went in sumptuous apparel, the which Mephostophiles stole from the mercers at Nuremberg, Augsburg, Frankfort, and Leipzig; for it was hard for them to find a lock to keep out such a thief. All their maintenance was but stolen and borrowed ware; and thus they lived an odious life in the sight of God, though as yet the world were unacquainted with their wickedness. It must be so, for their fruits be none other, as Christ saith through John where he calls the devil a thief and a murderer; and that found Faustus, for he stole him away both body and soul.

How Doctor Faustus would have married,
and how the Devil had almost
killed him for it. Chap. 9.

Doctor Faustus continued thus in his epicurish life day and night and believed not that there was a God, hell, or devil. He thought that body and soul died together and had quite forgotten divinity or the immortality of his soul, but stood in his damnable heresy day and night. And bethinking himself of a wife, called Mephostophiles to counsel, which would in no wise agree, demanding of him if he would break the covenant made with him or if he had forgot it. "Hast not thou," quoth Mephostophiles, "sworn thyself an enemy to God and all creatures? To this I answer thee, thou canst not marry; thou canst not serve two masters, God and my prince. For wedlock is a chief institution ordained of God, and that hast thou promised to defy, as we do all, and that hast thou also done; and moreover thou hast confirmed it with thy blood. Persuade thyself that what thou dost in contempt of wedlock, it is all to thine own delight. Therefore, Faustus, look well about thee and bethink thyself better, and I wish thee to change thy mind; for if thou keep not what thou hast promised in thy writing, we will tear thee in pieces like the dust under thy feet. Therefore, sweet Faustus, think with what unquiet life, anger, strife, and debate thou shalt live in when thou takest a wife; therefore change thy mind."

Doctor Faustus was with these speeches in despair; and as all that have forsaken the Lord can build upon no good foundation, so this wretched Faustus, having forsook the rock, fell in despair with himself, fearing if he should motion matrimony any more that the devil would tear him in pieces. "For this time," quoth he to Mephostophiles, "I am not minded to marry." "Then you do well," answered his spirit. But shortly, and that within two hours after, Faustus called his spirit, which came in his old manner like a friar. Then Faustus said unto him, "I am not able to resist nor bridle my fantasy; I must and will have a wife, and I pray thee give thy consent to it." Suddenly upon these words came such a whirlwind about the place that Faustus thought the whole house would come down; all the doors in the house flew off the hooks. After all this, his house was full of smoke and the floor covered over with ashes, which when Doctor Faustus perceived, he would have gone up the stairs. And flying up, he was taken and thrown into the hall, that he was not able to stir hand nor foot. Then round about him ran a monstrous circle of fire, never standing still, that Faustus fried as he lay and thought there to have been burned.

Then cried he out to his spirit Mephostophiles for help, promising him he would live in all things as he had vowed in his handwriting. Hereupon appeared unto him an ugly devil, so fearful and monstrous to behold that Faustus durst not look on him. The devil said, "What wouldst thou have, Faustus? How likest thou thy wedding? What mind art thou in now?" Faustus answered, he had forgot his promise, desiring him of pardon, and he would talk no more of such things. The devil answered, "Thou were best so to do," and so vanished.

After appeared unto him his friar Mephostophiles with a bell in his hand, and spake to Faustus: "It is no jesting with us. Hold thou that which thou hast vowed and we will perform as we have promised; and more than that, thou shalt have thy heart's desire of what woman soever thou wilt, be she alive or dead, and so long as thou wilt thou shalt keep her by thee."

These words pleased Faustus wonderfully well, and repented himself that he was so foolish to wish himself married that might have any woman in the whole city brought to him at his command, the which he practiced and persevered in a long time.

Questions put forth by Doctor Faustus unto his spirit Mephostophiles. Chap. 10.

Doctor Faustus, living in all manner of pleasure that his heart could desire, continuing in his amorous drifts, his delicate fare, and costly apparel, called on a time his Mephostophiles to him: which being come, brought with him a book in his hand of all manner of devilish and enchanted arts, the which he gave Faustus, saying "Hold, my Faustus, work now thy heart's desire." The copy of this enchanting book was afterwards found by his servant, Christopher Wagner. "Well," quoth Faustus to his spirit, "I have called thee to know what thou canst do if I have need of thy help." Then answered Mephostophiles and said, "My Lord Faustus, I am a flying spirit, yea, so swift as thought can think, to do whatsoever." Here Faustu

said, "But how came thy Lord and master Lucifer to have
so great a fall from heaven?" Mephostophiles answered,
"My Lord Lucifer was a fair angel, created of God as
immortal, and being placed in the seraphins, which are
above the cherubins, he would have presumed unto the
throne of God, with intent to have thrust God out of his
seat. Upon this presumption the Lord cast him down
headlong, and where before he was an angel of light, now
dwells he in darkness, not able to come near his first place
without God send for him to appear before him as
Raphael. But unto the lower degree of angels that have
their conversation with men he was come, but not unto
the second degree of heavens that is kept by the arch-
angels, namely Michael and Gabriel, for these are called
angels of God's wonders: yet are these far inferior places
to that from whence my Lord and Master Lucifer fell.
And thus far, Faustus, because thou art one of the beloved
children of my Lord Lucifer, following and feeding thy
mind in manner as he did his, I have shortly resolved
thy request, and more I will do for thee at thy pleasure."
"I thank thee, Mephostophiles," quoth Faustus. "Come
let us now go rest, for it is night." Upon this, they left
their communication.

How Doctor Faustus dreamed that he had seen hell in
his sleep, and how he questioned with his spirit of
matters as concerning hell, with the spirit's answer.
Chap. 11.

The night following, after Faustus his communication
had with Mephostophiles as concerning the fall of Lucifer,
Doctor Faustus dreamed that he had seen a part of hell;
but in what manner it was or in what place he knew not,
whereupon he was greatly troubled in mind and called
unto him Mephostophiles his spirit, saying to him, "My
Mephostophiles, I pray thee resolve me in this doubt.
What is hell, what substance is it of, in what place stands
it, and when was it made?" Mephostophiles answered,
"My Faustus, thou shalt know that before the fall of my

Lord Lucifer there was no hell, but even then was hell ordained. It is of no substance, but a confused thing. For I tell thee that before all elements were made, and the earth seen, the Spirit of God moved on the waters and darkness was over all; but when God said, 'Let it be light,' it was so at his word, and the light was on God's right hand, and God praised the light. Judge thou further: God stood in the middle, the darkness was on his left hand, in the which my Lord was bound in chains until the day of judgment: in this confused hell is nought to find but a filthy, sulphurish, fiery, stinking mist or fog. Further, we devils know not what substance it is of, but a confused thing. For as a bubble of water flieth before the wind, so doth hell before the breath of God. Further, we devils know not how God hath laid the foundation of our hell, nor whereof it is: but to be short with thee, Faustus, we know that hell hath neither bottom nor end."

Another question put forth by Doctor Faustus to his spirit concerning his Lord Lucifer, with the sorrow that Faustus fell afterwards into. Chap. 13.

Doctor Faustus began again to reason with Mephostophiles, requiring him to tell him in what form and shape and in what estimation his Lord Lucifer was when he was in favor with God. Whereupon his spirit required him of three days' respite, which Faustus granted. The three days being expired, Mephostophiles gave him this answer: "Faustus, my Lord Lucifer (so called now, for that he was banished out of the clear light of heaven) was at the first an angel of God, he sat on the cherubins, and saw all the wonderful works of God, yea he was so of God ordained, for shape, pomp, authority, worthiness, and dwelling, that he far exceeded all other the creatures of God, yea our gold and precious stones: and so illuminated that he far surpassed the brightness of the sun and all other stars; wherefore God placed him on the cherubins, where he had a kingly office, and was always before God's seat, to the end he might be the more perfect in all his beings: but when he began to be high minded, proud, and so presumptuous that he would usurp the seat of his Majesty, then was he banished out from amongst the heavenly powers, separated from their abiding into the manner of a fiery stone that no water is able to quench but continually burneth until the end of the world."

Doctor Faustus, when he had heard the words of his spirit, began to consider with himself, having diverse and sundry opinions in his head: and very pensively (saying nothing) unto his spirit, he went into his chamber and laid him on his bed, recording the words of Mephostophiles; which so pierced his heart that he fell into sighing and great lamentation, crying out "Alas, ah, woe is me! What have I done? Even so shall it come to pass with me. Am not I also a creature of God's making, bearing his own image and similitude, into whom he hath breathed the spirit of life and immortality, unto whom he hath made all things living subject? But woe is me; mine haughty mind, proud aspiring stomach, and filthy flesh hath brought my soul into perpetual damnation. Yea, pride hath abused my understanding, in so much that I have forgot my maker; the Spirit of God is departed from me. I have promised the devil my soul, and therefore it is but a folly for me to hope for grace, but it must be even with me as with Lucifer, thrown into perpetual burning fire. Ah, woe is me that ever I was born." In this perplexity lay this miserable Doctor Faustus, having quite forgot his faith in Christ, never falling to repentance truly, thereby to attain the grace and Holy Spirit of God again, the which would have been able to have resisted the strong assaults of Satan. For although he had made him a promise, yet he might have remembered through true repentance sinners come again into the favor of God; which faith the faithful firmly hold, knowing they that kill the body are not able to hurt the soul. But he was in all his opinions doubtful, without faith or hope, and so he continued.

Here followeth the second part of Doctor
Faustus, his life and practices, until his
end. Chap. 17.

Doctor Faustus, having received denial of his spirit to
be resolved any more in such like questions propounded
forgot all good works and fell to be a calendar maker
by help of his spirit, and also in short time to be a good
astronomer or astrologian. He had learned so perfectly
of his spirit the course of the sun, moon, and stars, that
he had the most famous name of all the mathematics that
lived in his time, as may well appear by his works dedi-
cated unto sundry dukes and lords; for he did nothing
without the advice of his spirit, which learned him to
presage of matters to come, which have come to pass
since his death. The like praise won he with his calendars
and almanacs making, for when he presaged upon any
change, operation, or alteration of the weather or elements—as wind, rain, fogs, snow, hail, moist, dry, warm
cold, thunder, lightning—it fell so duly out as if an ange
of heaven had forewarned it. He did not like the unskillfu
astronomers of our time, that set in winter cold, moist
airy, frosty; and in the dog days hot, dry, thunder, fire
and such like; but he set in all his works day and hour
when, where, and how it should happen. If anything
wonderful were at hand, as death, famine, plague, or wars
he would set the time and place in true and just order
when it should come to pass.

How Doctor Faustus fell into despair with himself:
for having put forth a question unto his spirit,
they fell at variance, whereupon the whole rout
of devils appeared unto him, threatening him
sharply. Chap. 19.

Doctor Faustus revolving with himself the speeches of
his spirit, he became so woeful and sorrowful in his cogitations that he thought himself already frying in the hottes

ames of hell; and lying in his muse, suddenly there
ppeared unto him his spirit, demanding what thing so
ieved and troubled his conscience, whereat Doctor
austus gave no answer: yet the spirit very earnestly lay
pon him to know the cause, and if it were possible, he
ould find remedy for his grief and ease him of his sor-
ows. To whom Faustus answered, "I have taken thee
nto me as a servant to do me service, and thy service
ill be very dear unto me; yet I cannot have any diligence
f thee farther than thou list thyself, neither dost thou
a anything as it becometh thee." The spirit replied, "My
austus, thou knowest that I was never against thy com-
aandments as yet, but ready to serve and resolve thy
uestions, although I am not bound unto thee in such
espects as concern the hurt of our kingdom, yet was I
lways willing to answer thee, and so I am still: therefore,
ay Faustus, say on boldly, what is thy will and pleasure?"
t which words, the spirit stole away the heart of Faustus,
ho spake in this sort: "Mephostophiles, tell me how and
fter what sort God made the world, and all the creatures
a them, and why man was made after the image of
iod."

The spirit, hearing this, answered, "Faustus, thou know-
st that all this is in vain for thee to ask. I know that thou
rt sorry for that thou hast done, but it availeth thee not,
or I will tear thee in thousands of pieces if thou change
ot thine opinions," and hereat he vanished away.
/hereat Faustus, all sorrowful for that he had put forth
ach a question, fell to weeping and to howling bitterly,
ot for his sins towards God but for that the devil was
eparted from him so suddenly and in such a rage. And
eing in this perplexity, he was suddenly taken in such an
xtreme cold as if he should have frozen in the place
here he sat, in which the greatest devil in hell appeared
nto him with certain of his hideous and infernal com-
any in the most ugliest shapes that it was possible to
aink upon, and traversing the chamber round about
here Faustus sat, Faustus thought to himself, now are
ney come for me though my time be not come, and that
ecause I have asked such questions of my servant

Mephostophiles. At whose cogitations, the chiefest de
which was his lord, unto whom he gave his soul, that w
Lucifer, spake in this sort: "Faustus, I have seen t
thoughts, which are not as thou hast vowed unto me
virtue of this letter," and showed him the obligation th
he had written with his own blood, "wherefore I am cor
to visit thee and to show thee some of our hellish pastime
in hope that will draw and confirm thy mind a little mo
steadfast unto us." "Content," quoth Faustus, "go to;
me see what pastime you can make." At which words, t
great devil in his likeness sat him down by Faustus, cor
manding the rest of the devils to appear in their form
if they were in hell. First entered Belial in form of
bear, with curled black hair to the ground, his ears stan
ing upright. Within the ear was as red as blood, out
which issued flames of fire. His teeth were a foot at lea
long, as white as snow; with a tail three ells long (at t
least); having two wings, one behind each arm. A
thus one after another they appeared to Faustus in for
as they were in hell. Lucifer himself sat in manner of
man, all hairy but of a brown color like a squirrel, curle
and his tail turning upwards on his back as the squirro
use; I think he could crack nuts too, like a squirrel. Aft
him came Beelzebub in curled hair of horse flesh cold
his head like the head of a bull with a mighty pair
horns and two long ears down to the ground, and tv
wings on his back, with pricking stings like thorns; out
his wings issued flames of fire; his tail was like a co
Then came Astaroth in form of a worm, going upright
his tail; he had no feet, but a tail like a slow-worm; und
his chaps grew two short hands, and his back was cc
black, his belly thick in the middle and yellow like gol
having many bristles on his back like a hedgehog. .
The rest of the devils were in form of unsensible beas
as swine, harts, bears, wolves, apes, buffaloes, goa
antelopes, elephants, dragons, horses, asses, lions, ca
snakes, toads, and all manner of ugly, odious serper
and worms: yet came in such sort that every one at I
entry into the hall made their reverence unto Lucifer, a
so took their places, standing in order as they came, un

ey had filled the whole hall. . . . Then said Faustus, "I
ke not so many of you together," whereupon Lucifer
ommanded them to depart except seven of the principal.
orthwith they presently vanished, which Faustus per-
eiving, he was somewhat better comforted, and spake
o Lucifer, "Where is my servant Mephostophiles? Let me
ee if he can do the like." Whereupon came a fierce
ragon, flying and spitting fire round about the house, and
oming towards Lucifer, made reverence, and then
hanged himself to the form of a friar, saying "Faustus,
hat wilt thou?" Saith Faustus, "I will that thou teach
e to transform myself in like sort as thou and the rest
ave done." Then Lucifer put forth his paw and gave
austus a book, saying "Hold. Do what thou wilt." Which
e looking upon, straightway changed himself into a hog,
en into a worm, then into a dragon, and finding this for
is purpose, it liked him well. . . .

*How Doctor Faustus was carried through the air up
to the heavens to see the world, and how the sky
and planets ruled: after the which he wrote one
letter to his friend of the same to Leipzig, how
he went about the world in eight days. Chap. 21.*

This letter was found by a freeman and citizen of Wit-
enberg, written with his own hand, and sent to his friend
t Leipzig a physician named Jove Victori, the contents
f which were as followeth. . . . I being once laid on my
ed, and could not sleep for thinking on my calendar and
ractice, I marveled with myself how it were possible that
e firmament should be known and so largely written of
en, or whether they write true or false, by their own
pinions, or supposition, or by due observations and true
ourse of the heavens. Behold, being in these my muses,
uddenly I heard a great noise, in so much that I thought
y house would have been blown down, so that all my
oors and chests flew open, whereas I was not a little
stonished, for withal I heard a groaning voice which said

"Get up. The desire of thy heart, mind, and thought sh
thou see." At the which I answered "What my he
desireth, that would I fain see, and to make proof, i
shall see I will away with thee." "Why then," quoth
"look out at thy window. There cometh a messenger
thee." That did I, and behold, there stood a wagon, w
two dragons before it to draw the same, and all the wag
was of a light burning fire, and for that the moon sho
I was the willinger at that time to depart. But the vo
spake again, "Sit up and let us away." "I will," said I, "
with thee, but upon this condition, that I may ask after
things that I see, hear, or think on." The voice answere
"I am content for this time." Hereupon I got me into t
wagon, so that the dragons carried me upright into t
air. The wagon had also four wheels which rattled so a
made such a noise as if we had been all this while runni
on the stones. And round about us flew out flames of fi
and the higher that I came the more the earth seemed
be darkened, so that methought I came out of a dungec
and looking down from heaven, behold, Mephostophil
my spirit and servant was behind me. And when
perceived that I saw him, he came and sat by me,
whom I said, "I pray thee, Mephostophiles, whither sh
I go now?" "Let not that trouble thy mind," said he, a
yet they carried us higher up. And now will I tell the
good friend and school fellow, what things I have se
and proved; for on the Tuesday went I out, and
Tuesday seven-nights following I came home again, th
is eight days, in which time I slept not, no, not one wi
came in mine eyes, and we went invisible of any man. A
as the day began to appear, after our first night's journe
I said to my spirit Mephostophiles, "I pray thee how f
have we now ridden? I am sure thou knowest: for m
thinks that we are ridden exceeding far, the world seeme
so little." Mephostophiles answered me, "My Faust
believe me, that from the place from whence thou can
unto this place where we are now is already forty-sev
leagues right in height." And as the day increased I look
down upon the world. There saw I many kingdoms a
provinces; likewise the whole world, Asia, Europe, a

Africa, I had a sight of. . . . Then looked I up to the
heavens, and behold, they went so swift that I thought
they would have sprung in thousands. Likewise it was so
clear and so hot that I could not long gaze into it, it so
dimmed my sight: and had not my spirit Mephostophiles
covered me as it were with a shadowing cloud, I had been
burnt with the extreme heat thereof; for the sky the which
we behold here when we look up from the earth is so fast
and thick as a wall, clear and shining bright as a crystal,
in the which is placed the sun, which casteth forth his
rays or beams over the universal world to the uttermost
confines of the earth. But we think that the sun is very
little: no, it is altogther as big as the world. Indeed the
body substantial is but little in compass, but the rays or
stream that it casteth forth, by reason of the thing wherein
is placed, maketh him to extend and show himself over
the whole world. And we think that the sun runneth his
course and that the heavens stand still: no, it is the
heavens that move his course and the sun abideth perpetually in his place. He is permanent and fixed in his
place, and although we see him beginning to ascend in
the orient or east, at the highest in the meridian or south,
setting in the occident or west, yet is he at the lowest in
septentrio or north, and yet he moveth not. It is the axle
of the heavens that moveth the whole firmament, being a
chaos or confused thing, and for that proof, I will show
thee this example: like as thou seest a bubble made of
water and soap blown forth of a quill, is in form of a
confused mass or chaos, and being in this form, is moved
at pleasure of the wind, which runneth round about that
chaos, and moveth him also round; even so is the whole
firmament or chaos, wherein are placed the sun, and the
rest of the planets turned and carried at the pleasure of
the Spirit of God, which is wind. . . . And like as I
showed before of the bubble or confused chaos made of
water and soap, through the wind and breath of man is
turned round and carried with every wind; even so the
firmament wherein the sun and the rest of the planets are
fixed, moved, turned, and carried with the wind, breath,
or Spirit of God; for the heavens and firmament are

movable as the chaos, but the sun is fixed in the firm
ment. And farther, my good schoolfellow, I was thus n
the heavens, where methought every planet was but
half the earth, and under the firmament ruled the spi
in the air, and as I came down I looked upon the wo
and the heavens, and methought that the earth was
closed in comparison within the firmament as the yolk
an egg within the white, and methought that the wh
length of the earth was not a span long. . . .

*How Doctor Faustus made his journey through
the principal and most famous lands in
the world. Chap. 22.*

Doctor Faustus having overrun fifteen years of
appointed time, he took upon him a journey, with f
pretence to see the whole world; and calling his sp
Mephostophiles unto him, he said, "Thou knowest tl
thou art bound unto me upon conditions, to perform a
fulfill my desire in all things, wherefore my pretence is
visit the whole face of the earth visible and invisible wl
it pleaseth me: wherefore, I enjoin and command thee
the same." Whereupon Mephostophiles answered, "I
ready, my lord, at thy command," and forthwith
spirit changed himself into the likeness of a flying hor
saying "Faustus, sit up, I am ready." Doctor Faus
loftily sat upon him, and forward they went. Faus
came through many a land and province. . . . He to
a little rest at home, and burning in desire to see m
at large and to behold the secrets of each kingdom,
set forward again on his journey upon his swift ho
Mephostophiles, and came to Treir, for that he chie
desired to see this town and the monuments thereof;
there he saw not many wonders except one fair palace tl
belonged unto the bishop, and also a mighty large ca:
that was built of brick, with three walls and three gr
trenches, so strong that it was impossible for any princ
power to win it. Then he saw a church wherein was bur
Simeon and the Bishop Popo; their tombs are of m

sumptuous large marble stone closed and joined together
with great bars of iron. From whence he departed to
Paris, where he liked well the Academy; and what place
or kingdom soever fell in his mind, the same he visited.
He came from Paris to Mentz, where the river of Main
falls into the Rhine; notwithstanding he tarried not long
there, but went to Campania in the kingdom of Naples,
in which he saw an innumerable sort of cloisters, nun-
neries, and churches, great and high houses of stone, the
streets fair and large, and straight forth from one end of
the town to the other as a line; and all the pavement of
the city was of brick, and the more it rained in the town
the fairer the streets were. There saw he the tomb of
Vergil and the highway that he cut through that mighty
hill of stone in one night, the whole length of an English
mile. Then he saw the number of galleys and argosies that
lay there at the city head, the windmill that stood in the
water, the castle in the water, and the houses above the
water where under the galleys might ride most safely
from rain or wind. Then he saw the castle on the hill over
the town and many monuments within, also the hill called
Vesuvius, whereon groweth all the Greekish wine and
most pleasant sweet olives. From thence he came to
Venice, whereas he wondered not a little to see a city so
famously built standing in the sea, where through every
street the water ran in such largeness that great ships and
barks might pass from one street to another, having yet
a way on both sides the water whereon men and horse
might pass. He marveled also how it was possible for so
much victual to be found in the town and so good cheap,
considering that for a whole league off nothing grew near
the same. He wondered not a little at the fairness of Saint
Mark's place and the sumptuous church standing therein
called Saint Mark's: how all the pavement was set with
colored stones and all the rood or loft of the church
doubly gilded over. Leaving this, he came to Padua, beholding the manner of their Academy, which is called the
mother or nurse of Christendom. There he heard the
doctors and saw the most monuments in the town, entered
his name into the university of the German nation, and

wrote himself Doctor Faustus, the insatiable speculator. Then saw he the worthiest monument in the world for a church, named Saint Anthony's Cloister, which for the pinnacles thereof and the contriving of the church hath not the like in Christendom. This town is fenced about with three mighty walls of stone and earth, betwixt the which runneth goodly ditches of water. Twice every twenty-four hours passeth boats betwixt Padua and Venice with passengers as they do here betwixt London and Gravesend, and even so far they differ in distance. Faustus beheld likewise the counsel house and the castle with no small wonder. Well, forward he went to Rome, which lay and doth yet lie on the river Tiber, the which divideth the city in two parts: over the river are four great stone bridges, and upon the one bridge called Ponte S. Angelo is the Castle of S. Angelo, wherein are so many great cast pieces as there are days in a year, and such pieces that will shoot seven bullets off with one fire; to this castle cometh a privy vault from the church and palace of Saint Peter, through the which the Pope (if any danger be) passeth from his palace to the castle for safegard. The city hath eleven gates, and a hill called Vaticinium whereon Saint Peter's church is built. In that church the holy fathers will hear no confession without the penitent bring money in his hand. Adjoining to this church is the Campo Santo, the which Carolus Magnus built, where every day thirteen pilgrims have their dinners served of the best: that is to say, Christ and his twelve Apostles. Hard by this he visited the churchyard of Saint Peter's, where he saw the pyramid that Julius Caesar brought out of Africa. It stood in Faustus' time leaning against the church wall of Saint Peter's, but now Papa Sixtus hath erected it in the middle of Saint Peter's churchyard. It is twenty-four fathom long and at the lower end six fathom foursquare, and so forth smaller upwards; on the top is a crucifix of beaten gold; the stone standeth on four lions of brass. Then he visited the seven churches of Rome, that were Saint Peter's, Saint Paul's, Saint Sebastian's, Saint John Lateran, St. Laurence, Saint Mary Magdalen, and Saint Marie Majora. Then went he without the town, where he saw the conduits of water that run level through hill and dale, bringing water into the town fifteen Italian miles off. Other monuments he saw, too many to recite, but amongst the rest he was desirous to see the pope's palace, and his manner of service at his table. Wherefore, he and his spirit made themselves invisible and came into the pope's court and privy chamber where he was. There saw he many servants attendant on his holiness, with many a flattering sycophant carrying of his meat, and there he marked the pope and the manner of his service, which he seeing to be so unmeasurable and sumptuous, "Fie," quoth Faustus, "why had not the devil made a pope of me?" Faustus saw notwithstanding in that place those that were like to himself, proud, stout, willful, gluttons, drunkards, whoremongers, breakers of wedlock, and followers of all manner of ungodly exercises. Wherefore he said to his spirit, "I thought that I had been alone a hog or pork of the devil's, but he must bear with me yet a little longer, for these hogs of Rome are already fattened and fitted to make his roast meat. The devil might do well now to spit them all and have them to the fire, and let him summon the nuns to turn the spits. For as none must confess the nun but the friar, so none should turn the roasting friar but the nun." Thus continued Faustus three days in the pope's palace, and yet had no lust to his meat, but stood still in the pope's chamber and saw everything whatsoever it was. On a time the pope would have a feast prepared for the Cardinal of Pavia, and for his first welcome the cardinal was bidden to dinner, and as he sat at meat the pope would ever be blessing and crossing over his mouth. Faustus could suffer it no longer, but up with his fist and smote the pope on the face, and withall he laughed that the whole house might hear him, yet none of them saw him nor knew where he was. The pope persuaded his company that it was a damned soul, commanding a mass presently to be said for his delivery out of purgatory, which was done. The pope sat still at meat, but when the latter mess came in to the pope's board, Doctor Faustus laid hands thereon, saying "This is mine." And so he took both dish and meat and fled unto the

Capitol or Campadolia, calling his spirit unto him, and said, "Come, let us be merry, for thou must fetch me some wine and the cup that the pope drinks of, and here upon Monte Caval will we make good cheer in spite of the pope and all his fat abbey lubbers." His spirit, hearing this, departed towards the pope's chamber, where he found them yet sitting and quaffing: wherefore he took from before the pope the fairest piece of plate or drinking goblet and a flagon of wine, and brought it to Faustus. But when the pope and the rest of his crew perceived they were robbed, and knew not after what sort, they persuaded themselves that it was the damned soul that before had vexed the pope so and that smote him on the face; wherefore he sent commandment through all the whole city of Rome that they should say mass in every church and ring all the bells for to lay the walking spirit, and to curse him with bell, book, and candle, that so invisibly had misused the pope's holiness, with the Cardinal of Pavia and the rest of their company. But Faustus notwithstanding made good cheer with that which he had beguiled the pope of, and in the midst of the order of Saint Barnard's barefooted friars, as they were going on procession through the market place called Campa de Fiore, he let fall his plate dishes and cup, and withall for a farewell he made such a thunderclap and a storm of rain as though heaven and earth should have met together, and so he left Rome. . . .

How the Emperor Carolus Quintus requested of Faustus to see some of his cunning, whereunto he agreed. Chap. 29.

The Emperor Carolus, the fifth of that name, was personally with the rest of his nobles and gentlemen at the town of Innsbruck where he kept his court; unto the which also Doctor Faustus resorted, and being there well known of divers nobles and gentlemen, he was invited into the court to meat, even in the presence of the emperor: whom when the emperor saw, he looked earnestly on him, thinking him by his looks to be some wonderful fellow, wherefore he asked one of his nobles whom he should be, who answered that he was called Doctor Faustus. Whereupon the emperor held his peace until he had taken his repast, after which he called unto him Faustus, into the privy chamber. Whither being come, he said unto him, "Faustus, I have heard much of thee, that thou art excelent in the black art, and none like thee in mine empire, for men say that thou hast a familiar spirit with thee and that thou canst do what thou list. It is therefore," saith the emperor, "my request of thee that thou let me see a proof of thine experience, and I vow unto thee by the honor of mine imperial crown, none evil shall happen unto thee for so doing." Hereupon Doctor Faustus answered his majesty that upon those conditions he was ready in anything that he could to do his highness's commandment in what service he would appoint him. "Well, then hear what I say," quoth the emperor. "Being once solitary in my house, I called to mind mine elders and ancestors, how it was possible for them to attain unto so great a degree of authority, yea so high that we the successors of that line are never able to come near. As for example, the great and mighty monarch of the world Alexander Magnus was such a lantern and spectacle to all his successors, as the chronicles make mention of so great riches, conquering, and subduing so many kingdoms, the which I and those that follow me (I fear) shall never be able to attain unto. Wherefore, Faustus, my hearty desire is that thou wouldst vouchsafe to let me see that Alexander, and his paramour, the which was praised to be so fair; and I pray thee show me them in such sort that I may see their personages, shape, gesture and apparel as they used in their lifetime, and that here before my face; to the end that I may say I have my long desire fulfilled and to praise thee to be a famous man in thine art and experience." Doctor Faustus answered, "My most excellent lord, I am ready to accomplish your request in all things, so far forth as I and my spirit are able to perform. Yet your majesty shall know that their dead bodies are not able substantially to be brought before

you, but such spirits as have seen Alexander and hi
paramour alive shall appear unto you in manner and forı
as they both lived in their most flourishing time; an
herewith I hope to please your imperial majesty." The
Faustus went a little aside to speak to his spirit, but h
returned again presently, saying "Now if it please you
majesty you shall see them, yet upon this condition tha
you demand no question of them nor speak unto them,
which the emperor agreed unto. Wherewith Docto
Faustus opened the privy chamber door, where presentl
entered the great and mighty Emperor Alexander Magnu;
in all things to look upon as if he had been alive, in prc
portion a strong thick-set man of a middle stature, blac
hair and that both thick and curled head and beard, re
cheeks, and a broad face, with eyes like a basilisk; h
had on a complete harness burnished and graven exceedin
rich to look upon. And so passing towards the Emperc
Carolus, he made low and reverent curtsy, whereat th
Emperor Carolus would have stood up to receive an
greet him with the like reverence, but Faustus took hol
of him and would not permit him to do it. Shortly afte
Alexander made humble reverence and went out agaiı
and coming to the door his paramour met him, she con
ing in. She made the emperor likewise reverence; she wa
clothed in blue velvet wrought and embroidered wit
pearl and gold; she was also excellent fair like milk an
blood mixed, tall and slender, with a face round as a
apple. And thus she passed certain times up and dow
the house, which the emperor marking, said to himsel
"Now have I seen two persons which my heart hath lon
wished for to behold, and sure it cannot otherwise be,
said he to himself, "but that the spirits have change
themselves into these forms and have not deceived me,
calling to his mind the woman that raised the proph
Samuel. And for that the emperor would be the moı
satisfied in the matter, he thought, "I have heard say tha
behind her neck she had a great wart or wen," wherefoı
he took Faustus by the hand without any words and wer
to see if it were also to be seen on her or not; but sh
perceiving that he came to her, bowed down her nec

where he saw a great wart, and hereupon she vanished, leaving the emperor and the rest well contented.

How Doctor Faustus in the sight of the emperor conjured a pair of hart's horns upon a knight's head that slept out of a casement. Chap. 30.

When Doctor Faustus had accomplished the emperor's desire in all things as he was requested, he went forth into a gallery, and leaning over a rail to look into the privy garden he saw many of the emperor's courtiers walking and talking together. And casting his eyes now this way, now that way, he espied a knight leaning out at a window of the great hall, who was fast asleep (for in those days it was hot) but the person shall be nameless that slept, for that he was a knight, although it was done to a little disgrace of the gentleman. It pleased Doctor Faustus, through the help of his spirit Mephostophiles, to firm upon his head as he slept a huge pair of hart's horns; and as the knight awoke, thinking to pull in his head he hit his horns against the glass that the panes thereof flew about his ears. Think here how this good gentleman was vexed, for he could neither get backward nor forward: which when the emperor heard all the courtiers laugh, and came forth to see what was happened, the emperor also, when he beheld the knight with so fair a head, laughed heartily thereat and was therewithal well pleased. At last Faustus made him quit of his horns again, but the knight perceived how they came, etc.

How the above-mentioned knight went about to be revenged of Doctor Faustus. Chap. 31.

Doctor Faustus took his leave of the emperor and the rest of the courtiers, at whose departure they were sorry, giving him many rewards and gifts. But being a league and a half from the city he came into a wood, where he beheld the knight that he had jested with at the court with other

in harness, mounted on fair palfreys, and running with
full charge towards Faustus. But he, seeing their intent
ran toward the bushes, and before he came amongst th
bushes he returned again, running as it were to mee
them that chased him; whereupon suddenly all the bushe
were turned into horsemen which also ran to encounte
with the knight and his company; and coming to them
they closed the knight and the rest and told them that the
must pay their ransom before they departed. Whereupo
the knight, seeing himself in such distress, besough
Faustus to be good to them, which he denied not, but le
them loose; yet he so charmed them that every one
knight and other, for the space of a whole month did wea
a pair of goat's horns on their brows, and every palfrey
pair of ox horns on their head; and this was their penanc
appointed by Faustus, etc.

How Doctor Faustus deceived an Horse-courser.
Chap. 34.

In like manner he served an horse-courser at a fai
called Pheiffring, for Doctor Faustus through his cunnin
had gotten an excellent fair horse, whereupon he rod
to the fair, where he had many chapmen that offere
him money. Lastly, he sold him for forty dollars, willin
him that bought him that in any wise he should not rid
him over any water. But the horse-courser marvele
with himself that Faustus bade him ride him over n
water, but quoth he, "I will prove," and forthwith he rod
him into the river. Presently the horse vanished fron
under him, and he sat on a bundle of straw, in so muc
that the man was almost drowned. The horse-course
knew well where he lay that had sold him his horse
wherefore he went angrily to his inn, where he foun
Doctor Faustus fast asleep and snorting on a bed. Bu
the horse-courser could no longer forbear him, took hin
by the leg and began to pull him off the bed; but he pulle
him so that he pulled his leg from his body, in so muc
that the horse-courser fell down backward in the place

hen began Doctor Faustus to cry with an open throat,
He hath murdered me!" Hereat the horse-courser was
fraid and gave the flight, thinking none other with
imself but that he had pulled his leg from his body. By
is means Doctor Faustus kept his money.

How Doctor Faustus ate a load of hay. Chap. 35.

Doctor Faustus being in a town of Germany called
wickau, where he was accompanied with many doctors
id masters, and going forth to walk after supper, they
et with a clown that drove a load of hay. "Good even,
od fellow," said Faustus to the clown, "what shall I
ve thee to let me eat my belly full of hay?" The clown
ought with himself, what a mad man is this to eat hay;
ought he with himself, thou wilt not each much. They
greed for three farthings he should eat as much as he
uld: wherefore Doctor Faustus began to eat, and that
 ravenously that all the rest of his company fell
 laughing, blinding so the poor clown that he was sorry
 his heart, for he seemed to have eaten more than the
alf of his hay. Wherefore the clown began to speak him
ir, for fear he should have eaten the other half also.
austus made as though he had had pity on the clown,
id went his way. When the clown came in place where
 would be, he had his hay again as he had before, a
ll load.

How Faustus served the drunken clowns. Chap. 37.

Doctor Faustus went into an inn wherein were many
bles full of clowns, the which were tippling can after can
 excellent wine, and to be short, they were all drunken.
nd as they sat, they so sung and hallooed that one could
t hear a man speak for them. This angered Doctor
austus, wherefore he said to those that had called him
, "Mark, my masters, I will show you a merry jest." The
owns continuing still hallooing and singing, he so con-

jured them that their mouths stood as wide open as it w
possible for them to hold them, and never a one of the
was able to close his mouth again. By and by the noi
was gone; the clowns notwithstanding looked earnes
one upon another and wist not what was happene
wherefore one by one they went out, and so soon as th
came without, they were as well as ever they were. B
none of them desired to go in any more.

How Doctor Faustus played a merry jest with the Duke of Anholt in his court. Chap. 39.

Doctor Faustus on a time came to the Duke of Anho
the which welcomed him very courteously, this was in t
month of January, where sitting at the table he perceiv
the duchess to be with child. And forbearing himself un
the meat was taken from the table and that they broug
in the banqueting dishes, said Doctor Faustus to t
duchess, "Gracious lady, I have always heard that t
great bellied women do always long for some dainties.
beseech therefore your grace hide not your mind fro
me, but tell me what you desire to eat." She answer
him, "Doctor Faustus now truly I will not hide from y
what my heart doth most desire, namely, that if it we
now harvest, I would eat my belly full of ripe grapes, a
other dainty fruit." Doctor Faustus answered hereupo
"Gracious lady, this is a small thing for me to do, for
can do more than this." Wherefore he took a plate a
made open one of the casements of the window, holdi
it forth, where incontinent he had his dish full of all ma
ner of fruits, as red and white grapes, pears, and appl
the which came from out of strange countries. All these
presented the duchess, saying "Madame, I pray y
vouchsafe to taste of this dainty fruit, the which car
from a far country, for there the summer is not y
ended." The duchess thanked Faustus highly, and s
fell to her fruit with full appetite. The Duke of Anh
notwithstanding could not withhold to ask Faustus wi
what reason there were such young fruit to be had

at time of the year. Doctor Faustus told him, "May it lease your grace to understand that the year is divided to two circles over the whole world, that when with us is winter, in the contrary circle it is notwithstanding ummer; for in India and Saba there falleth or setteth the un so that it is so warm that they have twice a year fruit. nd, gracious lord, I have a swift spirit, the which can in he twinkling of an eye fulfill my desire in anything, herefore I sent him into those countries, who hath rought this fruit as you see." Whereat the duke was in reat admiration.

How Doctor Faustus through his charms made a great castle in presence of the Duke of Anholt. Chap. 40.

Doctor Faustus desired the Duke of Anholt to walk a ttle forth of the court with him, wherefore they went oth together into the field, where Doctor Faustus through is skill had placed a mighty castle, which when the duke aw, he wondered thereat. So did the duchess, and all the eholders, that on that hill, which was called the Ro-umbuel, should on the sudden be so fair a castle. At last octor Faustus desired the duke and the duchess to walk ith him into the castle, which they denied not. This astle was so wonderfully strong, having about it a great nd deep trench of water, the which was full of fish and ll manner of water fowl as swans, ducks, geese, bitterns, nd such like. About the wall was five stone doors and vo other doors; also within was a great open court herein were enchanted all manner of wild beasts, espe-ally such as were not to be found in Germany, as apes, ears, buffalos, antelopes, and such like strange beasts. urthermore, there were other manner of beasts, as hart, ind, and wild swine, roe, and all manner of land fowl at any man could think on, the which flew from one ee to another. After all this, he set his guests to the ble, being the duke and duchess with their train, for he

had provided them a most sumptuous feast, both of m
and all manner of drinks. For he set nine messes of m
upon the board at once, and all this must his Wagner
place all things on the board, the which was brought u
him by the spirit invisibly of all things that their h
could desire, as wild fowl and venison with all manne
dainty fish that could be thought on; of wine also g
plenty, and of divers sorts, as French wine, Cullin w
Crabatsher wine, Rhenish wine, Spanish wine, Hunga
wine, Watzburg wine, malmsey and sack: in the wh
there were a hundred cans standing round about
house. This sumptuous banquet the duke took thankfu
and afterwards he departed homewards, and to t
thinking they had neither eaten nor drunk, so were t
blinded the while that they were in the castle. But as t
were in their palace they looked toward the castle,
behold, it was all in a flame of fire, and all those
beheld it wondered to hear so great a noise, as if it w
great ordnance should have been shot off; and thus
castle burned and consumed away clean. Which do
Doctor Faustus returned to the duke, who gave him g
thanks for showing them of so great courtesy, giving
a hundred dollars and liberty to depart or use his c
discretion therein.

How Doctor Faustus showed the fair Helena unto the students upon the Sunday following. Chap. 4

The Sunday following came these students home
Doctor Faustus' own house and brought their meat
drink with them. These men were right welcome gu
unto Faustus, wherefore they all fell to drinking of w
smoothly; and being merry, they began some of them
talk of the beauty of women, and everyone gave forth
verdict what he had seen and what he had heard. So
among the rest said, "I never was so desirous of anyth
in this world as to have a sight (if it were possible)
fair Helena of Greece for whom the worthy town
Troy was destroyed and razed down to the ground, th

fore" sayth he, "that in all men's judgment she was more
than commonly fair, because that when she was stolen
away from her husband there was for her recovery so great
bloodshed."

Doctor Faustus answered, "For that you are all my
friends and are so desirous to see that famous pearl of
Greece, fair Helena, the wife of King Menelaus and
daughter of Tindalus and Laeda, sister to Castor and
Pollux, who was the fairest lady in all Greece, I will
therefore bring her into your presence personally and in
the same form of attire as she used to go when she was
in her chiefest flower and pleasantest prime of youth. The
like have I done for the Emperor Carolus Quintus; at his
desire I showed him Alexander the Great and his paramour. But," said Doctor Faustus, "I charge you all that
upon your peril you speak not a word nor rise up from
the table so long as she is in your presence." And so he
went out of the hall, returning presently again, after
whom immediately followed the fair and beautiful Helena,
whose beauty was such that the students were all amazed
to see her, esteeming her rather to be a heavenly than an
earthly creature. This lady appeared before them in a
most sumptuous gown of purple velvet, richly embroidered; her hair hung down loose as fair as the beaten
gold and of such length that it reached down to her hams;
with amorous coal-black eyes, a sweet and pleasant round
face, her lips red as a cherry, her cheeks of rose all color,
her mouth small, her neck as white as the swan, tall and
slender of personage; and in sum, there was not one imperfect part in her. She looked roundabout her with a rolling hawk's eye, a smiling and wanton countenance, which
nearly had inflamed the hearts of the students but that
they persuaded themselves she was a spirit, wherefore
such fantasies passed away lightly with them. And thus
fair Helena and Doctor Faustus went out again one with
another. But the students at Doctor Faustus' entering
again into the hall requested of him to let them see her
again the next day, for that they would bring with them
a painter and so take her counterfeit, which he denied,
affirming that he could not always raise up her spirit, but

only at certain times. "Yet," said he, "I will give you her counterfeit, which shall be always as good to you as if yourselves should see the drawing thereof," which they received according to his promise but soon lost it again. The students departed from Faustus' home everyone to his house, but they were not able to sleep the whole night for thinking on the beauty of fair Helena. Wherefore a man may see that the devil blindeth and inflameth the heart with lust oftentimes, that men fall in love with harlots, nay even with furies, which afterward cannot lightly be removed.

How an old man, the neighbor of Faustus,
sought to persuade him to amend his evil
life and to fall unto repentance. Chap. 48.

A good Christian, an honest and virtuous old man, a lover of the holy Scriptures, who was neighbor unto Doctor Faustus, when he perceived that many students had their recourse in and out unto Doctor Faustus, he suspected his evil life. Wherefore like a friend he invited Doctor Faustus to supper unto his house, unto the which he agreed. And having ended their banquet, the old man began with these words. "My loving friend and neighbor Doctor Faustus, I have to desire of you a friendly and Christian request, beseeching you that you will vouchsafe not to be angry with me but friendly resolve me in my doubt and take my poor inviting in good part." To whom Doctor Faustus answered, "My loving neighbor, I pray you say your mind." Then began the old patron to say: "My good neighbor, you know in the beginning how that you have defied God and all the host [of] heaven and given your soul to the devil, wherewith you have incurred God's high displeasure and are become from a Christian far worse than a heathen person. Oh, consider what you have done. It is not only the pleasure of the body but the safety of the soul that you must have respect unto, of which if you be careless then are you cast away and shall remain in the anger of almighty God. But yet is it time

enough, Doctor Faustus, if you repent and call unto the
Lord for mercy, as we have example in the Acts of the
Apostles, the eighth chapter of Simon in Samaria, who
was led out of the way, affirming that he was Simon Homo
Sanctus. This man was notwithstanding in the end converted, after that he had heard the sermon of Philip, for
he was baptized and saw his sins and repented. Likewise
I beseech you, good brother Doctor Faustus, let my rude
sermon be unto you a conversion, and forget the filthy
life that you have led, repent, ask mercy, and live. For
Christ saith, 'Come unto me all ye that are weary and
heavy laden, and I will refresh you.' And in Ezekiel, 'I
desire not the death of a sinner, but rather that he convert
and live.' Let my words, good brother Faustus, pierce into
your adamant heart, and desire God for his Son Christ's
sake to forgive you. Wherefore have you so long lived
in your devilish practices, knowing that in the Old and
New Testament you are forbidden, and that men should
not suffer any such to live, neither have any conversation
with them, for it is an abomination unto the Lord, and
that such persons have no part in the Kingdom of God."
All this while Doctor Faustus heard him very attentively,
and replied: "Father, your persuasions like me wondrous
well, and I thank you with all my heart for your good
will and counsel, promising you so far as I may to follow
your discipline." Whereupon he took his leave. And being
come home, he laid him very pensive on his bed, bethinking himself of the words of the good old man, and in a
manner began to repent that he had given his soul to the
devil, intending to deny all that he had promised unto
Lucifer. Continuing in these cogitations, suddenly his
spirit appeared unto him clapping him upon the head,
and wrung it as though he would have pulled the head
from the shoulders, saying unto him "Thou knowest,
Faustus, that thou has given thyself body and soul unto
my lord Lucifer, and has vowed thyself an enemy unto
God and unto all men; and now thou beginnest to harken
to an old doting fool which persuadeth thee as it were
unto God, when indeed it is too late, for that thou art
the devil's, and he hath good power presently to fetch

thee: wherefore he hath sent me unto thee to tell thee, that seeing thou hast sorrowed for that thou hast done, begin again and write another writing with thine own blood; if not, then will I tear thee all to pieces." Hereat Doctor Faustus was sore afraid, and sayd, "My Mephostophiles, I will write again what thou wilt." Wherefore he sat him down and with his own blood he wrote as followeth, which writing was afterwards sent to a dear friend of the said Doctor Faustus being his kinsman.

How Doctor Faustus wrote the second time with his own blood and gave it to the Devil. Chap. 49.

I, Doctor John Faustus, acknowledge by this my deed and handwriting, that sith my first writing, which is seventeen years, that I have right willingly held, and have been an utter enemy unto God and all men, the which I once again confirm, and give fully and wholly my self unto the devil both body and soul, even unto the great Lucifer. And that at the end of seven years ensuing after the date of this letter, he shall have to do with me according as it pleaseth him, either to lengthen or shorten my life as liketh him. And hereupon I renounce all persuaders that seek to withdraw me from my purpose by the word of God, either ghostly or bodily. And further, I will never give ear unto any man, be he spiritual or temporal, that moveth any matter for the salvation of my soul. Of all this writing, and that therein contained, be witness, my own blood, the which with mine own hands I have begun and ended.

Dated at Wittenberg the 25 of July.

And presently upon the making of this letter, he became so great an enemy unto the poor old man that he sought his life by all means possible; but this godly man was strong in the Holy Ghost, that he could not be vanquished by any means. For about two days after that he had exhorted Faustus, as the poor man lay in his bed, suddenly there was a mighty rumbling in the chamber the which he was never wont to hear, and he heard as it had been the groaning of a sow, which lasted long. Whereupon the good old man began to jest and mock, and said "Oh, what barbarian cry is this, oh fair bird, what foul music is this of a fair angel that could not tarry two days in his place? Beginnest thou now to run into a poor man's house where thou hast no power and wert not able to keep thine own two days?" With these and such like words the spirit departed. And when he came home Faustus asked him how he had sped with the old man: to whom the spirit answered, the old man was harnessed, and that he could not once lay hold upon him. But he would not tell how the old man had mocked him, for the devils can never abide to hear of their fall. Thus doth God defend the hearts of all honest Christians that betake themselves under his tuition.

How Doctor Faustus gathered together a great army of men in his extremity against a knight that would have injured him on his journey. Chap. 52.

Doctor Faustus traveled towards Eisleben, and when he was nigh half the way he espied seven horsemen, and the chief of them he knew to be the knight to whom he had played a jest in the emperor's court, for he had set a huge pair of hart's horns upon his head. And when the knight now saw that he had fit opportunity to be revenged of Faustus, he ran upon him himself, and those that were with him, to mischief him, intending privily to shoot at him. Which when Doctor Faustus espied, he vanished away into the wood which was hard by them. But when the knight perceived that he was vanished away, he caused his men to stand still, where as they remained they heard all manner of warlike instruments of music, as drums, flutes, trumpets, and such like, and a certain troup of horsemen running towards them. Then they turned another way and there also were assaulted on the same side; then another way and yet they were freshly assaulted; so that which way soever they turned themselves he was

encountered, in so much that when the knight perceived
that he could escape no way, but that they his enemies
laid on him which way soever he offered to fly, he took
a good heart and ran amongst the thickest, and thought
with himself better to die than to live with so great an
infamy. Therefore, being at handy-blows with them, he
demanded the cause why they should so use them; but
none of them would give him answer until Doctor Faustus
showed himself unto the knight, where withal they en-
closed him round and Doctor Faustus said unto him, "Sir,
yield your weapon and yourself; otherwise it will go
hardly with you." The knight, that knew none other but
that he was environed with a host of men (where indeed
they were none other than devils), yielded. Then Faustus
took away his sword, his piece, and horse, with all the
rest of his companions. And further he said unto him,
"Sir, the chief general of our army hath commanded to
deal with you according to the law of arms; you shall
depart in peace whither you please." And then he gave
the knight a horse after the manner and set him thereon
so he rode. The rest went on foot until they came to their
inn, where being alighted his page rode on his horse to
the water, and presently the horse vanished away, the
page being almost sunk and drowned, but he escaped.
And coming home, the knight perceived his page so be-
mired and on foot, asked where his horse was become.
Who answered that he was vanished away; which when
the knight heard, he said, "Of a truth, this is Faustus'
doing, for he serveth me now as he did before at the
court, only to make me a scorn and a laughingstock."

How Doctor Faustus caused Mephostophiles to bring him
seven of the fairest women that he could find in all
those countries he had traveled in, in the twentieth year.
Chap. 53.

When Doctor Faustus called to mind that his time from
day to day drew nigh, he began to live a swinish and
epicurish life, wherefore he commanded his spirit Meph-

ostophiles to bring him seven of the fairest women that he had seen in all the time of his travel. Which being brought, first one and then another he lay with them all, insomuch that he liked them so well that he continued with them in all manner of love and made them to travel with him in all his journeys. These women were two Netherlanders, one Hungarian, one English, two Walloons, one Franklander; and with these sweet personages he continued long, yea even to his last end.

How Doctor Faustus made the spirit of fair Helena of Greece his own paramour and bedfellow in his twenty-third year. Chap. 55.

To the end that this miserable Faustus might fill the lust of his flesh and live in all manner of voluptuous pleasures, it came in his mind after he had slept his first sleep and in the twenty-third year past of his time, that he had a great desire to lie with fair Helena of Greece, especially her whom he had seen and showed unto the students of Wittenberg, wherefore he called unto him his spirit Mephostophiles, commanding him to bring him the fair Helena, which he also did. Whereupon he fell in love with her and made her his common concubine and bedfellow, for she was so beautiful and delightful a piece that he could not be one hour from her if he should therefore have suffered death, she had so stolen away his heart. And to his seeming, in time she was with child and in the end brought him a man child whom Faustus named Justus Faustus. This child told Doctor Faustus many things that were to come and what strange matters were done in foreign countries; but in the end when Faustus lost his life, the mother and the child vanished away both together.

How Doctor Faustus made his will, in the which he named his servant Wagner to be his heir. Chap. 56.

Doctor Faustus was now in his twenty-fourth and last year, and he had a pretty stripling to his servant, the which had studied also at the University of Wittenberg. This youth was very well acquainted with his knaveries and sorceries, so that he was hated as well for his own knaveries as also for his master's, for no man would give him entertainment into his service, because of his unhappiness, but Faustus. This Wagner was so well beloved with Faustus that he used him as his son, for do what he would his master was always therewith well content. And when the time drew nigh that Faustus should end, he called unto him a notary and certain masters the which were his friends and often conversant with him, in whose presence he gave this Wagner his house and garden. Item, he gave him in ready money sixteen hundred guilders. Item, a farm. Item, a gold chain, much plate, and other household stuff. This gave he all to his servant, and the rest of his time he meant to spend in inns and students' company, drinking and eating, with other jollity. And thus he finished his will for that time.

How Doctor Faustus having but one month of his appointed time to come, fell to mourning and sorrow with himself for his devilish exercise. Chap. 58.

Time ran away with Faustus, as the hourglass, for he had but one month to come of his twenty-four years, at the end whereof he had given himself to the devil body and soul, as is before specified. Here was the first token, for he was like a taken murderer or a thief, the which findeth himself guilty in conscience before the judge have given sentence, fearing every hour to die; for he was grieved, and wailing spent the time, went talking to himself, wringing of his hands, sobbing and sighing; he fell away from flesh and was very lean, and kept himself

lose. Neither could he abide to see or hear of his
Mephostophiles any more.

*How Doctor Faustus complained that he should in
his lusty time and youthful years die so miserably.
Chap. 59.*

This sorrowful time drawing near so troubled Doctor
Faustus that he began to write his mind, to the end he
might peruse it often and not forget it, and is in manner
as followeth.

Ah Faustus, thou sorrowful and woeful man, now must
thou go to the damned company in unquenchable fire,
whereas thou mightest have had the joyful immortality of
the soul, the which thou now hast lost. Ah gross understanding and willful will, what seizeth on my limbs other
than a robbing of my life? Bewail with me my sound and
healthful body, wit and soul, bewail with me my senses,
for you have had your part and pleasure as well as I. Oh
envy and disdain, how have you crept both at once into
me, and now for your sakes I must suffer all these torments? Ah whither is pity and mercy fled? Upon what
occasion hath heaven repaid me with this reward by suf-
ferance to suffer me to perish? Wherefore was I created
a man? The punishment that I see prepared for me of
myself now must I suffer. Ah miserable wretch, there is
nothing in this world to show me comfort: then woe is
me, what helpeth my wailing.

Another complaint of Doctor Faustus. Chap. 60.

Oh poor, woeful and weary wretch, oh sorrowful soul
of Faustus, now art thou in the number of the damned.
For now must I wait for unmeasurable pains of death,
yea far more lamentable than ever yet any creature hath
suffered. Ah senseless, willful and desperate forgetfulness!
O cursed and unstable life! O blind and careless wretch,
that so hast abused thy body, sense and soul! O foolish

pleasure, into what a weary labyrinth hast thou broug
me, blinding mine eyes in the clearest day! Ah weak hea
O troubled soul, where is become thy knowledge to con
fort thee? O pitiful weariness! Oh desperate hope, no
shall I never more be thought upon! Oh, care upon car
fulness, and sorrows on heaps; ah grievous pains th
pierce my panting heart, whom is there now that can d
liver me? Would God that I knew where to hide me,
into what place to creep or fly. Ah, woe, woe is me,
where I will, yet am I taken. Herewith poor Faustus w
so sorrowfully troubled that he could not speak or utt
his mind any further.

How Doctor Faustus bewailed to think on hell, and of the miserable pains therein provided for him. Chap. 6

Now thou Faustus, damned wretch, how happy wert tho
if as an unreasonable beast thou mightest die without sou
so shouldst thou not feel any more doubts! But now t
devil will take thee away both body and soul and set th
in an unspeakable place of darkness. For although oth
souls have rest and peace, yet I, poor damned wretc
must suffer all manner of filthy stench, pains, cold, hunge
thirst, heat, freezing, burning, hissing, gnashing, and
the wrath and curse of God, yea all the creatures th
God hath created are enemies to me. And now too late
remember that my spirit Mephostophiles did once tell n
there was a great difference amongst the damned, for t
greater the sin, the greater the torment. For as the twi
of the tree make greater flame than the trunk thereof, an
yet the trunk continueth longer in burning, even so t
more that a man is rooted in sin the greater is his punis
ment. Ah thou perpetual damned wretch, now art tho
thrown into the everlasting fiery lake that never shall
quenched; there must I dwell in all manner of wailin
sorrow, misery, pain, torment, grief, howling, sighin
sobbing, blubbering, running of eyes, stinking at nos
gnashing of teeth, fear to the ears, horror to the co
science, and shaking both of hand and foot. Ah that

ould carry the heavens on my shoulders, so that there
were time at last to quit me of this everlasting damna-
on! Oh who can deliver me out of these fearful torment-
ng flames, the which I see prepared for me? Oh there is
o help, nor any man that can deliver me, nor any wailing
f sins can help me, neither is there rest to be found for
he day nor night. Oh woe is me, for there is no help for
he, no shield, no defense, no comfort. Where is my hold?
Knowledge dare I not trust, and for a soul to God wards
hat have I not, for I shame to speak unto him. If I do,
o answer shall be made me, but he will hide his face
rom me, to the end that I should not behold the joys of
he chosen. What mean I then to complain where no help
s? No, I know no hope resteth in my groanings. I have
lesired that it should be so, and God hath said Amen to
hy misdoings: for now I must have shame to comfort me
n my calamities.

An oration of Faustus to the students. Chap. 63.

My trusty and well beloved friends, the cause why I
have invited you into this place is this: Forasmuch as you
have known me this many years, in what manner of life
have lived, practicing all manner of conjurations and
wicked exercises, the which I have obtained through the
help of the devil, into whose devilish fellowship they have
brought me, the which use the like art and practice, urged
by the detestable provocation of my flesh, my stiff-necked
nd rebellious will, with my filthy infernal thoughts, the
which were ever before me, pricking me forward so
arnestly that I must perforce have the consent of the
levil to aid me in my devices. And to the end I might the
better bring my purpose to pass, to have the devil's aid
nd furtherance, which I never have wanted in mine
ctions, I have promised unto him at the end and ac-
omplishing of twenty-four years, both body and soul,
o do therewith at his pleasure. And this day, this dismal
lay, those twenty-four years are fully expired, for night
beginning my hourglass is at an end, the direful finishing

whereof I carefully expect. For out of all doubt this nig'
he will fetch me, to whom I have given myself in recom
pense of his service, both body and soul, and twice co
firmed writings with my proper blood. Now have I call
you, my well beloved lords, friends, brethren, and fellow
before that fatal hour to take my friendly farewell, to th
end that my departing may not hereafter be hidden fro
you; beseeching you herewith courteous and loving lor
and brethren, not to take in evil part anything done t
me, but with friendly commendations to salute all n
friends and companions wheresoever, desiring both yc
and them, if ever I have trespassed against your minds
anything, that you would all heartily forgive me. And
for those lewd practices the which this full twenty-fov
years I have followed, you shall hereafter find them
writing. And I beseech you let this my lamentable er
to the residue of your lives be a sufficient warning, th
you have God always before your eyes, praying un
him that he would ever defend you from the temptatic
of the devil and all his false deceits, not falling altogeth
from God as I, wretched and ungodly damned creatur
have done, having denied and defied baptism, the sacr
ments of Christ's body, God himself, all heavenly power
and earthly men, yea, I have denied such a God th:
desireth not to have one lost. Neither let the evil fellov
ship of wicked companions mislead you as it hath do
me. Visit earnestly and oft the church, war and striv
continually against the devil with a good and steadfa
belief on God and Jesus Christ, and use your vocation
holiness. Lastly, to knit up my troubled oration, this is m
friendly request, that you would to rest, and let nothir
trouble you. Also, if you chance to hear any noise (
rumbling about the house, be not therewith afraid, f
there shall no evil happen unto you. Also, I pray yo
arise not out of your beds. But above all things I entre:
you, if you hereafter find my dead carcass, convey it un
the earth, for I die both a good and bad Christian: a goo
Christian for that I am heartily sorry and in my hea
always pray for mercy that my soul may be delivered;
bad Christian for that I know the devil will have my bod

ıd that would I willingly give him so that he would
ave my soul in quiet. Wherefore I pray you that you
ʹould depart to bed, and so I wish you a quiet night,
ʹhich unto me notwithstanding will be horrible and
:arful.

This oration or declaration was made by Doctor
ʹaustus, and that with a hearty and resolute mind, to the
nd he might not discomfort them. But the students
ʹondered greatly thereat, that he was so blinded, for
navery, conjuration, and such like foolish things, to give
is body and soul unto the devil; for they loved him en-
rely and never suspected any such thing before he had
pened his mind to them. Wherefore one of them said
nto him, "Ah, friend Faustus, what have you done to
onceal this matter so long from us? We would by the
ıelp of good divines and the grace of God have brought
ou out of this net and have torn you out of the bondage
nd chains of Satan, whereas now we fear it is too late,
ɔ the utter ruin of your body and soul." Doctor Faustus
nswered, "I durst never do it, although I often minded,
ɔ settle myself unto godly people, to desire counsel and
ıelp, as once mine old neighbor counselled me that I
ıould follow his learning and leave all my conjurations.
ʹet when I was minded to amend and to follow that good
ıan's counsel, then came the devil and would have had
ıe away, as this night he is like to do, and said so soon
s I turned again to God he would dispatch me altogether.
ʹhus, even thus, good gentlemen and my dear friends, was
enthralled in that Satanical band, all good desires
lrowned, all piety banished, all purpose of amendment
.tterly exiled by the tyrannous threatenings of my deadly
nemy." But when the students heard his words, they gave
ıim counsel to do naught else but call upon God, desiring
ıim for the love of his sweet Son Jesus Christ's sake, to
ıave mercy upon him, teaching him this form of prayer:
) God be merciful unto me, poor and miserable sinner,
nd enter not into judgment with me, for no flesh is able
ɔ stand before thee. Although, O Lord, I must leave my
inful body unto the devil, being by him deluded, yet thou
n mercy mayest preserve my soul.

This they repeated unto him, yet it could take no hol
but even as Cain he also said his sins were greater tha
God was able to forgive; for all his thought was on h
writing, he meant he had made it too filthy in writing
with his own blood. The students and the others that we
there, when they had prayed for him they wept and
went forth, but Faustus tarried in the hall. And when tl
gentlemen were laid in bed, none of them could sleep fo
that they attended to hear if they might be privy of h
end. It happened between twelve and one o'clock
midnight; there blew a mighty storm of wind against tl
house as though it would have blown the foundatic
thereof out of his place. Hereupon the students began
fear, and got out of their beds, comforting one anothe
but they would not stir out of the chamber; and the ho
of the house ran out of doors, thinking the house wou
fall. The students lay near unto that hall wherein Doct
Faustus lay, and they heard a mighty noise and hissi
as if the hall had been full of snakes and adders. Wi
that, the hall door flew open wherein Doctor Faust
was; then he began to cry for help, saying "Murde
murder," but it came forth with half a voice hollowl
Shortly after, they heard him no more. But when it w
day, the students that had taken no rest that night arose ar
went into the hall in the which they left Doctor Faustu
where notwithstanding they found no Faustus, but all tl
hall lay besprinkled with blood, his brains cleaving to tl
wall. For the devil had beaten him from one wall again
another: in one corner lay his eyes, in another his teet
a pitiful and fearful sight to behold. Then began tl
students to bewail and weep for him and sought for h
body in many places. Lastly they came into the yar
where they found his body lying on the horse dung, mo
monstrously torn and fearful to behold, for his head an
all his joints were dashed in pieces.

The forenamed students and masters that were at h
death, have obtained so much, that they buried him i
the village where he was so grievously tormented. Aft
the which, they returned to Wittenberg, and coming in
the house of Faustus, they found the servant of Faustu

ery sad, unto whom they opened all the matter, who
ook it exceeding heavily. There found they also this his-
ory of Doctor Faustus noted, and of him written as is
efore declared, all save only his end, the which was after
y the students thereto annexed; further, what his servant
ad noted thereof was made in another book. And you
ave heard that he held by him in his life the spirit of fair
Helena, the which had by him one son, the which he
amed Justus Faustus. Even the same day of his death
they vanished away, both mother and son. The house
efore was so dark that scarce anybody could abide
therein. The same night Doctor Faustus appeared unto
his servant lively, and showed unto him many secret
things the which he had done and hidden in his lifetime.
Likewise there were certain which saw Doctor Faustus
ook out of the window by night as they passed by the
house.

And thus ended the whole history of Doctor Faustus
his conjuration and other acts that he did in his life, out
f the which example every Christian may learn. But
chiefly the stiff-necked and high-minded may thereby learn
to fear God, and to be careful of their vocation, and to
be at defiance with all devilish works, as God hath most
precisely forbidden, to the end we should not invite the
devil as a guest nor give him place as that wicked Faustus
hath done. For here we have a fearful example of his
writing, promise, and end, that we may remember him:
that we go not astray, but take God always before our
eyes, to call alone upon him, and to honor him all the
days of our life with heart and hearty prayer, and with
all our strength and soul to glorify his holy name, defying
the devil and all his works, to the end we remain with
Christ in all endless joy. Amen, amen, that wish I unto
every Christian heart, and God's name to be glorified.
Amen.

FINIS

Commentaries

RICHARD B. SEWALL

The Tragic Form

A discussion of tragedy is confronted at the outset with
the strenuous objections of Croce, who would have no
truck with the genres. "Art is one," he wrote in his famous
Britannica article,[1] "and cannot be divided." For convenience, he would allow the division of Shakespeare's
plays into tragedies, comedies, and histories, but he
warned of the dogmatism that lay in any further refining
of distinctions. He made a special point of tragedy, which
as usual was the fighting issue. No artist, he said, will
submit to the servitude of the traditional definition: that
a tragedy must have a subject of a certain kind, characters
of a certain kind, and a plot of a certain kind and length.
Each work of art is a world in itself, "a creation, not a
reflection, a monument, not a document." The concepts
of aesthetics do not exist "in a transcendent region" but
only in innumerable specific works. To ask of a given
work "is it a tragedy?" or "does it obey the laws of
tragedy?" is irrelevant and impertinent.

From *Essays in Criticism*, IV (1954), 345–58. Reprinted by permission
of *Essays in Criticism: A Quarterly Journal of Literary Criticism.* This
essay includes no specific comment on Marlowe's play, but its examination
of the tragic cosmos, tragic man, and tragic society provides much relevant
material. The footnotes have been renumbered consecutively.

1 Eleventh edition, article "Aesthetics."

Although this may be substituting one dogmatism for another, there is sense in it. Nothing is more dreary than the textbook categories; and their tendency, if carried too far, would rationalize art out of existence. The dilemma is one of critical means, not ends: Croce would preserve tragedy by insuring the autonomy of the artist; the school men would preserve it by insuring the autonomy of the form.

But the dilemma is not insurmountable, as Eliot and a number of others have pointed out. There is a life-giving relationship between tradition and the individual talent, "wooing both ways" (in R. P. Blackmur's phrase) between the form which the artist inherits and the new content he brings to it. This wooing both ways has been especially true of the development of tragedy, where values have been incremental, where (for instance) each new tragic protagonist is in some degree a lesser Job and each new tragic work owes an indispensable element to the Greek idea of the chorus. So I should say that, provided we can get beyond the stereotypes Croce seems to have had in mind, we should continue to talk about tragedy, to make it grow in meaning, impel more artists and attract a greater and more discerning audience.

But we must first get a suitable idea of form. Blackmur's article[2] from which I have just quoted provides, I think, a useful suggestion. It is the concept of "theoretic form," which he distinguishes from technical or "executive" form. "Technical form," he writes, "is our means of getting at . . . and then making something of, what we feel the form of life itself is: the tensions, the stresses, the deep relations and the terrible disrelations that inhabit them. . . . This is the form that underlies the forms we merely practice. . . ." This (and here Croce's full concept of form is more adequately represented) is "what Croce means by theoretic form for feeling, intuition, insight, what I mean by the theoretic form of life itself."

2 "The Loose and Baggy Monsters of Henry James: Notes on the Underlying Classic Form in the Novel," *Accent*, Summer, 1951; see also Eliseo Vivas, "Literature and Knowledge," *Sewanee Review*, Autumn 1952.

Discussion of the "form" of tragedy in this sense need be neither prescriptive nor inhibiting, but it may define a little more precisely a vital area of thought and feeling.

Here is the kind of situation in which such a discussion might be helpful: Two years ago, in *Essays in Criticism* (October 1952), Miss K. M. Burton defended what she called the "political tragedies" of Ben Jonson and George Chapman as legitimate tragedies, although non-Aristotelian. *Sejanus* was perhaps the clearest case in point. Herford and Simpson, in their commentary, had set the play down as at best "the tragedy of a satirist" a "proximate" tragedy, with no tragic hero and with no cathartic effect. "Whatever effect [Jonson] aimed at," they wrote, "it was not the purifying pity excited by the fatal errors of a noble nature." Miss Burton's reply lay in her concept of political tragedy. She saw Jonson's tragic theme as "the manner in which evil penetrates the political structure." The "flaw" that concerned him lay "within the social order," and whatever purifying pity we feel would come from contemplating the ordeal of society, not the fatal errors of a noble nature. The play for her had "tragic intensity"; it was both "dramatic, and a tragedy."

Whether one agrees with her or not, the question, despite Croce, is out: "Is the play a tragedy?" And many others follow. Can there be a tragedy without a tragic hero? Can "the social order" play his traditional role? Is catharsis the first, or only, or even a reliable test? In a recent article, Professor Pottle wrote, "I shall be told Aristotle settled all that." And added, "I wish he had." The disagreement on *Sejanus* is symptomatic. F. L. Lucas once pointed out that (on much the same issues) Hegel thought only the Greeks wrote true tragedy; and I. A. Richards, only Shakespeare. Joseph Wood Krutch ruled out the moderns, like Hardy, Ibsen and O'Neill; and Mark Harris ruled them in.[3] The question arises about

---

[3] F. A. Pottle, "Catharsis," *Yale Review*, Summer, 1951; F. L. Lucas, *Tragedy in Relation to Aristotle's Poetics*, N.Y., 1928; Joseph Wood Krutch, *The Modern Temper*, N.Y., 1929; Mark Harris, *The Case for Tragedy*, N.Y., 1932.

every new "serious" play or novel; we seem to care
great deal about whether it is, or is not, a tragedy.

I have little hope of settling all this, but I am persuade
that progress lies in the direction of theoretic form,
Blackmur uses the term. Is it not possible to bring tl
dominant feelings, intuitions, insights that we meet in s
called tragic writings into some coherent relationship
which the word "form" could be applied without too gre
violence? This is not to tell artists what to do, nor to s
up strict *a priori* formulae, nor to legislate among tl
major genres. The problem of evaluating the total exce
lence of a given work involves much more than determi
ing its status as a tragedy, or as a "proximate" traged
or as a non-tragedy. It involves, among other things, tl
verbal management within the work and the ordering
the parts. Furthermore, our discussion need not imp
the superiority of tragedy over comedy (certainly not
Dante conceived of comedy) or over epic, although,
we look upon these major forms as presenting total inte
pretations of life, the less inclusive forms (lyric, satire
would seem to occupy inferior categories. But as we ent
the world of any play or novel to which the term traged
is at all applicable, we may well judge it by what v
know about the possibilities of the form, without insistir
that our judgment is absolute. If, set against the fu
dimensions of the tragic form, Jonson's *Sejanus* or Hen
ingway's *A Farewell to Arms* (for instance) reveal ur
developed possibilities or contrary elements, we can st
respect their particular modes of expression.

In indicating these dimensions of tragedy, I shall l
mindful of Unamuno's warning[4] that tragedy is not
matter, ultimately, to be systematized. He speaks truly,
think, about "the tragic sense of life." He describes it as
sub-philosophy, "more or less formulated, more or le
conscious," reaching deep down into temperament, not
much "flowing from ideas as determining them." It is tl
sense of ancient evil, of the mystery of human sufferin

[4] *The Tragic Sense of Life,* tr. J. E. C. Flitch, London, 1921, pp. 17–1

of the gulf between aspiration and achievement. It colours the tragic artist's vision of life (his theoretic form) and gives his works their peculiar shade and tone. It speaks, not the language of systematic thought, but through symbolic action, symbol and figure, diction and image, sound and rhythm. Such a recognition should precede any attempt to talk "systematically" about tragedy, while not denying the value of the attempt itself.

Two more comments remain to be made about method. The first is the problem of circular evidence,[5] the use of tragedies to define tragedy. I am assuming that we can talk meaningfully about a body of literature which reveals certain generic qualities and which can be distinguished from the body of literature called comedy, epic, satire, or the literature of pathos. My purpose is to isolate these qualities and to refer to the works themselves as illustrations rather than proof.

The second comment involves the problem of affectivism, which is the problem of catharsis: "This play is a tragedy because it makes me feel thus and so." As Max Scheler puts it, this method would bring us ultimately to the contemplation of our own ego. Thus, I would reverse the order of F. L. Lucas's discussion, which assumes that we must know what tragedy does before we can tell what it is: "We cannot fully discuss the means," Lucas wrote, "until we are clear about the ends." It is true that the usual or "scientific" way is to define natures by effects, which are observable. But rather than found a definition of tragedy on the infinite variables of an audience's reactions, I would consider first the works themselves as the "effects" and look in them for evidences of an efficient cause: a world-view, a form that "underlies the forms we merely practice." What are the generic qualities of these effects? Do they comprise a "form"? I think they do; and for convenience I shall use the term from the start as if I had already proved its legitimacy.

5 Cf. Max Scheler, "On the Tragic," *Cross Currents*, Winter, 1954. This is a selection from Scheler's *Vom Umsturz der Werte*, vol. I (1923), tr. Bernard Stambler.

Basic to the tragic form is its recognition of the inevitability of paradox, of unresolved tensions and ambiguities, of opposites in precarious balance. Like the arch, tragedy never rests—or never comes to rest, with all losses restored and sorrows ended. Problems are put and pressed, but not solved. An occasional "happy ending," as in *The Oresteia* or *Crime and Punishment,* does not mean a full resolution. Though there may be intermittences, there is no ultimate discharge in that war. Although this suggests formlessness, as it must in contrast with certain types of religious orthodoxy or philosophical system, it would seem the essence of the tragic form. Surely it is more form than chaos. For out of all these tensions and paradoxes, these feelings, intuitions, insights, there emerges a fairly coherent attitude towards the universe and man. Tragedy makes certain distinguishable and characteristic affirmations, as well as denials, about (I) the cosmos and man's relation to it; (II) the nature of the individual and his relation to himself; (III) the individual in society.

(I) *The tragic cosmos.* In using the term cosmos to signify a theory of the universe and man's relation to it, I have, of course, made a statement about tragedy: that tragedy affirms a cosmos of which man is a meaningful part. To be sure, the characteristic locale of tragedy is not the empyrean. Tragedy is primarily humanistic. Its focus is an event in this world; it is uncommitted as to questions of ultimate destiny, and it is non-religious in its attitude toward revelation. But it speaks, however vaguely or variously, of an order that transcends time, space and matter.[6] It assumes man's connection with some supersensory or supernatural, or metaphysical being or principle, whether it be the Olympians, Job's Jehovah or the Christian God; Fate, Fortune's Wheel, the "elements" that Lear invoked, or Koestler's "oceanic sense," which comes in so tentatively (and pathetically) at the end of

---

[6] Cf. Susan Taubes, "The Nature of Tragedy," *Review of Metaphysics,* December 1953.

Darkness at Noon. The first thing that tragedy says about the cosmos is that, for good or ill, it *is*; and in this respect tragedy's theoretic opposite is naturalism or mechanism. Tragedy is witness (secondly) to the cosmic mystery, to the "wonderful" surrounding our lives; and in literature the opposite of tragedy is not only writing based upon naturalistic theory but also upon the four-square, "probable"[7] world of satire and rationalistic comedy. Finally, what distinguishes tragedy from other forms which bespeak this cosmic sense—for tragedy of course is not unique in this—is its peculiar and intense preoccupation with the *evil* in the universe, whatever it is in the stars that compels, harasses, and bears man down. Tragedy wrestles with the evil of the mystery—and the mystery of the evil. And the contest never ends.

But, paradoxically, its view of the cosmos is what sustains tragedy. Tragedy discerns a principle of goodness that coexists with the evil. This principle need be nothing so pat as The Moral Order, the "armies of unalterable law," and it is nothing so sure as the orthodox Christian God. It is nearer the folk sense that justice exists somewhere in the universe, or what Nietzsche describes as the orgiastic, mystical sense of oneness, of life as "indestructibly powerful and pleasurable." It may be a vision of some transcendent beauty and dignity against which the present evil may be seen as evil and the welter as welter. This is what keeps tragedy from giving up the whole human experiment, and in this respect its opposite is not comedy or satire but cynicism and nihilism, as in Schopenhauer's theory of resignation. The "problem of the good" plays as vital a part in tragedy as the "problem of evil." It provides the living tension without which tragedy ceases to exist.

Thus tragedy contemplates a universe in which man is not the measure of all things. It confronts a mystery. W.

---

7 The "wonderful" and the "probable" are the basic categories in Albert Cook's distinction between tragedy and comedy. (*The Dark Voyage and the Golden Mean*, Cambridge, Mass., 1949, chap. 1.)

Macneile Dixon[8] pointed out that tragedy started as "an affair with the gods"; and the extent to which literature has become "secularized and humanized," he wrote, is a sign of its departure from (to use our present term) the tragic form. While agreeing with him as to the tendency, one may question the wholesale verdict which he implies. The affair with the gods has not, in the minds of all our artists, been reduced to an affair with the social order, or the environment, or the glands. But certainly where it becomes so, the muse of tragedy walks out; the universe loses its mystery and (to invoke catharsis for a moment) its terror.

The terms "pessimism" and "optimism" in the view of the universe as conceived in the tragic form, do not suggest adequate categories, as Nietzsche first pointed out.[9] Tragedy contains them both, goes beyond both, illuminates both, but comes to no conclusion. Tragedy could, it is true, be called pessimistic in its view of the evil in the universe as unremitting and irremediable, the blight man was born for, the necessary condition of existence. It is pessimistic, also, in its view of the overwhelming proportion of evil to good and in its awareness of the mystery of why this should be—the "unfathomable element" in which Ahab foundered. But it is optimistic in what might be called its vitalism, which is in some sense mystical, not

8 *Tragedy*, London, 1924. The extent of my indebtedness to this book, and to the other discussions of tragedy mentioned in this paper, is poorly indicated by such passing references as this. Since observations on tragedy and the theory of tragedy appear in innumerable discussions of particular authors, eras, and related critical problems, a complete list would be far too cumbersome. Among them would be, surely, the standard work of A. C. Bradley and Willard Farnham on Shakespearean tragedy; C. M. Bowra and Cedric Whitman on Sophocles; W. L. Courtney (*The Idea of Tragedy*, London, 1900); Maxwell Anderson, *The Essence of Tragedy*, Washington, 1939; Northrop Frye, "The Archetypes of Literature," *Kenyon Review*, Winter, 1951; Moody Prior, *The Language of Tragedy*, N.Y., 1947; and Herbert Weisinger, *Tragedy and the Paradox of the Fortunate Fall*, Michigan State College Press, 1953, which makes rich use of the archaeological and mythographic studies of the origin of tragedy (Cornford, Harrison, Murray). I am indebted, also, to my colleague Laurence Michel, for frequent conversations and helpful criticism.

9 See also Reinhold Niebuhr, *Beyond Tragedy*, London, 1938.

arth-bound; in its faith in a cosmic good; in its vision,
owever fleeting, of a world in which all questions could
e answered.

(II) *Tragic man.* If the tragic form asserts a cosmos,
ome order behind the immediate disorder, what does it
ssert about the nature of man, other than that he is a
eing capable of cosmic affinities? What is tragic man as
e lives and moves on this earth? Can he be distinguished
eaningfully from the man of comedy, satire, epic or
ric? How does he differ from "pathetic man" or "re-
gious man"? or from man as conceived by the material-
tic psychologies? Tragic man shares some qualities, of
ourse, with each of these. I shall stress differences in the
ppropriate contexts.

Like the cosmos which he views, tragic man is a para-
ox and a mystery. He is no child of God; yet he feels
imself more than a child of earth. He is not the plaything
f Fate, but he is not entirely free. He is "both creature
nd creator" (in Niebuhr's phrase)—"fatefully free and
eely fated" (in George Schrader's). He recognizes "the
ct of guilt" while cherishing the "dream of innocence"
Fiedler), and he never fully abandons either position. He
plagued by the ambiguity of his own nature and of the
orld he lives in. He is torn between the sense in common-
nse (which is the norm of satire and rationalistic, or
orrective, comedy) and his own uncommon sense. Aware
f the just but irreconcilable claims within and without, he
conscious of the immorality of his own morality and
ffers in the knowledge of his own recalcitrance.

The dynamic of this recalcitrance is pride. It sustains
is belief, however humbled he may become by later ex-
erience, in his own freedom, in his innocence, and in his
ncommon sense. Tragic man is man at his most prideful
nd independent, man glorying in his humanity. Tragic
ride, like everything else about tragedy, is ambiguous; it
an be tainted with arrogance and have its petty side; but
is not to be equated with sin or weakness. The Greeks
ared it when it threatened the gods or slipped into arro-
ance, but they honoured it and even worshipped it in

their heroes. It was the common folk, the chorus, w⌐
had no pride, or were "flawless."[10] The chorus invariat
argue against pride, urging caution and moderation, t
cause they know it leads to suffering; but tragedy as su
does not prejudge it.

While many of these things, again, might be said
other than tragic man, it is in the peculiar nature of l
suffering, and in his capacity for suffering and appropri
ing his suffering, that his distinguishing quality lies. F
instance (to ring changes on the Cartesian formula), tra
man would not define himself, like the man of correcti
comedy or satire, "I think, therefore I am"; nor like t
man of achievement (epic): "I act, or conquer, therefo
I am": nor like the man of sensibility (lyric): "I fe
therefore I am": nor like the religious man: "I believ
therefore I am." Although he has all these qualities (
thought, achievement, sensibility, and belief) in vario
forms and degrees, the essence of his nature is broug
out by suffering: "I suffer, I will to suffer, I learn
suffering; therefore I am." The classic statement,
course, is Aeschylus's: "Wisdom comes alone throu
suffering" (Lattimore's translation); perhaps the mo
radical is Dostoevski's: "Suffering is the sole origin
consciousness."[11]

This is not to say that only tragic man suffers or th
he who suffers is tragic. Saints and martyrs suffer a
learn by suffering; Odysseus suffered and learned; Dar
suffered and learned on his journey with Virgil. But tra
man, I think, is distinguishable from these others in t
nature of his suffering as conditioned by its source a
locus, in its characteristic course and consequences (th
is, the ultimate disaster and the "knowledge" it leads to
and in his intense preoccupation with his own suffering.

But to consider these matters in turn and to illustra
them briefly:

I have already suggested the main sources and locus

10 Cf. Arthur Miller, "Tragedy and the Common Man," New Yo
Times, February 27th, 1949.
11 Notes from Underground, tr. B. G. Guerney.

ragic man's suffering. He suffers because he is more than
usually sensitive to the "terrible disrelations" he sees about
im and experiences in himself. He is more than usually
ware of the mighty opposites in the universe and in man,
f the gulf between desire and fulfilment, between what is
nd what should be. This kind of suffering is suffering on
 high level, beyond the reach of the immature or brutish,
nd for ever closed to the extreme optimist, the extreme
essimist,[12] or the merely indifferent. It was Job on the
sh-heap, the proto-type of tragic man, who was first
truck by the incongruity between Jehovah's nature and
Iis actions, between desert and reward in this life; and
 was he who first asked, not so much for a release from
hysical suffering as a reasonable explanation of it. But
bove all, the source of tragic suffering is the sense, in the
onsciousness of tragic man, of simultaneous guilt and
uiltlessness. Tillich called tragedy "a mixture of guilt and
ecessity." If tragic man could say, "I sinned, therefore
 suffer" or "He (or They or God) sinned, therefore I
uffer," his problem would be resolved, and the peculiar
oignancy of his suffering would be removed. If he felt
imself entirely free or entirely determined, he would
ease to be tragic. But he is neither—he is, in short, a
aradox and mystery, the "riddle of the world."

To draw further distinctions: The element of guilt in
ragic suffering distinguishes it from the pathetic suffering
f the guiltless and from the suffering of the sentimental-
t's bleeding heart. On the other hand, tragic man's sense
f fate, and of the mystery of fate, distinguishes his suffer-
ig from the suffering (which is little more than embar-
assment) of the man of corrective comedy and satire.
he suffering of the epic hero has little of the element of
afflement or enigma; it is not, characteristically, spiritual
uffering. The Christian in his suffering can confess *total*
uilt and look to the promise of redemption through
race.[13] The martyr seeks suffering, accepts it gladly,

12 Cf. William Van O'Connor, *Climates of Tragedy*, Baton Rouge, La.,
)43.

13 Cf. Karl Jaspers, *Tragedy is Not Enough*, tr. Reiche, Moore, Deutsch;
oston, 1952.

"glories in tribulation." Tragic man knows nothing
grace and never glories in his suffering. Although he m
come to acquiesce in it partly and "learn" from it (a sta
I shall discuss below), his characteristic mood is reser
ment and dogged endurance. He has not the stoic's p
tience, although this may be part of what he lear
Characteristically, he is restless, intense, probing a
questioning the universe and his own soul (Job, Le
Ahab). It is true that, from Greek tragedy to trage
written in the Christian era (Shakespeare and beyon
emphasis shifts from the universe to the soul, from t
cosmic to the psychological. But Prometheus had an inn
life; Antigone, for all her composure, suffered an ultima
doubt; Oedipus suffered spiritually as he grew to unde
stand the dark ambiguities in his own nature. And v
should be mistaken if we tried to interpret the divi
powers in the plays of Shakespeare simply as "allegori
symbols for psychological realities."[14]

Tragic man, then, placed in a universe of irreconc
ables, acting in a situation in which he is both innoce
and guilty, and peculiarly sensitive to the "cursèd spite"
his condition, suffers. What in the tragic view is t
characteristic course of this suffering and what furth
aspects of tragic man are revealed by it? The tragic fo
develops, not only the partial outlines of a cosmology a
a psychology, but of an ethic.

(III) *Tragic man and society*. The tragic sufferer m
now be viewed in his social and moral relationships.
the tragic world there are several alternatives. A man c
default from the human condition—"Curse God and di
—and bring his suffering to an end: he can endure a
be silent; he can turn cynic. Tragic man understands the
alternatives, feels their attractions, but chooses a differe
way. Rising in his pride, he protests: he pits himself
some way against whatever, in the heavens above and
the earth beneath, seems to him to be wrong, oppressi
or personally thwarting. This is the hero's commitme
made early or late, but involving him necessarily in soci

14 Susan Taubes, op. cit., p. 196.

nd in action—with Prometheus and Antigone early, with
Hamlet late. What to the orthodox mind would appear
o be the wisdom or folly, the goodness or badness, of the
ommitment is not, in the beginning, the essence of the
natter. In the first phase of his course of suffering, the
ero's position may be anarchic, individual, romantic.
Herein tragedy tests all norms—as, by contrast, satire,[15]
omedy, or epic tend to confirm them. The commitment
nay even be expressed in what society knows as a crime,
ut, as with tragic pride (of which the commitment is in
art the expression) tragedy does not prejudge it. Thus it
s said that tragedy studies "the great offenders," and
Dostoevski sought among criminals and outcasts for his
reatest spiritual discoveries. But the commitment must
row in meaning to include the more-than-personal. Ul-
imately, and ideally, the tragic hero stands as universal
nan, speaking for all men. The tragic sufferer, emerging
rom his early stage of lament or rebellion (Job's opening
peech; the first scenes of Prometheus; Lear's early bursts
f temper), moves beyond the "intermittences" of his own
eart and makes a "pact with the world that is unremit-
ing and sealed."[16]

Since the commitment cannot lead in the direction of
scape or compromise, it must involve head-on collision
vith the forces that would oppress or frustrate. Conscious
f the ambiguities without and within, which are the
ource of his peculiar suffering, tragic man accepts the
onflict. It is horrible to do it, he says, but it is more hor-
ible to leave it undone. He is now in the main phase of
is suffering—the "passion."[17]

In his passion he differs from the rebel, who would
nerely smash; or the romantic hero, who is not conscious
f guilt; or the epic hero, who deals with emergencies

---

[15] Cf. Maynard Mack, "The Muse of Satire," *Yale Review, Spring,* 1952.
[16] Wallace Fowlie, "Swann and Hamlet: A Note on the Contemporary
Hero," *Partisan Review,* 1942.
[17] Cf. Francis Fergusson, *The Idea of a Theatre,* Princeton, N.J., 1949,
hap. 1, "The Tragic Rhythm of Action." Fergusson translates Kenneth
urke's formulation *"Poiema, Pathema, Mathema"* into "Purpose, Passion,
erception." (See *A Grammar of Motives,* pp. 38ff.) Cf. also Susan Taubes,
p. cit., p. 199.

rather than dilemmas. Odysseus and Aeneas, to be sure
face moral problems, but they proceed in a clear ethica
light. Their social norms are secure. But the tragic her
sees a sudden, unexpected evil at the heart of things tha
infects all things. His secure and settled world has gon
wrong, and he must oppose his own ambiguous natur
against what he loves. Doing so involves total risk, as th
chorus and his friends remind him. He may brood an
pause, like Hamlet, or he may proceed with Ahab's fur;
but proceed he must.

He proceeds, suffers, and in his suffering "learns." Th'
is the phase of "perception." Although it often culminate
in a single apocalyptic scene, a moment of "recognition,
as in *Oedipus* and *Othello,* it need not be separate in tim
from the passion phase. Rather, perception is all that ca
be summed up in the spiritual and moral change that th
hero undergoes from first to last and in the simil:
change wrought by his actions or by his example in thos
about him.

For the hero, perception may involve an all-but-con
plete transformation in character, as with Lear an
Oedipus; or a gradual development in poise and sel
mastery (Prometheus, Hamlet); or the softening an
humanizing of the hard outlines of a character like A;
tigone's. It may appear in the hero's change from mood
isolation and self-pity to a sense of his sharing in th
general human condition, of his responsibility for it an
to it. This was one stage in Lear's pilgrimage ("I ha·
ta'en too little care of this") and as far as Dostoevski
Dmitri Karamazov ever got. In all the manifestations ·
this perception there is an element of Hamlet's "read
ness," of an acceptance of destiny that is not merely resi,
nation. At its most luminous it is Lear's and Oedipus
hard-won humility and new understanding of love. It m:
transform or merely inform, but a change there must b

And it is more, of course, than merely a moral chang
just as the hero's problem is always more than a moral on
His affair is still with the gods. In taking up arms again
the ancient cosmic evil, he transcends the human situatio
mediating between the human and the divine. It w

Orestes's suffering that, in the end, made the heavens more
just. In the defeat or death which is the usual lot of the
tragic hero, he becomes a citizen of a larger city, still
defiant but in a new mood, a "calm of mind," a partial
acquiescence. Having at first resented his destiny, he has
lived it out, found unexpected meanings in it, carried his
case to a more-than-human tribunal. He sees his own
destiny, and man's destiny, in its ultimate perspective.

But the perception which completes the tragic form is
not dramatized solely through the hero's change, although
his pilgrimage provides the traditional tragic structure.[18]
The full nature and extent of the new vision is measured
also by what happens to the other figures in the total
symbolic situation—to the hero's antagonists (King Creon,
Claudius, Iago); to his opposites (the trimmers and
hangers-on, the Osrics); to his approximates (Ismene,
Horatio, Kent, the Chorus). Some he moves, some do
not change at all. But his suffering must make a difference
somewhere outside himself. After Antigone's death the
community (even Creon) re-forms around her; the "new
acquist" at the end of *Samson Agonistes* is the common
note, also, at the end of the Shakespearean tragedies. For
the lookers-on there is no sudden rending of the veil of
day, no triumphant assertion of The Moral Order. There
has been suffering and disaster, ultimate and irredeemable
loss, and there is promise of more to come. But all who

---

[18] Indeed, it has been pointed out that, in an age when the symbol of the
hero as the dominating centre of the play seems to have lost its validity
with artist and audience, the role is taken over by the artist himself, who
is his own tragic hero. That is, "perception" is conveyed more generally, in
the total movement of the piece and through all the parts. The "pact with
the world" and the suffering are not objectified in a hero's ordeal but seem
peculiarly the author's. This quality has been noted in Joyce's *Ulysses*;
Berdiaev saw it in Dostoevski; Hardy, Conrad, Faulkner are examples
that come to mind. At any rate, the distinction may be useful in determining matters of tone, although it is not clear cut, as distinctions in tone
seldom are. But it is one way of pointing to the difference between the
tragic tone and the Olympian distance of Meredithian comedy, the
harmony of the final phase of Dantesque comedy, or the ironic detachment
of satire. Nietzsche spoke of the difference between the Dionysian (or
tragic) artist and "the poet of the dramatized epos . . . the calm, unmoved
embodiment of Contemplation, whose wide eyes see the picture before
them." (*Birth of Tragedy* in *Works*, ed. O. Levy, Edinburgh and London,
1909, III, p. 96.)

are involved have been witness to new revelations abo
human existence, the evil of evil and the goodness of goo
They are more "ready." The same old paradoxes a
ambiguities remain, but for the moment they are tra
scended in the higher vision.

G. K. HUNTER

Five-Act Structure in "Doctor Faustus"

The original and substantive texts of Marlowe's *Doctor Faustus* (the Quartos of 1604 and 1616) present the play completely without the punctuation of act division or scene enumeration. This is common enough in the play-texts of the period. Indeed it is much the commonest form in plays written for the public theatres.[1] Shakespeare's *Henry V* and *Pericles* are without divisions in their quarto texts, but we know that they were written with a five-act structure in mind—the choruses tell us that.

What is exceptional in the textual history of *Doctor Faustus* is not the lack of division in the original texts; it is rather the reluctance of modern editors to impose an act-structure on the modern texts. This is curious, but it seems possible to discern why the reluctance exists and a survey of the modern editions of *Faustus* throws some interesting light on critical attitudes to the subject matter of the play.

Marlowe (like other Elizabethan dramatists) was "rediscovered" by the educated English public in an atmosphere which played down his specifically dramatic and theatrical powers. Charles Lamb's *Specimens of the*

First published in the *Tulane Drama Review*, Vol. 8, No. 4 (T24 Summer 1964) © Copyright 1964, *Tulane Drama Review;* © Copyright, 1967 *The Drama Review*. Reprinted by permission of the publisher and author.
[1] W. T. Jewkes notes that "of the 134 plays written for the public stage [*and printed before 1616*], 30 are divided, as against 104 undivided." *Act division in Elizabethan and Jacobean Plays, 1583–1616,* [Hamden, Conn.: 1958], p. 96.)

*English dramatic poets who lived about the time c
Shakespeare* (1808) established him primarily as a poe
This, as I say, did not distinguish him from other drama
tists of the period. But the attitudes implied by Lamb'
volume were more difficult to shake off in the case c
Doctor Faustus than in other Elizabethan plays; for her
they were reinforced, later in the century, by a secon
wave of anti-theatrical (or at least a-theatrical) influenc
In 1887 the young Havelock Ellis (then a medical str
dent) suggested to Henry Vizetelly, well known in "ac
vanced" circles as a courageous though rather *risqu*
publisher, that he should put out a series of unexpurgate
(key word!) texts of the Elizabethan dramatists—th
famous "Mermaid" series. The *Marlowe,* the first volun
in the series, was edited by Ellis himself, and may l
taken as a manifesto of the whole new movement. It bor
proudly on the title-page the legend *Unexpurgated,* n
simply because the usual casual indecencies of clown cor
versations were preserved, but rather because an append
carried the full testimony of the informer Richard Bain
"concernynge [Marlowe's] damnable opinions and jud,
ment of Religion and scorne of Gods worde," to whic
Ellis added the even more offensive comment that suc
"damnable opinions . . . have, without exception, bee
substantially held, more or less widely, by students
science and the Bible in our own days." To say this
remarks like "Moses was but a juggler," "that Christ be
ter deserved to die than Barabas," etc., was to pu
Marlowe into the front line of the late Victorian batt
against bourgeois values. Marlowe appears as a soci
rebel and religious freethinker (like Ellis himself) and th
comes to reinforce the earlier view that he was primari
a poet. The two attitudes join together, in fact, to sugge
that he was a poet *because* he was a freethinker, rejectir
social conventions in order to achieve his individual ar
personal vision. He becomes the morning-star of t
nineties, a harder and more gem-like Oscar Wilde.

In order to preserve the image of Marlowe as a cu
figure of this kind it is necessary to discount the theatric
and so popular, provenance of his work. If he was t

laureate of the atheistical imagination, he must have stood at a considerable distance from his rudely Christian audience; and this assumption presses especially heavily upon *Doctor Faustus,* whose hero is himself a freethinker and (by implication at least) a poet. It is not surprising therefore to find Ellis saying in his headnote to *Faustus:* "I have retained the excellent plan introduced by Professor Ward and adopted by Mr. Bullen, of dividing the play into scenes only; it is a dramatic poem rather than a regular drama." In the face of this critical assurance, and with the *Zeitgeist* exerting the kind of pressure that I have described, the earlier editorial practice of presenting the play in five acts, derived from the 1663 Quarto by Robinson (1826) and continued in Cunningham (1870), Wagner (1877), and Morley (1883), withered away. It was not until the bibliographical breakthrough[2] of Boas, Kirschbaum, and Greg (1932, 1946, 1950) that the play reappeared in the five-act form. Even after their labors the old attitudes persist. The edition by Kocher (1950) is divided into scenes only, and the recent replacement of Boas by the "Revels" edition of J. D. Jump (1962) avoids the act divisions: "Neither A1 [1604] nor B1 [1616] makes any attempt to divide the play into acts and scenes, so no such distribution is given prominence in the present edition" (xxxv). It may be sufficient reply to this to quote the recent comment of W. T. Jewkes, who has analyzed the act structure of all the plays in the period:

The plays of the "University wits," however, appear

---

2 I mean the perception that the 1616 text must be the basis of any modern recension. In this text the nature of the structure is much clearer; and it was, in fact, the reading of Greg's *editio minor* that first made clear to me the precision with which the play moved. Greg himself, however, hedges his bets. He finds the act division "convenient in discussing the construction of the play" (parallel text edition, p. 153) and so presents it to the reader; but he confides to us in a footnote that "I see no reason to suppose that any act division was originally contemplated" (p. 153 n.5). His argument is that there is too great a disproportion between the numbers of lines to be found in the different acts for these to make just divisions. A rereading of *The Winter's Tale,* in which Act IV is two and a half times as long as Act III, ought to convince us of the insignificance of this mode of assessment.

both undivided and divided. On a closer inspection it was evident that the clearly divided texts from this group were those which showed least sign of playhouse annotation, while those which retained fragmentary division, or none at all, showed signs of adaptation for performance. It is evident then that these dramatists divided their plays originally, but that adaptation for the stage resulted in either the total or partial loss of act headings.[3]

This argument might well be augmented, in the particula case of *Doctor Faustus,* by reference to the choruses whicl mark the beginnings of some of the acts, or by repeatin; Boas' observations about the material taken from th Faustbook. But it is not my purpose here to argue th textual or theatrical probability that *Faustus* is in five-ac form. I rather wish to look at the developing movemen of the play to see if the act divisions accepted by Boas an others correspond to anything in the inner economy of th work, marking progressive stages in an organized advanc through the material. Since Goethe remarked, "Hov greatly is it all planned" in 1829,[4] many have been foun to repeat his encomium, but few to justify it. I woul suggest that the play *is* planned greatly, even precisely in five clear stages (or acts), moving forward continuousl in a single direction. I am assuming, when I say this, tha the text as we have it in the 1616 Quarto is the produc of a unified organizing intelligence. Marlowe *may* hav had a collaborator, but I do not believe that we ca detect his work—and a stroke of Occam's razor make him disappear.

The first point I should like to make is that the actio (I deal only with the main plot at the moment) move through clearly separable stages. Act I is concerned (as i usual) with setting up the situation and introducing th principal characters. Here we learn the nature of Faustus desires, set against the limiting factor of his nature; w meet Mephistophilis and the contrast between the two i

---

[3] *Op. cit.,* p. 97.
[4] Recorded in the *Diary* of H. Crabb Robinson, for 2nd August, 182?

made evident. Act II begins with a preliminary reminder (found before each act of the play) of the stage at which the action has arrived:

> Now Faustus must thou needs be damned,
> And canst thou not be saved.
> What boots it then to think on God or heaven?
>   (II, i, 1–3)

In Act I, the temptation to think of heaven is hardly present; but the subject here announced is the warp on which much of the main-plot action of Act II is woven. The conflict is entered upon in real earnest. The introductory note to Act III is more obvious, being handled by the "Chorus." He tells us that "Learned Faustus," having searched into the secrets of Astronomy, now is gone to prove Cosmography. He is in fact completing his Grand Tour when we meet him, having taken in Paris, Mainz, Naples, Venice, and Padua, and is newly arrived in Rome, "Queen of the Earth" as Milton calls it,[5] and the summation of worldly grandeur. Mephistophilis describes the sights, and then conducts his master into the highest social circles in the city, and so in the world.

Act III is spent in Rome; Act IV in the courts of Germany. The introductory Chorus makes clear the distinction between "the view/Of rarest things" which is the substance of Act III and the "trial of his art" which is what we are to see in Act IV. The introductory speech to Act V is spoken by Wagner, Faustus' servant, who is confused in one text with the Chorus, and who is exercising here what is clearly a choric function. His first line marks the change of key: "I think my master means to die shortly." Act V is concerned with preparations and prevarications in the face of death.

It is obvious enough, I suggest, that each act handles a separate stage in Faustus' career. But it is not obvious from what I have said that the stages move forward in any single and significant line of development. To see that

---

[5] Cf. William Thomas, who calls Rome "the onelie jewell, myrrour, maistres, and beautie of the worlde" (*Historie of Italie* [1549]).

they do requires a fairly laborious retracing of the action, seen now in the light of what was more obvious to Marlowe and his audience than to us—the supposed hierarchy of studies.

The opening lines of the play show us Faustus trying to *settle his studies;* the opening speech, with this aim in mind, moves in an orthodox direction through the academic disciplines, beginning with logic, here representative of the whole undergraduate course of Liberal Arts, through the *Noble Sciences* of Medicine and Law and so to the *Queen of Sciences,* Divinity. So far, the movement has been, as I say, completely orthodox, and a frame of reference has been neatly established. But, having reached Divinity, Faustus still hopes to advance, and can only do so in reverse:

> . . . Divinity, adieu!
> These metaphysics of magicians
> And negromantic books are heavenly.[6]
> (I, i, 46–48)

At this point he passes, as it were, through the looking glass; he goes on trying to evaluate experience, but his words of value (like "heavenly") now mean the opposite of what they should. The "profit and delight . . . power . . . honor . . . omnipotence" that he promises himself through the practice of magic are all devalued in advance. By embracing negromancy he ensures that worthwhile ends cannot be reached; and the rest of the play is a demonstration of this, moving as it does in a steadily downward direction.

The route taken by Faustus in his descent through human activities was, I think, intended to be easily understood by the original audience, and again I suggest that it is the structure of knowledge as at that time understood that provides the key. Divinity was, as I have

---

[6] I preserve the original form *negromantic,* though most modernizing editors change it to *necromantic.* This seems to me to be a greater change than is warranted by a licence to modernize. It is the "black art" in general that Faustus is welcoming, not the power to raise the dead.

noted, the "Queen of the Sciences." Not only so, but it was the discipline which gave meaning to all other knowledge and experience. Hugh of St. Victor expresses the idea succinctly: "all the natural arts serve divine science, and the lower order leads to the higher."[7] In Marlowe's own day the same point is made, more elaborately, in the popular *French Academy* of La Primaudaye:

> What would it availe or profit us to have and attaine unto the knowledge and understanding of all humane and morall Philosophy, Logicke, Phisicke, Metaphisicke, and Mathematick . . . not to bee ignorant of any thing, which the liberall arts and sciences teach us, therewith to content the curious minds of men and by that means to give them a tast, and to make them enjoy some kind of transitory good in this life: and in the meane time to be altogether and wholy ignorant, or badly instructed, in the true and onely science of divine Philosophy, whereat all the rest ought to aime.
>
> (Preface to Book IV)

But if one rejects the final cause here supposed, what happens to the rest of knowledge? This is the question that the play asks and pursues. In what direction does the Icarus of learning fall when he abandons the orthodox methods of flight? The order of topics in the medieval encyclopaedias gives one some clue here. These regularly begin with God and divine matters. Vincent of Beauvais' *Speculum* starts from the Creator, then moves to "the empyrean heaven and the nature of angels," then to "the formless material and the making of the world; the nature and the properties of things created," then to the human state and its ramifications. The *De Rerum Natura* attributed to Bede and William of Conches' *Philosophia Mundi*[8] have the same four-book order. Book I deals with God; Book II with the heavens; Book III with the lower atmosphere; Book IV with the earth, so down to man and

---

7 *De Sacramentis* (Prologue), in Migne's *Patrologia Latina* Vol. CLXXVI, col. 185.

8 The first is to be found in *Patrologia Latina* XC, cols. 1127 ff., and the second (attributed to Honorius Augustodunensis) in vol. CLXXII, cols. 39 ff. I am indebted to Dr. Hans Liebeschütz for pointing these out to me.

his human activities. The *Proem* to Book IV (identica
in both works) gives a fair indication of the nature o
the movement assumed:

> The series of books which began with the First Cause
> has now descended to The Earth, not catering for itch-
> ing ears nor loitering in the minds of fools, but dealing
> with what is useful to the reader. For now is that verse
> fulfilled: "For the time will come when they will not
> endure sound doctrine; but after their own lusts shall
> they heap to themselves teachers, having itching ears."
> (2 Timothy, IV,3). But since the mind of the honest
> man does not turn after wickedness, but conforms itself
> to the better way, let us turn to the remaining subjects,
> in the interest of a mind of this kind, estranged from
> wickedness and conformable to virtue.

In Marlowe's own day this order of topics appeared
in works as popular as the Baldwin-Palfreyman *Treatise
of Moral Philosophy* (innumerable editions from 1557 to
1640), in Palfreyman's companion *Treatise of Heavenly
Philosophy,* and in William Vaughan's *The Golden Grove*
(1600; 1608). *The French Academy,* which Marlowe
has been supposed to have known, uses the same or-
ganization of topics but treats them in reverse order,
upwards from (1) "the institution of manners and call-
ings of all estates," through (2) "concerning the soule
and body of man," and (3) "a notable description of
the whole world . . . Angels . . . the foure elements
. . . fowles, fishes, beasts . . . etc." to (4) "Christian
philosophy, instructing the true and onely meanes to
eternall life." It seems reasonable to suppose that Marlowe
knew this system of knowledge; and it is my assertion that
he used it to plan the relationship of the parts of *Doctor
Faustus.*

When Faustus has signed away his soul, the first fruits
of his new "power . . . honor . . . omnipotence" appear
in the knowledge of astronomy that he seeks. Astronomy
is a heavenly art, no doubt—it appears early in the encyclopaedias—but it is one that is not obviously de-
pendent on divinity. Yet here it leads by the natural

rocess that the encyclopaedists describe to the question
f first cause. If the heavens involve more than the tedium
f mechanics ("these slender questions Wagner can de-
de") then astronomy leads straight back to the funda-
ental question: Who made the world? But, under the
onditions of knowledge that Faustus has embraced, this
asic question cannot be answered, for it is "against our
ngdom." The trap closes on the pseudo-scholar and
rces him backwards and downwards.

This is the movement—backwards into ever more su-
erficial shallows of knowledge and experience—which
ontinues inexorably throughout the whole play, as it
ust, given the initial choice. Balked in Act II from the
ll pursuit of astronomy, in Act III Faustus turns to
osmography, from the heavens to the earth. But the
arms of sightseeing pall, and a magical entrée even to
e "best" society in the world involves only a tediously
perficial contact. Marlowe's age had serious doubts
out the importance of cosmography (or geography) as
a object of human endeavor. *The French Academy*
eats it under the heading of "curiosity and novelty," as
destructively unserious pursuit. The drop in the status
f Faustus' activities is nicely caught by the change of
one between the Chorus at the beginning of Act III
nd that introducing Act IV. The first tells us that

> Learnèd Faustus
> To find the secrets of astronomy
> Graven in the book of Jove's high firmament
> Did mount him up to scale Olympus' top.
> (III, Prol., 1–4)

Ve seem here still to be dealing with a genuine search
r knowledge. But in the second chorus we hear only
nat:

> When Faustus had *with pleasure*[9] ta'en the view
> Of rarest things and royal courts of kings,
> He stay'd his course and so returnèd home.
> (IV, Prol., 1–3)

9 My italics.

The emphasis is no longer on the search after knowledg
with discovery, presumably, as the aimed-for end, b
with what is more appropriate to the diabolical premi
("that is not against our kingdom"), with pleasure tak
and then given up, without reaching forward to the fir
causes. Faustus' merry japes among the cardinals are e
joyed by the protagonist, and are clearly meant to
enjoyed by the audience; but nothing more than pleasu
is involved, and given the giant pretensions of the fir
act, the omission is bound to be a factor in our vie
of the Roman scenes.

Faustus not only views Rome. He also dabbles in stat
craft, rescuing the Antipope Bruno and transporting hi
back to his supporters in Germany. The step from co
mography to statecraft is similar to that from astronom
to cosmography. In each case we have a reduction
the area covered, an increasing remoteness from fir
causes. The panoply of state is not here (as it usually
in Shakespeare) an awesome and a righteous thing. It
not approached through the lives of those who must li
and suffer inside the system, but via the structure
knowledge, so that it is the relationship to divinity rath
than the power over individual lives that is the determi
ing factor in our attitude. The ludicrous antics at t
Papal court have usually been seen as a simple piece
Protestant propaganda, pleasing to the groundlings a
inserted for no better reason. Yet one can see that t
episode (placed where it is) has its own unique part
play in the total economy of the work. It is proper
start Faustus' descent through the world from the high
point, in Rome; it is equally proper to begin his social a
political descent with the Vicar of Christ (and so do
to Emperor, to Duke, and back to private life). By tur
ing the conduct of the papal court into farce Marlo
devalues *all* sovereignty and political activity in advan
Bruno (and his tiara) are saved; but there is no sugg
tion that *he* has any more virtue to recommend him;
has no real function in the play except to reduce t
title and state of the Pope to a mere name.

There is no suggestion in this act that Faustus hims

aware of the startling discrepancy between the actual
appenings and the promises he made to himself (and to
s) at the beginning of the play. The audience, however,
an hardly forget so soon; and our memory is reinforced
a the papal palace by the ritual threats of damnation ut-
ered by the Pope and friars. It is no doubt comic that
e Pope should be boxed on the ear and exclaim,
Damn'd be this soul for ever for this deed," but we
ould not fail to notice the sinister echo reverberating
ehind the horseplay; the curse is comic at this point, but
nister in the context of the whole action.

Act IV carries the descent of Faustus one more clear
ep, by still further reducing the importance of the area
a which he operates. I have mentioned the social descent
o the secular courts of Emperor and Duke of Vanholt.
t the same time there is a descent in terms of the kind
f activity that the magic procures. Faustus' anti-Papal
ctivities can be seen as political action of a kind, and
is aspect would be more obvious to the Elizabethans
an it is to us (involved, as they were, in the kind of
ruggle depicted). But in Act IV he is presented quite
rankly as a court entertainer or hired conjurer. In the
ourt of Charles V, of course, there is still some intel-
ectual dignity in his activities. Charles's longing, to see
that famous conqueror, Great Alexander, and his para-
our," is a kingly interest in a paragon of kingship. But
hen Faustus goes on to the court of the Duke of Van-
olt he is reduced to satisfying nothing more dignified
an the pregnant "longings" of the duchess for out-of-
eason grapes. At the same time his side activities are
rought down by a parallel route. At the court of the
mperor he was matched against the disbelieving knights,
rederick, Benvolio, etc.; at Vanholt his opponents are
lowns, the Horse-courser, the Hostess.[10]

---

10 I find that this general point has been made by Kirschbaum in his
aperback *The Plays of Christopher Marlowe* (New York: Meridian,
962): "Surely Marlowe means to stress the magician's continuing degra-
ation by showing him first playing his tricks with the spiritual head of
Roman Christendom and then ultimately declining, to play them with
e clowns" (p. 119).

The last act of *Faustus* is often thought of as involvi
restoration of dignity and brilliance to the sadly tarnish
magician. In terms of poetic power there is something
be said on this side; but the poetry that Faustus is giv
in this act serves to do more than simply glorify t
speaker. The fiery brilliance of the Helen speech is lit I
the Fire of Hell (as has been pointed out by Kirschbaun
and others). The imminence of eternal damnation giv
strength and urgency to the action, but the actions th
Faustus himself can initiate are as trivial and as restrict
as one would expect, given the moral development th
I have described as operating throughout the rest of t
play. There is no change of direction. In Acts III a
IV we saw Faustus sink steadily from political intrig
at the Curia to fruit-fetching for a longing duchess. T
last act shows a consistent extension of this movemer
It picks up the role of Faustus as entertainer, but reduc
the area of its exercise still further; it is now confin
to the enjoyment of some "two or three" private frienc
and as an epilogue to what Wagner characterizes I
"banquet . . . carouse . . . swill . . . belly-cheer." Hel
appears, in short, at the point where one might have e
pected dancing-girls.

The nature of the object conjured in Act V, no le
than the occasion of the conjuring, shows the same logic
development of the movement in the preceding ac
Charles V had longed to satisfy an intellectual interes
the Duchess of Vanholt longed for the satisfaction of
carnal but perfectly natural appetite; but the desire
view Helen of Troy is both carnal and (as the iron
word *blessed* should warn us) reprehensible, and lea
logically to the further and final depravity of:

> One thing, good servant, let me crave of thee
> To glut the longing of my heart's desire—
> That I may have unto my paramour
> That heavenly Helen which I saw of late,
> Whose sweet embraces may extinguish clear

11 "Marlowe's Faustus: a Reconsideration," *R.E.S.* XIX (1943).

Those thoughts that do dissuade me from my vow,
And keep mine oath I made to Lucifer.
(V, i, 87–93)

The circle in which Faustus conjures has now shrunk
from the *urbs et orbis* of Rome to the smallest circle of
all—that which contains only himself. When the dream of
power was lost, the gift of entertainment remained; but
even this has now faded. The conjuring here exists for
an exclusively self-interested and clearly damnable purpose. The loneliness of the damned, summed up in Meph-
tophilis' cryptic *"Solamen miseris socios habuisse
doloris,"* this now is clearly Faustus' lot. Left alone with
himself and the mirror of his own damnation[12] in Helen
("Her lips suck forth my soul: see where it flies"), he
is in a situation that cannot be reached by either the Old
Man or the students. His descent has taken him below
the reach of human aid; and there is a certain terrible
splendor in this, as the poetry conveys, but the moral
level of this splendor is never in doubt; it is something
that the whole weight of the play's momentum presses
on our attention, moving steadily as it does, through the
clearly defined stages of its act-structure, away from the
deluded dream of power and knowledge and downward,
inevitably, coherently, and logically, into the sordid reality
of damnation.

I have sought to show that the movement of the main
plot of *Faustus* is controlled and splendidly meaningful.
It moves in a single direction (downwards) through a
series of definite stages which it would be wilfully ob-
scurantist not to call acts. Indeed it conforms, by and
large, to the strict form of five-act structure which was
taught in Tudor grammar schools, out of the example
of Terence. The structural paradigm was, of course, concerned with comedy, and especially the comedy of intrigue,
and could not be applied very exactly to a moralistic tragedy like *Faustus*. But it is easy to see that Act I of *Faustus*
gives us the introductory materials, Act II the first moves
in the central conflict (Faustus versus the Devil), Acts

12 See W. W. Greg, "The Damnation of Faustus," *M.L.R.* XLI (1946).

III and IV the swaying back and forward of this confli and Act V the catastrophe.

What is more, these stages of the main plot are rei forced or underlined by a parallel movement going simultaneously in the subplot. The general relation b tween the two levels of the plot, the level of spiritu struggle and that of carnal opportunism, is one of paro —a mode of connection that was common in the perio And I should state that by "parody" I do not mean t feeble modern reduction of characteristics to caricatu but rather that multiple presentation of serious themes which relates them both to the man of affairs and to t light-minded clown.

It is not only in the detail of individual scenes that t subplot parodies the main plot: the whole movement the subplot mirrors that social and intellectual desce that I have traced in the career of Faustus. The first su plot scene concerns Wagner, a man close to Faustus hin self. The second comic scene involves Wagner and h servants, Robin and Dick. The third and subsequent scen show Robin and Dick by themselves, Wagner having di appeared (he reappears—though not as part of the su plot—in V, i). It has been argued that this very descen and the disappearance of Wagner, "suggests a differe hand" [*not Marlowe's*] for the Robin and Dick scenes. This provides an interesting parallel to the assumption th Marlowe cannot be responsible for the main plot scen in the middle of the play. At both levels the action d scends to trivialities, and the critics close their eyes dissent. But if the movement is deliberate at one level seems likely that it is so at the other level also.

Even more impressive than this general movement the subplot is the accumulation of details in which t action of the subplot scene mirrors that of the contiguo main plot. Thus Act I, scene one shows us Faustus usin his virtuosity in logic to deceive himself. Scene two show

---

13 See G. K. Hunter, *John Lyly* (Cambridge: Harvard University Pre 1962), pp. 135–40. The significance of the parody in *Faustus* is denied Jump (*op. cit.* lix–lx).

14 *Doctor Faustus*, ed. F. S. Boas (London: Methuen, 1932), p. 27.

s Wagner as no less able to chop logic and so to avoid
he plain meaning of words. As a development from this
ve see Faustus raising Mephistophilis and arranging that
ie should be his servant. The following scene shows us
Vagner trying to control Robin, who would not "give
ais soul to the devil for a shoulder of mutton," unless it
vere "well roasted, and good sauce to it, if I pay so
lear." Wagner too has learned how to raise spirits and
aakes Robin his servant by a parody compact, promising
o teach him "to turn thyself to a dog, or a cat, or a
nouse, or a rat, or anything." It may be noted that the
general effect of this and the preceding comic scene is
o reduce in status and to "place" for us Faustus' pre-
ensions to have conquered a new art by the force of his
earning, and to have gained important new powers. When
uch as Wagner can raise Banio and Belcher, and all
'or the sake of terrifying Robin, then neither the means
ior the ends of magic can be considered sufficient, by
hemselves, to make the magician a hero.

In Act II, scenes one and two, Faustus signs his pact
vith the Devil and has the first fruits of his "new" knowledge. In scene three we meet Robin again. The power of
aising spirits has declined from Faustus' servant Wagner
o Wagner's servant, Robin. He and his fellow, Dick,
olan to use one of the conjuring books to get free drink.
In Act III the first two scenes show Doctor Faustus sur-
eying the great cities of Europe and conjuring at Rome.
The third scene shows Robin and Dick enjoying *themselves* in their own clownish way; but it is not now a
way that is so remote from that of Faustus. He "took
iway his Holiness' wine," "stole his Holiness' meat from
:he table," "took Friar Sandelo a blow on the pate"; they
:tole the Vintner's cup, and when pursued for it they rely
(as Faustus does) on magic, as a rescue from their scape.

The play began with Faustus and Robin at opposite
ends of the spectrum. One was "glutted with learning's
golden gifts," powerful and renowned; the other was ig-
norant, "out of service," and "hungry." But the process
of logical development in the main plot, as I have described it, has by the end of Act III brought Faustus down

through the diminishing circles of his capacity to t
point where his powers and Robin's are no longer incon
mensurate. Up to this point, of course, Faustus and t
clowns have never appeared together in any one scen
Such a conjunction would be unthinkable at the beginni
of the play. But by Act IV Faustus has himself sunk
the level of a comic entertainer. His relationship to Fre
erick, Martino, and Benvolio is entirely without digni
or intellectual pretension, and the intrusion of the clown
Robin, Dick, Carter, Horse-courser, Hostess, into t
court of the Duke of Vanholt marks a natural and ine
table climax in the downward movement of the main pl
The comic "Doctor Fustian" is now all the figure th
Faustus can cut in the world; the "success" that he h
bought so dearly is to be the leader of a troupe of clown

There is no doubt a *frisson* intended between the la
line of Act IV and the first line of Act V—between t
duchess's appreciation of Faustus' powers: "His artf
sport drives all sad thoughts away," and (set against tha
Wagner's "I think my master means to die shortly." T
contrast between the two lines catches much of the mov
ment from Act IV to Act V. Act IV is the climax
the subplot interest. Almost the whole act is taken
with triviality of one kind or another, and it ends wi
the confrontation of main plot and subplot character
reducing them to one level. Act V, on the other han
is without comic relief; and one can see why, in the tern
I have outlined, this should be so. Through Act IV
see Faustus' life enmeshed in the triviality that was i
herent in the original stipulation of "any thing . . . th
is not against our kingdom." Act V, as it begins wi
the mention of death, so continues to move in the shado
of a tragic conclusion. Faustus has now fallen *beneath* t
level of the clowns and horse-courser:

> Why wert thou not a creature wanting soul?
> . . . .
> Ah, Pythagoras' *metempsychosis*, were that true,
> This soul should fly from me and I be changed
> Unto some brutish beast. All beasts are happy,

For when they die
Their souls are soon dissolv'd in elements.

(V, ii, 179, 181–85)

The movement of the subplot helps to confirm this view of the general direction of Faustus' development. The constant looming presence of the clownish common man, with his attention set on immediate comforts, serves as a norm against which we may observe and judge the splendors and the miseries of the overweening intellectual.

JOHN RUSSELL BROWN

"Doctor Faustus" at *Stratford-upon-Avon, 1968*

Nine editions of Marlowe's *Faustus* before 1640, performances in Germany in the early seventeenth century, and in England until a year or two before the closure of the theaters for the Civil War in 1642—all attest the play's immediate popularity with audiences. And today it is one of the very few Elizabethan plays still to be seen on our stages: of plays written in England before 1600, its nearest rivals in popularity are the anonymous *Everyman*, first printed in the second decade of the sixteenth century, and Dekker's ebullient *Shoemakers' Holiday* written in the summer of 1599.

Productions today must lack much of the direct excitement of the earliest performances, for their audiences were accustomed to a belief in witchcraft and the sight of men and women convicted and burned for these practices. Several accounts of *Doctor Faustus* have survived, such as the Puritan, William Prynne's report in 1633 of the

> visible apparition of the devil on the stage at the Belsavage Playhouse, in Queen Elizabeth's days (to the great amazement both of the actors and spectators) whiles they were there prophanely playing the History of Faustus, the truth of which I have heard from many now alive, who well remember it, there being some distracted with that fearful sight.

Two versions of this story say that the actors themselves

"Dr. Faustus" at Stratford-upon-Avon, 1968," Copyright © 1969 by John Russell Brown. Used by permission of the author.

fell to prayer and piety. This is not a twentieth-century phenomenon, but nevertheless the devilry, which may seem to be such a wasted asset or, even, liability in the play today, is one of the two main reasons for present revivals: it provides a large and fascinating opportunity for the scene and costume designer, working with lights and special-effects consultants. The enchantments, splendors and tortures displayed in a sequence of eye-catching *coups de théâtre* take possession of the audience's senses and make it forget its disbelief in acceptance of a fantastic reality. The audience watches the play in something of the same mind as we might explore a painting by Hieronymus Bosch, his "Earthly Paradise" or "Seven Deadly Sins"; costume designs for productions of *Faustus* are often undisguised borrowings from these pictures. If a modern audience cannot take the devils with intellectual assurance, it can respond eagerly to visual realizations of fantasies of desire and guilt.

The other major hold that the play has over modern audiences is the star role: the opportunity for an actor to dominate the production, speak magniloquent verse, and attempt to create an outsized characterization that can confront devils, sins, scholars, emperors, Helen of Troy, and death.

At Stratford-upon-Avon in the summer of 1968, a production designed by Abd'Elkader Farrah and directed, for the Royal Shakespeare Company, by Clifford Williams, blazed and threatened with sumptuous theatricality. Many of the stage directions of the original quarto editions were cues for technological invention. Mephostophilis first appeared as a disembodied head with a shock of wild hair, vibrating in lurid light and with strange rhythmic sound in support; for perhaps as long as one minute its silent presence suggested a strange, unthinkable reality about to be released upon the stage. The Seven Deadly Sins had gross, distorted, distended, and discolored limbs, and were again supported with electronically doctored sound. The comic enchantments were staged rapidly and with seemingly endless resource: exploding grapes, a realisti-

cally articulated hand appearing from the center of a dish
of food, wine that squirted up into the face of the Pope.
Alexander and his paramour were lit in a circle of blue
light and dressed in silver paint and silver spangles; they
danced slowly to soft and lucid music. Maggie Wright,
playing the mute Helen, was bronzed and gleaming; as
she walked onstage naked, partly like a conventionally
pretty nude and partly like a Cellini Venus, an unfamiliar
quiet showed the audience to be held and perhaps dis-
concerted. At the end of the play there was a further
moment of effective silence—when attention has been
gained by visual means a director can readily take such
liberties—which seemed to give Faustus a hope of sur-
vival after his last words, and then the squarish bulkheads
at the back of the stage moved forward slowly, motivated
by unseen power, and, still slowly, they then fell forward
to reveal great gray spikes; through these came a crowd
of silent devils. There was an enormous sound, with cries
of pain and pleasure amplified stereophonically, as they
encircled Faustus. When they moved away their satisfaction was only a murmur, and the stage was bare.

The text of the play was taken as an invitation to
sensationalism. But it must be firmly controlled. Harold
Hobson, writing in *The Sunday Times* (June 30, 1968),
found the Stratford production inconsistent and therefore
unsatisfying:

> Let [Helen] be naked by all means, if that is how Mr.
> Williams wants her, but to normal eyes she should, if
> the production is consistent, be hideous, like the Seven
> Deadly Sins which Faustus finds so lovely and enticing.

The action of the play and Marlowe's keen verbal intelligence implicit in its words necessitate a careful significance for every detail, just proportion and a proper
relation between each element.

For example, when Faustus has signed his pact with
Lucifer in his blood, Mephostophilis on his own initiative
decides to "fetch him somewhat to delight his mind" and
a stage direction follows:

Enter Devils giving crowns and rich apparel to Faustus.
    They dance and then depart.

It is this sight and the promise that he may raise such
spirits when he pleases that persuade Faustus to hand
the deed of gift of body and of soul into Mephostophilis'
keeping. This is the first of a sequence of "shows"—
pageant-like clarifications of the action—the most natural
of them all and the one most directly "speaking" to
Faustus. Its staging must mark all this; and the other
"shows" must be graded in contrast both in splendor and
realism. The she-devil who comes when Faustus asks for
a wife may be both ridiculous and offensive as Faustus'
response suggests, but the Seven Deadly Sins must be
compelling as well so that they give "delight" to Faustus'
soul as he instinctively exclaims.

The Stratford production failed noticeably in the papal
scenes when compared to an earlier production by Michael Benthall for the Old Vic in 1961. Clifford Williams
followed the demands for tricky practical jokes, but he
disregarded the further insistence of both Quarto texts
on the "pride" and high "solemnity" of the Vatican's
ceremonies; his friars and prelates entered as if for farcical
business. In contrast, the Old Vic production started here
with "magnificence":

> The contrast between the fusty study and the riot of
> colour when [Faustus] gets loose as a magician is ex-
> tremely effective. (*Punch,* August 30, 1961)

> When the papal court has been gradually assembled . . .
> the scene is so impressive in its solemnity that almost
> any joke would seem tellingly out of place, and the
> final wrecking of all this grandeur by Faustus and
> Mephistophilis seems indeed a devilish outrage. (The
> London *Times,* August 23, 1961)

Marlowe uses spectacle, or "shows" as he would say, to
very precise and, often, ironic effect. Contrasts and sequence are of crucial importance.

The Stratford production was perhaps too freely an
consistently fantastic, without sufficient ordinary realit
Its careful staging of Faustus cutting his own arm fc
blood with which to sign, and the chafing of it in flam
showed how effective small-scale realism could be. B
other opportunities were missed. It was incredible that th
Emperor of Germany should wish to embrace the silvere
phantoms of Alexander and his paramour, as he does i
the Quarto of 1616; still less that he should wonde
whether the lady had a wart or mole on her neck as h
does in both Quartos. Yet the illusion of reality here
important as a preparation for Helen's entry, the awe
silence with which she is greeted by Faustus on her fir
appearance and his unresisted kiss on her reappearanc
Possibly the director wished the play to become progre
sively unreal, for the Old Man, who simply and bravel
calls Faustus to repentance just before his last hour, er
tered in a red spotlight and had a woolly beard like ar
other less resourceful stage-phantom: yet he should b
clearly a man and not a spirit, one who can resist th
torments of Mephostophilis. Even the Chorus, who speal
from outside the play's time and place, lacked a distinc
tive reality: the Stratford stage was theatrical spac
without boundaries or permanent structure, and th
Chorus was just one more illusory figure with no speci
point of vantage.

The director and designer must make their audienc
accept fantastic illusions, but they must also mark clearl
the varying reality of each moment in the drama. N
must they overwhelm the audience with large scale ser
sationalism. Some of the most significant moments ar
simply histrionic. When Faustus "pants and quivers" a
he remembers his youth, when he finds "Heaven" i
Helen's lips or boasts that he will sack Wittenberg fc
her sake, the physical transformations must be enacte
and must dominate all other impressions. For the clari
of the play, and for its full excitement, Faustus must b
seen to change from merriment to despair, to fear, t
cruelty, and to sensual desire, all within a hundred or s
lines at the beginning of the last scene. The spectac

must not overwhelm the acting, as it frequently does in twentieth-century theaters and as it did at Stratford.

For all its obvious attractions, the central role of *Faustus* poses serious problems for most twentieth-century actors. A common mistake is to choose a single definite "through-line" or an individual distinguishing mark for characterization; it will be too small a basis. For Irving Wardle, the drama critic of the London *Times,* Richard Burton's performance at the Oxford Playhouse and subsequently for a film version in 1967, was both plausible and "unsatisfactory" in "showing a bandy-legged little scholar seizing on magic to act out his frustrated sensual fantasies" (The London *Times,* June 28, 1968). Eric Porter at Stratford chose a dry, ascetic tone, dressed always in black and played with disdain rather than pride, quiet relish rather than delight or glutting pleasure as the text demands. In effect most actors lack weight: for the 1961 Old Vic production, "Paul Daneman . . . began in much too cavalier a manner; the entry into this dark world of ghostly temptation and deep doubt needs to be more subtle and awed. He dashed his books aside like a naughty schoolboy. The Latin he spouted seemed to mean nothing to him" (*The Guardian,* August 23, 1961). A seriousness is required, by both the theme and style of the play. So many large positive reactions are required—pleasure, fear, pride, humiliation, intellectual and imaginative energy—that the first and almost the last effort of the actor should be to find the reality, and a suitably clear, assured and true-to-life expression, for each element.

Edward Alleyn, who first created the role, was especially famed for his interpretation of Marlowe's earlier hero, Tamburlaine.[1] In a pamphlet of 1597, a man who "bent his brows and fetched stations up and down the room" was said to do so with "such furious gesture as

[1] Alleyn's style has been discussed by W. A. Armstrong and A. J. Gurr in *Shakespeare Survey,* VII (1954) and XVI (1963); both articles usefully quote contemporary assessments.

if he had been playing Tamburlaine on a stage." Clearl
Alleyn's acting was violent, stalking, astounding. Whe
fashions changed and Alleyn's Tamburlaine was remem
bered as "flying from all humanity," it still was praise
for the hold it kept over an audience: Joseph Hall's satir
(1597) on "some upreared, high-aspiring swain" like "th
turkish Tamburlaine" attests:

> He vaunts his voice upon an hired stage,
> With high-set steps, and princely carriage:
> Now swooping in side robes of royalty,
> That erst did scrub in lousy brokery.
> There if he can with terms italianate,
> Big-sounding sentences, and words of state,
> Fair patch me up his pure iambic verse,
> He ravishes the gazing scaffolders . . .

Alleyn's acting was broad and violent, but while it coul
command popular attention it could also give specia
pleasure at Elizabeth's court where he was recalled fror
retirement to act before the Queen in 1600. Thoma
Nashe, a dramatist and university-trained writer, said tha
his very name was "able to make an ill matter good" an
that not even the famed Roman actor, Roscius, "coul
ever perform more in action than famous Ned Alleyn."

Alleyn did not act in Shakespeare's plays, and it i
arguable that he could never have done so with suc
success. Marlowe's effects are not Shakespeare's, his "Big
sounding sentences and words of state" are quite unlik
the developing and complex expressiveness of Shake
speare's mature verse. Quote any long speech from *Faustu*
and Hamlet's advice will seem out of place: "Speak th
speech . . . as I pronounced it to you, trippingly on th
tongue." But the opposite, a thundering Herod, is als
wrong. Marlowe spoke of "working words," of "disputes,
"concise syllogisms," words that "win," "incantations.
Energy is the most important requirement, composed o
force, clarity or control, and speed. When the situatio
and reactions are complex, as they often are, Marlow
does not write lines of allusive complexity or multipl

meaning; he divides to express the complexity, following one clear thought with another, perhaps its opposite. Frequently two or three contrasted characters speak successively about a single occurrence, as do the scholars and the Good and Bad Angels who attend on Faustus, or the speaker varies his reaction widely within a single speech. Brecht's dramaturgy is more relevant here than Shakespeare's: he asked for boldness, clarity, contradictions; he displayed complicated action and reactions through "montage" rather than "growth"; the event is "not to be read between the lines" but "directly stated."

The physical demands of Faustus on the actor are at one with the verbal; they need the same qualities. It is instructive to observe how successive scenes start with clearly contrasted moods, each requiring an entry in strict contrast to previous ones, and an immediate effect. For his second scene Faustus enters, as he says, "resolute" (I.iii.14); his long study is already completed and his prayers and sacrifice to devils: he is committed. For his third scene (II.i) he is revealed *"in his study,"* not living in speculation of his art as he had left the stage, but exclaiming that he must "needs be damned"; we are not shown this change taking place, but its full effect; how it is, not how it happens. Marlowe wishes us to observe, wonder and question at the changes in Faustus not share in the process of them. For his fourth scene, he is in debate with Mephostophilis, the first entry in duologue. In the fifth scene, he starts by telling Mephostophilis of the wonders of his travels, and the actor is set the task of appearing as if he has just ridden across the firmament on a dragon-drawn chariot. And so on through the play, completing a series of appearances that give by montage the complex impression of the mind and being of a man whose dominion "stretcheth as far as doth the mind of man."

The montage effect and the great economy in presentation of the central character may be illustrated by the soliloquy when Faustus is discovered in his study after the pact with Lucifer:

> Now, Faustus, must thou needs be damned;
> Canst thou not be saved:—

The statement, sharpened by the emphasis on *Now* and *must,* is in two sections each representing a different involvement: *needs,* and then *canst.* The next line is a question, referring to thoughts immediately released:

> What boots it then to think of God or heaven?

There is nothing irresolute or nervous in the expression of any of these first lines; but an ejaculation follows defining the wildness and uncertainty that is another facet of Faustus' complicated state of mind and being:

> Away with such vain fancies, and despair.

Then at once there is a counterstatement, for two lines breaking the full run of the iambic pentameter with shorter thrusts and rhythms:

> Despair in God and trust in Belzebub!
> Now go not backward. Faustus, be resolute!

And again a counterstatement: back to a question which expresses, not strength and purpose, but irresolution:

> Why waver'st thou?

Then a description of a sudden sense of a different reality: Faustus' mind is impelled by a force he cannot control: this is experienced, described, rapidly questioned, and then almost as rapidly counterstated. Each of these short elements demands different vocal and physical representations for the varying emotional, intellectual, and physical realities implied:

> Why waver'st thou? O something soundeth in mine ear,
> "Abjure this magic, turn to God again."
> Ay, and Faustus will turn to God again.
> To God? He loves thee not. . . .

The speech does not build in effect: each element is self-contained and from this we gain an impression of a man of great energy and complexity. The soliloquy concludes with, first, a more sustained and temperate description of his new allegiance:

> The God thou serv'st is thine own appetite
> Wherein is fixed the love of Belzebub!

and then a new concern with *future* activity, in two stages, of which the second represents in one line a hitherto unknown element of cruelty and callowness:

> To him I'll build an altar and a church,
> And offer lukewarm blood of newborn babes!

The Good and Bad Angels enter on either side of the stage, to express visually and verbally the contrary possibilities that are available to Faustus; when they go, Faustus expresses yet further facets of his being. Here, rapidly, are love of wealth, sense of triumph, feelings of security, warmth and eagerness, and then committal and incantation:

> Wealth!
> Why, the signory of Emden shall be mine!
> When Mephostophilis shall stand by me
> What power can hurt me? Faustus, thou art safe.
> Cast no more doubts! Mephostophilis, come,
> And bring glad tidings from great Lucifer.
> Is't not midnight? Come Mephostophilis,
> *Veni, veni Mephostophile!*

The greatest challenge to the actor is the last soliloquy of the play. At Stratford, Eric Porter tried to sustain and unify it by a sense of terror and physical struggle. Most of it was spoken in white heat; Faustus writhed on the door as if wrestling with a devil. In this way the astonishing variety of its demands was lessened and the play robbed of its climactic representation of Faustus' "do-

minion that . . . Stretcheth as far as doth the mind o
man," which realizes that dominion with economy, energy
and sensuous fullness. The actor should play the con
tradictions and the contrasts; he must not represent :
general state of being which the audience may recogniz
and share, but open out the character's variety of impulse
sensation, and thought, anatomize him for the audience t
see plainly and to wonder at, and not fully comprehend

Clifford Williams' direction at Stratford had one ex
pected success, and one unexpected. Most other produc
tions have shown how effective is the contrast betwee
Mephostophilis and Faustus, the spirit usually terse an
often unvaried in his reactions, and independent eve
when obeying the magician's commands. For Harold Hob
son, "The controlled Mephistophilis of Terence Hardiman
occasionally allowing a flicker of torment to pass ove
his quiet face, is what does most to hold the productio
together" (The London *Sunday Times,* June 30, 1968)
For Irving Wardle, "It is a pity that Terence Hardiman'
Mephistophilis, as quiet and powerful as a coiled spring
did not meet a more challenging adversary" (The Londo
Times, June 28, 1968).

The dramatic device of contrast is what justifies th
comic subplots and the comic episodes of the main action
justifies them to the scholar and critic knowledgeable c
the scriptural, medieval, and early Renaissance love o
analogy, and able to mark the verbal connections betwee
the comic and serious elements. But in performance th
validity of the comedy, as practicable theater, has ofte
been questionable. Mr. Williams, by encouraging robus
and inventive performances by the minor characters
showed that these scenes are eminently playable; indee
that their verbal simplicity, in comparison with the ob
scurity of many of Shakespeare's low comedy episodes
makes them more immediately effective for twentieth
century audiences. For Irving Wardle, there was "goo
phallic fun between Robin (Bruce Myers) and Ralph.
Ronald Bryden, writing in *The Observer* (June 30, 1968)
noted with some surprise that "Richard Moore manage

make the servant Wagner's scenes of crude supernatural slapstick genuinely funny." These are not parts
that play themselves: they require something of the independent and scene-stealing qualities of the Elizabethan
personality comics. A renewal of interest in improvisa-
tional techniques and in popular, music-hall comedy is
showing our actors the way toward, literally, reviving
these parts.

But the problem that remains is how to relate Faustus'
part in the comedy to his role as a whole. Why should
he bother with the trivial concerns of the Duke and
Duchess of Vanholt or the comic stubbornness of the
Horse-courser? How can the audience accept from the
same character metaphysical doubt and courtly subservi-
ence, sensitivity to beauty and childish exploitation of
human absurdity? If the presentation of Faustus in his
most obviously effective scenes is any clue, the answer
must be to accept the contrasts and play them for all
their local worth, to play each episode for itself (in the
Brechtian manner) and leave the coherence to Marlowe,
to the inward unity of the actor's performance (based
as it must be in one individual man and his possibilities
of suggestion), and to the audience's realization that
however dignified or important a man may be there are
usually absurdities and surprises deep within him. In full
possession of magical powers, Faustus might well become
irresponsible and childish; he might well play with the
Emperor and the Duke of Vanholt in rather the same
way as Mephostophilis has played with him. The practice
of power may cause him to lose a sense of proportion.
Familiarization with devilish practices and indulgence of
his fancies may cause him to lose both his appearance
of serious purpose and his sense of relevance.

Even in the height of the comedy in IV.v, Faustus
returns for one speech to the earlier manner of obvious
seriousness and high-pressured consciousness:

What art thou, Faustus, but a man condemned to die?
Thy fatal time draws to a final end;
Despair doth drive distrust into my thoughts.

Confound these passions with a quiet sleep.
Tush, Christ did call the thief upon the cross!
Then rest thee Faustus, quiet in conceit.

If the actor of Faustus creates this moment clearly ar
strongly, with its sharp transitions, with the firm, extende
rhythm of the second line enforced with alliteration ar
monosyllabic stress, with the abrupt "Tush" followed t
the simple New Testament reference, and with, lastly, tl
punning ambiguity of "rest," "quiet," and "conceit," tl
audience may sense the deep inward knowledge of jud;
ment, confusion, and longing that in the comic scenes
banished from Faustus' consciousness by his petty a
tivity.

The object of director and actors, and of scene design
and technicians, must be to reveal all with clarity, trutl
and power, to give each element its own full effect ar
allow Marlowe's astonishingly varied and comprehensiv
drama to appear in meaningful sequence before tl
audience. To seek an easy unity, or to play one characte
emotion, spectacle, or incident overwhelmingly, is to fig!
against the style in which the play was written. It is n
an easy play for audience or performers: its subjec
treated by an imaginative, speculative ironist, must wa
us not to expect that; a study of its style must warn
that the audience should be continually alerted and th;
a sense of unity should be created by each member i
his own imagination rather than made obvious and i
escapable on the stage. Marlowe provides excitemen
confrontation, and questions in plenty: he does not lea
by the nose. *Doctor Faustus* is dialectic drama, in Brecht
sense; it is spectacular; and it lives in the imaginatio
freely and with complexity.

Suggested References

Among modern editions of the play, two are especially valuable: *Marlowe's Doctor Faustus 1604-1616: Parallel Texts*, ed. W. W. Greg (Oxford, 1950), gives the A and B texts on facing pages, and contains a long discussion of the textual problems; *Doctor Faustus*, ed. John D. Jump (London, 1962), is abundantly annotated.

Among numerous critical studies, the following may provide a useful beginning:

Barber, C. L., " 'The Form of Faustus' Fortunes good or bad,' " *Tulane Drama Review*, 8, no. 4 (Summer, 1964), 92–119.

Brockbank, J. P., *Marlowe: Dr. Faustus* (London, 1962).

Craik, T. W., "Faustus' Damnation Reconsidered," *Renaissance Drama*, new series, 2 (1969), 189–96.

Farnham, Willard, ed., *Twentieth Century Interpretation of Doctor Faustus* (Englewood Cliffs, New Jersey, 1969).

Kernan, Alvin, ed., *Two Renaissance Mythmakers: Christopher Marlowe and Ben Jonson* (Baltimore, 1977).

Levin, Harry, *The Overreacher* (Cambridge, Mass., 1952).

Maclure, Millar, ed., *Marlowe: The Critical Heritage* (London, 1979).

Manley, Frank, "The Nature of Faustus," *Modern Philology*, 66 (1969), 218–31.

Ornstein, Robert, "Marlowe and God: The Tragic Theology of Dr. Faustus," *PMLA*, 83 (1968), 1378–85.

Sewall, Richard B., *The Vision of Tragedy* (New Haven, Conn., 1959).

Steane, J. B., *Marlowe: A Critical Study* (Cambridge, 1964).

Weil, Judith, *Christopher Marlowe: Merlin's Prophet* (Cambridge, 1977).

Westlund, Joseph, "The Orthodox Christian Framework of Marlowe's *Faustus*," *Studies in English Literature*, 3 (1963), 191–205.

ℂ SIGNET CLASSICS (04

Enduring British Classics

☐ **CHANCE by Joseph Conrad.** With an Introduction by Alfred Kazin.
psychologically penetrating portrait of a young woman's metamorph
from a tragic figure to a self-respecting woman.   (525574—$4.

☐ **THE SECRET AGENT by Joseph Conrad.** In this world of plot
counterplot, where identities are deceptions and glowing slogans m
savage realities, each character becomes an ever more helpless pu
of forces beyond control—until one woman's love, grief, and anger
through the entire fabric of the conspiracy with a passionate, profou
human act.   (524160—$3.

☐ **THE PICTURE OF DORIAN GRAY by Oscar Wilde,** with *Lord Arthur Savi*
Crime, **The Happy Prince,** and *The Birthday of the Infanta.* The cont
versial novel of a youth whose features, year after year, retain the sa
yo   de
vic $3.

WGRL-HQ NONFIC
31057100170482
822.3 MARLO
Marlowe, Christopher
Doctor Faustus

☐ PR   op
ior   am
no   ng
fa $2.

☐ TH   Th
tw   P
TV $4.
Pri

Buy them at your local bookstore or use this convenient coupon for ordering.

PENGUIN USA
P.O. Box 999 – Dept. #17109
Bergenfield, New Jersey 07621

Please send me the books I have checked above.
I am enclosing $_____ (please add $2.00 to cover postage and handli
Send check or money order (no cash or C.O.D.'s) or charge by Mastercard
VISA (with a $15.00 minimum). Prices and numbers are subject to change with
notice.

Card #_____ Exp. Date _____
Signature_____
Name_____
Address_____
City _____ State _____ Zip Code _____

For faster service when ordering by credit card call **1-800-253-6476**

Allow a minimum of 4-6 weeks for delivery. This offer is subject to change without not